Faith stared at Zach in shock.

"There's no father listed on his birth certificate!" she blurted out.

He met her gaze. "It doesn't surprise me. I don't think Annette wanted me to be part of our child's life."

Her heart pounding, she moved even closer. "And why would that be?"

Regret tautened his handsome features. "Because we had ended our relationship. And I'm gone more than I'm around."

How well she knew that lifestyle. Pushing the old bitterness and remembered loneliness aside, she forced herself to lower her voice. "You're a navy SEAL?"

"Yes."

Which meant he'd gone through some of the toughest training around and would be a formidable adversary. If it came to that. It might not. This could all be a terrible mistake.

She moved away from him. Stood with her back to the late-autumn sunshine streaming in through the windows. "Why haven't you claimed your child before now?"

"I didn't know I had a child until a few weeks ago."

Dear Reader,

There are times when it is easy to know what to do. There are other times when trying to figure out what is right is a lot more elusive.

This is the situation that Faith Lockhart Hewitt and Lieutenant Zach Callahan find themselves in. Faith has been fostering five-month-old Quinn ever since his birth mother died. She is days away from adopting him when Zach Callahan arrives on the scene. The navy SEAL has just discovered he has a baby boy, and he very much wants to be part of Quinn's life. But there is a hitch. He is still active-duty military and will not be there to care for his son. The only fair thing to do—the only right thing—is to let Faith help him raise Quinn.

Unfortunately, their plan is not as easy to implement as they had hoped. Before they know it, they are married. That, too, seems simple enough. They won't be together more than a few weeks or months a year. So it ought to be easy to just be coparents, and friends, and leave it at that...right?

I hope you enjoy this Christmas story as much as I enjoyed writing it. Happy holidays to everyone!

Best wishes,

Cathy Gillen Thacker

cathygillenthacker.com

Their Texas Christmas Gift

CATHY GILLEN THACKER

Recycling programs for this product may not exist in your area.

ISBN-13: 978-1-335-40824-2

Their Texas Christmas Gift

This edition published by arrangement with Harlequin Books S.A.

For questions and comments about the quality of this book, please contact us at CustomerService@Harlequin.com.

Harlequin Enterprises ULC
22 Adelaide St. West, 40th Floor
Toronto, Ontario M5H 4E3, Canada
www.Harlequin.com

Printed in U.S.A.

Cathy Gillen Thacker is a married mother of three. She and her husband reside in North Carolina. Her stories have made numerous appearances on bestseller lists, but her best reward is knowing one of her books made someone's day a little brighter. A popular Harlequin author, she loves telling passionate stories with happy endings and thinks nothing beats a good romance and a hot cup of tea! Visit her at cathygillenthacker.com for information on her books, recipes and a list of her favorite things.

Books by Cathy Gillen Thacker

Harlequin Special Edition

Lockharts Lost & Found

His Plan for the Quadruplets
Four Christmas Matchmakers
The Twin Proposal
Their Texas Triplets

Texas Legends: The McCabes

The Texas Cowboy's Quadruplets
His Baby Bargain
Their Inherited Triplets

Harlequin Western Romance

Texas Legends: The McCabes

The Texas Cowboy's Triplets
The Texas Cowboy's Baby Rescue

Visit the Author Profile page at Harlequin.com for more titles.

Chapter One

"There's another fella here to see you!" Miss Mim announced merrily.

Faith Lockhart-Hewitt looked up from the accounts-receivable spreadsheet she was working on. And asked, from the way the petite, red-haired senior was beaming, "In military uniform?"

The retired librarian and longtime resident of Laramie Gardens sighed and fanned her face, as if she was about to faint. "Oh, my, yes…!"

Faith grimaced. She knew the Navy SEALs that kept coming to see her meant well. But these visits were hard as heck on her nevertheless.

Evidently recalling just how many visitors she'd had, now that Thanksgiving was almost here, Miss Mim offered sympathetically, "I could tell the lieutenant you don't have time to see him this afternoon."

Faith vetoed the kind offer with a shake of her head. "No. He'll just come back tomorrow or the next day." Figuring she might as well get the condolence call over with, she cast a fond glance at the infant sleeping soundly in the buggy beside her, then rose reluctantly.

"Did he give his name?" she asked.

"Zach Callahan."

No one she knew then. Although whether that would make this meeting easier or harder was impossible to say.

"Want me to keep an eye on Quinn?" the older woman asked eagerly.

"Please." Faith shut down her computer screen, then stepped out from behind her desk. "He shouldn't wake up for at least another half an hour, but if he does..."

"I'll wheel your sweet baby boy to you right away!"

"Thanks." She ran a hand through her hair. Wondering if she should at least hazard a look in the mirror before she met the man, then figured there was no point. It wasn't like she would ever see him again after today. "Where is the soldier?"

"The solarium in the west wing."

One of the most comfortable rooms in the assisted-living facility, it was generally used for private family meetings, or quiet activities like knitting and reading. "Anyone else in there?"

Miss Mim waved her hand. "A few. Not to worry, dear. I cleared the room for you."

Faith was grateful for the privacy. These meet-and-greets could get abruptly awkward or emotional or both. "Thank you." She squared her shoulders and gathered her courage, then promised, "I won't be long."

"Don't worry about us, dear." Miss Mim paused to give her a reassuring hug and a gentle pat on the back. "Take your time."

Faith walked through the halls, past the large community room, the art studio and the dining hall, her steps slowing and her heartbeat increasing with every step. She could tell by the hopeful smiles of some of the female residents that they had seen her visitor. What no one seemed to understand was that she wasn't interested in another romance. She'd already had the love of her life. And now, the baby boy she was going to adopt in just a few short days…

Squaring her shoulders, she rounded the corner and caught her first glimpse of her visitor.

He was standing with his back to her, legs braced apart, hands on his hips.

Like most special operators, he was hard, rippling muscle from head to toe. His dark brown hair was cut to regulation, and the military-issue fatigues that adorned his six-foot-four-inch frame only seemed to emphasize the width of his broad shoulders, taut middle and long, sturdy limbs. Yet despite this man's huge, imposing figure, his big body was quiet as he continued to stare out the window, oblivious to her presence.

She had half a mind to run, but Faith forced herself to move just past the threshold. She stopped and said, "Lieutenant Callahan?"

That caught his attention.

He turned to face her. And she felt the full impact of his masculine strength.

Damn, but he was good-looking! With chiseled features, a wide unsmiling mouth and eyes that were a deep sea-blue, and oh, so familiar to her.

If Zach Callahan hadn't known better, he would have thought Faith Lockhart-Hewitt knew exactly why he was here. But that was ridiculous. No one knew but him, and the private investigator he had hired.

He moved toward her, extending a hand and unable to help but note how incredibly beautiful she was. She was a good seven or eight inches shorter than him. Slender-framed. Her white sweater clung to her full breasts, and her brown skirt showed off her narrow waist, hips and shapely legs. But it was her chin-length strawberry blonde hair, feminine features and long-lashed emerald eyes that really caught his attention. Made him realize he really needed to get on with this. Tough as it was going to be.

He clasped her palm. "Mrs. Hewitt. I'm Lieutenant Zach Callahan."

She returned his grasp politely before abruptly letting go and taking a step back. Huffing out a breath, she looked him in the eye. "Here to pay your condolences. I know."

Actually, he hadn't planned to bring that up. Not right away, anyway. But now that she had, he nodded soberly. "I'm sorry for your loss."

She surveyed him dispassionately. "Did you know my husband?"

"Yes. We attended a six-week training course together, several years ago."

"I see." Her eyes clouded over.

Compelled to say something comforting, Zach continued, "He was a fearless soldier. Smart. Dedicated. Quick to react, no matter what the situation."

Her expression grew even more remote. She didn't seem to want to hear how admired her late spouse had been. "Yes, well, thank you for stopping by, Lieutenant Callahan. I appreciate your condolences." She moved as if to show him the door.

He lifted a hand. "But that's not why I'm here," he said.

She stopped. Waited. Somewhat impatiently.

"I'm here to talk about the child you are adopting."

Every inch of her delectable body went still. For a second, she barely seemed to breathe. "Quinn?"

A mixture of guilt and determination roared through him. “Yes.”

She came toward him once again. Looking every inch the fiercely protective mama bear now. Eyes sparkling with emotion, she lifted her chin in challenge. Which did not surprise Zach one bit. For four months now, she had been caring for the infant, whose mother had died in a car accident while in the middle of moving across the country. “What about him?” she demanded in a tone that said she had become *far* more than a temporary foster mother to the boy.

There was no easy way to say it.

“I think he’s mine.”

Faith stared at Zach in shock. Certain this must be some very bad joke. “There’s no father listed on his birth certificate!” she blurted before she could stop herself.

He met her gaze equably. “It doesn’t surprise me. I don’t think Annette wanted me to be part of our child’s life.”

Her heart pounding, she folded her arms militantly across her chest. “And why would that be?”

Acceptance tautened his handsome features. “Because we had ended our relationship,” he stated with a tinge of regret. “And I’m gone more than I’m around.”

How well she knew that lifestyle. Pushing aside the old bitterness and remembered loneliness, she took a closer look at the insignia patch on his camo uniform and forced herself to lower her voice. “You’re a Navy SEAL?”

“Yes.”

Which meant he had gone through some of the

toughest training around and would be a formidable adversary. If it came to that. But it might not. This could all be just a terrible mistake.

She moved away from him, her back to the late autumn sunshine streaming in through the windows. "Assuming what you suspect is correct, why haven't you claimed your child before now?"

"I didn't *know* I had a child until a few weeks ago, when I got back from a three-month mission."

She knew about those, too. "In which you were incommunicado the whole time," she mused.

He nodded curtly.

That explained part of it, she thought sympathetically. But not all. She straightened. "What about the two months prior to that?" she persisted. "The time around when Quinn was actually born? Annette gave birth to him nearly *five* months ago."

He leveled his gaze on hers. "And we broke up *six months* before that."

Faith did some fast calculations. "So she would have been pregnant?"

"While we were still together? Yes." He squinted. "Annette had to have been in her first trimester."

Wary of letting him into her and Quinn's lives in even the slightest way, she declared, "And you had no idea."

He went very still. "All I can tell you is that after years of her saying being tied down was the *last thing* she desired…that she suddenly wanted to get married. Pronto. *But only* if I resigned my commission and went with her wherever she found a job after she completed her surgical residency, which was set to happen in another month."

Faith didn't care much for ultimatums, either. "Which you weren't willing to do."

His jaw tightened. Broad shoulders flexing, he folded his arms in front of him. "She knew I was career military when we first got involved."

And still was, from the looks of it. Restless, she paced the cozy solarium, catching a whiff of his brisk, masculine scent as she moved. Damn, but he was physically fit. Not that she should be noticing… "Who ended it?"

Seemingly oblivious to the unexpected jolt of physical awareness he aroused in her, he grimaced. "She did." Then his gaze narrowed. "But we had taken a break a couple of times before, when one of our careers got too demanding. I figured when Annette cooled off, she might want us to be on again. So, when I got back from my last assignment, I went to see her. And found out she'd had a baby on her own, and then had left Virginia, to take a job elsewhere. 'Start over,' she said. She had promised her friends she would get in touch with them when she got settled, but then she never did. No one thought too much about it at the time. Everyone in her residency program was starting over somewhere, and she had always been something of a loner. I had to hire a private investigator to find out what had happened to her. Which led me here."

She studied his contained expression, the fatigue bracketing his eyes that said this had been quite the emotional ordeal for him. Learning Annette had died, and then finding out he might have a son she hadn't bothered to tell him about, must have upended his entire world. How could it *not*? Despite everything, her heart went out to him. "How long were you involved with her?" she asked softly.

He scrubbed a weary hand over his face. Let his hand drop to his side. "Ten years, off and on. Since shortly after we both graduated from college."

She shifted her gaze over his strong, suntanned neck, past the grim set of his lips, to his intent blue eyes. "That's a long time to be with someone."

He shrugged. "We were apart more than we were ever together."

A tension-fraught silence fell between them. Faith drew a deep, stabilizing breath. She had to know a lot more about this man, if he was here to lay claim to *her* little boy. Because no way was she going to give up Quinn now, to a soldier who would seldom be around. Needing to see what she was missing, she said, "I still don't understand why Annette wouldn't have told you if she were having your child."

"I don't, either. She had to know I would have done the honorable thing."

She looked him over critically. "And married her." *Out of duty.*

He nodded with no hesitation whatsoever. "Yes."

"Well, maybe Annette didn't want a marriage born out of obligation." She watched Zach's frown deepen.

"Or," she continued, her mood sobering all the more, even as hope that this would work out for her and her son flared again, "maybe you aren't Quinn's biological father after all." Maybe that was why Annette hadn't told Zach she was pregnant!

The same possibility had clearly occurred to him, too. He inhaled sharply. "Either way, I have to know."

Was it getting hot in here or what? Willing herself to cool off, she said, "Which is why you're here."

Another curt nod. He kept his gaze locked with hers. "I want to do a DNA test."

Panic roiled through her. She had no idea what rights she had, if any, as a foster mother in a situation like this. "And if I say no?" she challenged quietly, not about to back down, either.

The formidable Navy SEAL was back. "I can hire a lawyer, and go to court to assert my paternity, and then force you, or social services, to allow one."

How well she knew that. So she threw herself on his mercy instead. "I'm going to adopt Quinn in a few days."

He nodded. Apparently, his private investigator had told him that, too. "And I'll be the first to cheer you on," he promised her, "*if* it turns out I'm wrong about this."

Another quiver of fear rippled through her. "And if you're right in your assumption?" she demanded anxiously. "Then what?"

Chapter Two

Faith waited nervously to hear what the handsome SEAL's plan was.

To her relief, Zach Callahan held up a staying hand. "Let's not get ahead of ourselves," he cautioned matter-of-factly.

In an effort to still the sudden trembling in her knees, she took a deep, bolstering breath.

He tilted his head to one side, his demeanor becoming less formidable. "Like you said…for all we know, the baby you have been raising for the last four months is not mine."

A light bulb went on in Faith's head as she thought about her brother's wife, Susannah, who'd had her quintuplets via in vitro. "Do you think she might have had a baby courtesy of a sperm or embryo donor?"

"I don't know. I don't think the private investigator I hired even looked at that possibility, but it would certainly explain why Annette never told me she was pregnant or listed my name, or anyone else's, on Quinn's birth certificate."

Yes, it would, Faith rationalized, as she began to relax. Still… "But if Quinn is your son?" she asked, forcing out the question.

"Then I'll do the right thing."

She stared at the rugged planes of Zach's face and

the sensual slant of his lips, and wished he wasn't so damn confident. Or *noble*. "Which is?"

He folded his arms in front of him. "Make sure he's provided for. Legally and financially."

Faith waited but nothing else was forthcoming. "You're not thinking about raising him yourself?" she asked, swallowing around the parched feeling in her throat.

He stepped even closer. When he spoke, his voice was a deep, sexy rumble. "It would be a little hard, since I'm not married or even romantically involved with anyone."

She could feel the heat emanating from his body. She drew another breath, taking in the scent of him. Aware that standing so close to him was making her tingle in a way that was not the least bit appropriate, she knew she had to nip this in the bud. Pronto. Which meant she was definitely *not* going to wonder what it would be like to feel the force of all that testosterone. Or fantasize about what it would be like to feel the skill of his big, manly hands, or hot, sensual lips… "Is that the only reason you don't wish to retain custody yourself? Because you're single?" she asked, forcibly shaking off her errant thoughts.

His gaze moved over her in another long, thoughtful survey. "That, and the fact I know nothing about babies."

If there was anything Faith hated, it was lame excuses. She retorted, just as smoothly, "Childcare can be learned." *Wait! Why was she making his argument for him? Pushing him to take on a responsibility he didn't seem to want?* But she kept right on going, anyway, assuming the role of devil's advocate, to see what he would do if backed into a corner. "And you look like a quick study to me."

His brow lifting, he seemed to reserve judgment on her fickle heart. "I am. But it wouldn't be fair to Quinn, given that I'm out of country more than I'm in. Often on assignments where no communication with loved ones is possible until the mission is concluded."

So he wasn't self-centered or selfish. Good to know. "You don't have extended family that would raise Quinn for you?" *People who would be all too willing to take Quinn from me, should the paternity question turn out in your favor.*

Sorrow came and went in his gorgeous sea-blue eyes. He lifted one broad shoulder in a careless shrug. "My dad wasn't around to even raise me. And my mom is pretty wrapped up in her new family."

Faith regarded him questioningly.

With a heavy sigh, he went on, "They're divorced. Have been for about twenty-five years now."

"I'm sorry."

"Don't be." A muscle ticked in his jaw. "It was for the best. All they ever did when I was growing up was fight. It was actually a relief when they ended their marriage, when I was ten. They both found their happily-ever-afters, when they married other people they were more suited for."

So on top of being unselfish, he was also pragmatic and sensitive. A combination that had always really appealed to her. Faith fought back her attraction and pushed on. "So what are you thinking then—about Quinn's care—if it does turn out he is yours after all?" she asked, aware how very much there was on the line.

He shoved a hand over his hair. Grimaced in a way

that told her he was as upset about the situation as she was. "You have been fostering him, and from what I understand, you *wanted* to adopt him—"

He made it sound so tenuous. Cutting him off with a scowl, she said sternly, "I'm *going* to adopt him. I have already been through all the parenting classes, been fostering him for four months and have a court date on Monday to officially make the petition."

It would be at least six months after that until the adoption would become final. Six months, she worried silently, where a lot could still go wrong. "Unless," she added, her mouth suddenly going as dry as her parched throat, "you do something to stop that. Which, you obviously could," she admitted reluctantly, abruptly feeling near tears.

He regarded her steadily, his expression as implacably masculine as the rest of him. "I have no plans to take Quinn away from you. But, that said, for a whole host of reasons, I do need to know if he is my son or not. And so do you," he added.

He had a point there, Faith conceded. Nothing would be legal until the full truth surrounding Quinn's birth had been properly addressed.

The sound of high heels echoed in the hall outside the solarium. Seconds later, Miss Mim breezed in, pushing the buggy. She had applied a fresh coat of lipstick, and newly fluffed her red bouffant. "I hate to interrupt," she said cheerfully, "but your darling baby boy woke up as soon as you were gone. I think he sensed your absence…" Miss Mim pushed the pram closer, then gloated to the lieutenant. "Faith is such a wonderful mother! We're all in awe of her!"

Zach Callahan nodded and forced a polite smile, quietly absorbing the information.

"Any man would be lucky to have her!" she continued enthusiastically.

Faith flushed with embarrassment. She wished this was a one-off, but it wasn't. The seniors were always trying to pair her up with a new man. "Okay, Miss Mim," she chided. "Sorry to disappoint, but he's not here to marry me."

"Of course not!" the older woman scoffed. "The two of you just met, didn't you?"

"Yes," she and Zach said in unison.

Faith looked over at him, glad they were both of one mind. They needed to end this. *Now.*

"But there's always love at first sight!" Miss Mim added, romantic as ever.

It was all Faith could do not to sink through the floor.

"Good to know," Zach said in a way that ended that line of conversation.

"Well! I'll leave you two be!" Miss Mim waggled her eyebrows and backed from the room.

Another incredibly awkward silence stretched between them. Zach turned to her. "Miss Mim can't possibly know why I'm here. *Can she?* I mean, the place isn't bugged, is it?"

"You mean besides the security cameras that keep the residents safe? Of course not! She and all the other women here just think that I am one of those women that needs to have a husband to be happy." She blew out a breath, then admitted softly, "And it's no secret how much I have always wanted a family of my own. So a few months after Harm passed, they began encouraging me to start going out again. And hopefully find someone to have children with." She rolled her eyes. "And to that end, they have sung my praises to every eligible man of an even remotely compatible age. So as *shocking* as this might be to hear, soldier...you are nothing special."

Mischief sparkled in his eyes. He chuckled and ran a hand beneath his jaw. "So how's that working for you?" he drawled.

Not good. Until now. Aware his teasing had hit the mark, she waved a hand, sidestepping the question. "I've already got the love of my life," she declared passionately. "This little guy right here." She turned the buggy so he could see the baby inside.

Zach hadn't ever considered himself a baby person. But something about this little guy damn near stopped his heart—he was just *that* remarkable. With long lashes, big blue eyes, tufts of dark wispy hair and a cherubic face, he was cute enough to adorn a diaper box. Not too thin, not too husky—Quinn was just perfect.

In every way.

And Faith Lockhart-Hewitt thought so, too, he realized, his chest squeezing.

"Do you want to hold Quinn?" she whispered.

He had an idea what it was costing her to offer him that, given the fact she seemed to fear he was there to rob her of the baby she had taken into her home and her heart.

He shook his head. It was going to be hard enough to walk away from the little tyke as it was.

Not that he had any intention of physically caring for him. Or even really getting to know him, if it meant he would be breaking the little fella's heart every time he had to walk away again.

No, she was what this baby needed.

And he would make sure that she got the motherhood she had earned.

Faith picked up Quinn and held him in her arms. He watched her stare adoringly into his face, while the baby looked back at her with the same deep affection, smiling and babbling nonsensically.

Damn if she hadn't become the little man's mommy in every way that counted. He cleared his throat. Worked to get them back on track. "All I need is a paternity test…"

"I can call my brother-in-law Griff a lawyer in Fort Worth. It's not his field but he'll know how we should proceed."

"Okay."

She started to ease Quinn back into the pram. But the baby let out a howl of protest. His lower lip slid out, and his eyes grew fierce.

Wow. The little guy really knew what he wanted, and how to go for it, Zach thought in amusement. He had never seen a five-month-old baby with such an outgoing personality!

Faith eased her cell phone out of the holder she had clipped to the waistband of her skirt.

Sensing once again he wasn't the center of her attention, Quinn began to squirm. Unable to handle both the phone and baby simultaneously, she shot a quick, furtive look at Zach. He knew what she wanted to ask, but that she *wouldn't.* Not after having been rebuffed once already. Duty reigned. "I'll take him." Zach held out his hands. Anything to get this task complete and get the hell out of there.

Trying not to get too worked up about the fact he

might be holding his own firstborn son in his arms, he walked over to the window and turned so Quinn could see the residents sitting in the garden as they chatted with a group of high-school students doing some sort of community-service project.

Behind him, Faith talked on the phone.

But everything else faded into the background as he gazed down at the precious child cuddled against him. A tenderness Zach hadn't expected to feel welled up inside him. Quinn was so vulnerable. Yet strong… And was it his imagination, or did the boy have Zach's granddad's chin?

Fortunately, it didn't take Faith long to get the information they needed. "Thanks, Griff," she said, then ended the call. "He said, in Texas, to prove paternity, you are going to need both blood work from the father, mother and baby, and a DNA sample from both you and Quinn. And that Quinn's and Annette's blood type will be in the hospital birth records. Do you have them?"

"No." That information was privileged, as far as Zach knew. "Just the birth certificate the private investigator got for me."

"Well, Griff said he can help us obtain those. Although it might take a couple of weeks and will likely require a subpoena, unless Laramie County already has them in their records, and they might, since those kinds of records are all connected these days. In the meantime, we can all go over to the hospital and get the lab work on you and Quinn done there."

"Won't we need an appointment?"

She shook her head, suddenly looking as anxious to have this all resolved as he was. "I have a brother,

Gabe, who is a physician there. I'm sure he will write the orders for us if we just ask."

Zach nodded, aware he was still holding Quinn, who was snuggled against his chest. Faith held out her hands. The baby lurched forward into her waiting arms. Although he had been content in Zach's arms, he was deliriously happy in Faith's.

Zach felt oddly bereft. Not that he should have expected anything different. Doing his best to tamp down his emotions, he asked, "How many brothers do you have?"

"Four. Three sisters."

"Big family."

"Lieutenant—" Faith smiled and shook her head, then reached for her phone as she transferred Quinn to Zach's arms again "—you have no idea..."

Faith expected her oldest brother to be as helpful as her brother-in-law. She wasn't disappointed. Gabe listened to her dilemma, then told her to come right over to the hospital. When all three of them arrived, he had a tech obtain Zach's DNA and then send Zach on to the lab for the necessary blood work, while he took her and Quinn into an unused ER bay.

As her brother prepared to do Quinn's DNA test, Faith began to have second thoughts. Although she had no reason to doubt Zach's story, or his assertion that he was not there to take Quinn from her, it was still all happening awfully fast. Was this yet another instance of her trying to put everyone else's needs above her own?

"How come you're not trying to talk me out of this?" she asked Gabe suspiciously. The former Physicians

Without Borders doctor, who was now an ER doc and infectious-disease specialist at Laramie Community Hospital, had always been a little too free with advice, as far as she was concerned. Maybe because he saw her as vulnerable in a way the rest of their siblings weren't.

"What would be the point?" Gabe asked, while she held Quinn in her arms and watched as he swabbed the inside of her infant son's cheek, then put the DNA sample into the sterile specimen bag. "I mean, Zach's right. You-all do need to know the truth."

Did they? Suddenly, Faith wasn't so sure. "Even if it could cost me my son?"

Gabe paired the sample with the one Zach had already left a short while ago.

"I thought you said he wasn't planning to take the baby from you."

"He feels that way *now*." She recalled the way the handsome soldier's face had changed, the tenderness in his eyes, when he had looked at Quinn for the very first time. The depth of emotion in his expression as he held him in his arms…

Zach Callahan might think he wasn't a baby person. He was wrong. Worriedly, she continued, "That could change if he discovers there is a match." And had a little more time to think about it.

Gabe put the samples into a plastic tray for outgoing lab tests. "From what I know about Navy SEALs, there's not much chance of that, if it means prematurely giving up his career."

She thought about her late husband, and how fiercely Harm had loved his work as a SEAL. How reluctant he had been to give it up, even to have a family with her. She sighed. "True."

"And isn't it better this way?" her brother continued. "Than getting lawyers involved?"

"Yes." Custody fights could be ugly. Plus, maybe there would be no need for one. Maybe Zach was right. Maybe the reason Annette had run off like that, without ever telling him she was pregnant, was because she had found another way to start a family. And the baby boy she'd given birth to hadn't been Zach's.

Bolstered by the hope that her life might not be crashing down again, after all, she shifted Quinn a little higher in her arms and asked, "How long before we know the results?"

Gabe slid his pen back in the pocket of his white coat. "A DNA paternity test usually takes two days if I put a rush on it. But with tomorrow being Thanksgiving, it will probably be Saturday before we hear."

A few days. She could do this. "Okay. Thanks."

"Are you going to tell the folks?"

She really didn't want to, but... "I know we put up a fire wall between us when I made the decision to foster-adopt, but I think I'm going to have to at least speak to Mom, since I might need her advice if it becomes a Department of Child and Family Services problem."

A longtime social worker, Carol was not just compassionate, but quick with a remedy for whatever people in crisis faced, too.

Her older brother nodded approvingly. "Let me know if there is anything else I can do." He gave her a one-handed hug, bussed Quinn on the head and escorted her out.

Zach was waiting in one of the straight-backed chairs. He rose when she walked out and looked right at her. She saw several staff members shoot curious glances his way. Which wasn't surprising. He wasn't just an out-of-towner; he was damn sexy. And military to boot, which just added another layer of intoxicating allure.

Not wanting an audience, she motioned for him to follow and headed outside into the November sunshine. The day was warm, with the temperature hovering in the low seventies.

Faith turned to face him, on the sidewalk, out of earshot of the electronic glass door. "So. We won't know until Saturday," she informed him.

"That's what your brother said to me, too."

They studied each other in silence. "So what are your plans until then?" she asked eventually. "Going to visit your folks?"

He gestured noncommittally. "I didn't know how this was going to go, so… I didn't make any plans. I'll probably just stay in Laramie County."

"For the holiday?" she asked, aghast.

He shrugged. "The clerk at the Laramie Inn told me there is a cafeteria in San Angelo that has a pretty good turkey buffet. I'll probably hit that."

SEALs had so few opportunities to be stateside for Thanksgiving and Christmas. He really shouldn't be stuck alone! Before she could stop herself, she said, "Listen. My family is having a big get-together out at my folks' ranch tomorrow. Why don't you come along?"

That he actually looked tempted told her he hadn't been anticipating celebrating Thanksgiving alone. "You're sure?"

Still cradling Quinn in one arm, she handed over her phone. "Put your information in there for me and I'll text you the details."

* * *

Faith had plenty of time to regret her impulsiveness over the next eighteen hours. But once issued, the invitation was unable to be rescinded. Not nicely, anyway, so she stuck with it. Even going so far as to invite him to drive out to the Circle L Ranch with her and Quinn.

He arrived on her doorstep at twelve sharp. Looking incredibly handsome in dark slacks and a burgundy crew-neck sweater that molded nicely over his broad shoulders, and draped loosely over his taut abs. He smelled incredible, too. Of brisk winter and spice.

Ridiculously glad she had taken the time to put on her favorite dark brown knit dress and matching tights, and sweep her hair up into a loose topknot, she ushered him in. Past her Norwich terrier, Tinkerbelle.

"She always sit by the door, with a leash in her mouth?" he asked, kneeling to pet her.

Faith admired the sight of the big man and the small dog. Sighed. "Tinkerbelle knows we're getting ready to go somewhere besides work, or something quick, like the grocery."

Zach smiled wryly. "She can tell all that?"

"Well, I've been exceptionally busy all morning. Baking the pies I'm taking to the dinner. Getting Quinn and myself ready…"

Zach gazed tenderly down at the infant seat, where a strapped-in Quinn snoozed. "He's out like a light."

Faith nodded. Her son had drifted off an hour before. She had gone ahead and put him in his infant seat, so she wouldn't have to wake him to put him in the car, if he was still asleep, which he was.

"We lucked out there, soldier. He gets pretty cranky when he doesn't have a late-morning nap."

Amusement sparkled in his blue eyes. He stepped closer, poised and ready for whatever she needed.

Making her aware that the grief she had felt when her husband had passed had faded more than she had let herself realize. Was she ready to move on? Or was this just nerves on her part? The uncertainty of the situation making her so hyper-conscious of him? All she knew for certain was that for now, anyway, she felt they were in this together.

That could, and would, change if the paternity results were negative.

"What can I do to help?" he asked in a low, gravelly voice that sent shivers through her.

It had been so long since she had a man underfoot. Never mind one as attractive as this. But that didn't mean she should get physically—or emotionally—involved with him! Especially when the situation was already so complicated. "Just help me get everything and everyone loaded in my SUV?"

He touched two fingers to his brow in a sexy salute. "Sure thing."

Another ribbon of awareness sifted through her as they exchanged smiles. It was too bad they had met the way they had, Faith thought. Otherwise, she might have been interested in him, the way she had promised herself that she would never be again. Not with another SEAL, anyway.

Twenty minutes later, they arrived at her parents' Circle L Ranch. "Nice place," Zach remarked as they parked in front of the sprawling white-stone-and-cedar ranch house.

Faith nodded in agreement. Her folks' home was beautiful. The split-rail fences and Western vibe of the house and barns perfectly suited the ten-thousand-acre cattle ranch.

"If you can get Tinkerbelle, I'll get Quinn. We'll come back for the pies later."

He paused next to the car, then shut the door for her. "Does the rest of your family know about the DNA test…?"

The million-dollar question. Wondering how he was going to take this information—Harm always preferred that her family stay completely out of their business—she looked him in the eye and said, "I told them all, yes."

His expression remained completely inscrutable, even as his gaze moved over her face, lingering on the heart-shaped pendant she wore on her neck before returning with slow deliberation to her eyes. "Everyone?" he rasped.

Faith nodded in acknowledgment. "It wasn't a secret that was going to be able to be kept." Plus, she had needed the emotional support.

Because it was too much of a leap for the small terrier, Zach lifted Tinkerbelle out and gently set her on the ground. She settled next to him, tail wagging, as if they were longtime friends instead of new acquaintances. Noticing, Zach reached down to give her pet's ears a friendly rub.

Straightening, he looked at Faith. "And how do they feel about it?" he asked warily.

She tried to focus on the beauty of the November afternoon, instead of the potentially tricky-to-navigate ordeal ahead of them. It was a perfect fall day—the temperature was in the low fifties, and the blue sky was dotted with fluffy white clouds. The trees were losing their leaves—what remained was a symphony of gold, red, brown and orange—and the air was scented with a combination of slow-burning oak and roasting turkey from the smokers out back. Sighing, she gave Zach a look that let him know he did not have to worry about anyone's manners. "They're happy to have you join us. Along with our other guests that don't have family nearby."

In fact, there would be so many people, with all eight Lockhart kids, various spouses and offspring, and a few friends, that any private conversations would be near impossible. At least that was what she hoped.

Zach's steady gaze never wavered. She felt it like a heat laser from the top of her head to the tips of her toes. Faith drew a stabilizing breath. Aware that, like it or not, there might soon come a day when she would have to go toe-to-toe with him over what was best for Quinn.

Because he still seemed wary, she added, "Everyone is very nice. And you've already met Gabe. I think you'll be very comfortable."

"That's not what I meant," he countered quietly. Suddenly demonstrating the Navy SEAL in him. The soldier who never ever gave up. Fortunately, Faith thought, the hardships in her life had made her just as headstrong. "How do they feel about the fact I could be Quinn's father?"

That's right. *Could* be, Faith reminded herself. Not definitely was.

Shrugging, she answered his question with an easygoing attitude she didn't completely feel. "Like me, they're just waiting to see what comes next."

Chapter Three

"Admit it," Jillian said, helping to carry the pumpkin and pecan pies into the dining room. She set them on the buffet already stuffed with sumptuous-looking desserts. "You had an ulterior motive for inviting Zach Callahan out here today."

Faith set down the apple- and cherry-filled pastries.

"You mean the fact he's insanely hot?" Mackenzie teased. She wanted everyone to be happily involved since she had gotten hitched to her best friend, Griff, and had their twins.

Gabe's wife, Susannah, continued setting the long plank table. "I don't think Faith is looking for romance right now."

Allie, their brother Cade's wife, folded white damask napkins. "No one is. Until sparks hit. Then all bets are off."

The relentlessly single, but still hopelessly romantic, Emma set down the last of the candles and came over to offer a hug of support. "It can be good to be on your own." She gave her sister an empathetic look, acknowledging her recent widowhood. "At least for now."

Faith nodded. "That's absolutely true," she said firmly. She was not looking for romance!

All six women entered the kitchen, where the holiday dinner was in progress. "The point is..." She looked out the window and saw Zach, accompanied by her father, walking Tinkerbelle on a leash. Yikes. Probably not a good sign. Knowing how protective her dad could be.

Checking in on Quinn, who was still sleeping in his baby carrier in a corner of the kitchen, she reached for an apron and tied it on. "Even if I found the lieutenant attractive, and I don't," she continued, telling a fib, "the situation would still be impossible."

Mackenzie, who had found love as an offshoot of a yearslong friendship with a boy she had met in foster care, before she and her siblings were all adopted by Carol and Robert Lockhart, looked doubtful. "You sure? Because if the lieutenant is Quinn's biological daddy, then it would certainly be advantageous for all three of you if you and Zach did have some chemistry."

Carol walked in, just in time to hear the tail end of the conversation. She gave the simmering potatoes a stir then lifted the lid on a big pot of green beans. "I don't think you should even consider going there. The situation is complicated enough as it is. Plus, I have a feeling that's not why Faith invited Zach here today."

Leave it to her always astute mom to discover her real reason.

"Then why *did* she?" Emma, the youngest sister, asked, bending to adjust the closures on a pair of leather ankle boots she had designed and made herself.

Carol Lockhart turned to Faith, one eyebrow raised. Commanding her to confess.

She lifted her hands in self-defense. "First of all, he's a serviceman with nowhere to go on a holiday."

Mackenzie shook her head in disagreement. "Not exactly true. You could easily have set him up with the buffet dinner over at the West Texas Warriors Association in Laramie today, where there would be plenty of current and ex-military."

"That seems a little cold, don't you think?" Faith countered. She couldn't say why, exactly. There was no reason she needed to be protective of Zach Callahan, even if he was Quinn's biological daddy. But for some reason, deep down, she was…

Dubious looks were exchanged all around, and with good reason, since the WTWA was a warm and welcoming place.

"Okay," she conceded finally, the heat of embarrassment creeping from her chest into her neck. She gave an excuse she knew everyone would accept. "I might have wanted to get to know him a little better, just in case Quinn is his son. Biologically."

"And?" Susannah, who'd bravely had quintuplets on her own, with her deceased sister's embryos, asked.

The way everyone was looking at her forced Faith to come clean. She cleared her throat. "I might *also* have wanted him to see what Quinn would have if he stayed with me, in terms of a big, loving extended family and the financial resources to meet his every need."

Carol's expression gentled.

"Does that make me a bad person?" Faith asked, suddenly near tears. She had thought the days of her reacting selfishly to potential loss were over. Perhaps not.

"No." Her mom engulfed her in a hug. "It makes you human. But you are still going to have to be careful," she warned softly. "This is a very, very difficult situation you are in."

Outside, Robert Lockhart finished showing Zach around the stables and the barns. All of which were as meticulously kept up as the Circle L ranch house and grounds.

As they started back to join the others, Robert gave Zach a man-to-man look that held nothing back. "Faith told us what was going on."

Bracing himself for whatever came next, Zach nodded. "She said as much."

The older man frowned, taking on the air of an experienced father and respected rancher. "I want you to know, son," he added compassionately, "we all empathize with everything you're going through."

"Thank you."

"We understand you have to do what you have to do. Especially if it turns out that you are indeed little Quinn's father. Which is why I have to advise you..." He paused, pressing his lips into a thin line. "If you think there is a chance you will want to raise this child on your own, or give him to another family member of yours to raise, that you let Faith know that immediately after paternity is confirmed. Because her heart is already fully involved with that little boy. And we don't want to see her hurt."

Zach thought about the close bond between foster mother and son, and knew he could never do anything to disrupt that. "I don't either, sir."

Robert studied him in silence.

"In fact," he went on soberly, "I'd like her to remain a big part of Quinn's life, no matter what the DNA tests show."

But instead of that declaration reassuring her dad, like he'd hoped, Zach was dismayed to see Robert's expression turn even more skeptical. "Things can change rapidly when you find out for certain that you're a child's father," he predicted.

Would they?

Zach couldn't imagine it now. But he also hadn't anticipated how he would feel the first time he had held Quinn in his arms. How immediately enthralled and emotionally connected he had felt. Would his parents feel that way about their first grandchild?

Robert's gaze narrowed. "It's not too early for you to start talking to your own family and figuring out exactly what you are going to do, if that is the case."

It was good advice.

Zach continued thinking about his talk with Robert Lockhart all through dinner and dessert. They stayed long enough to lend a hand with the dishes, then said good-night and hit the road around 8:00 p.m.

Instead of falling immediately asleep, this time, Quinn fussed as they began the drive back to town. Tinkerbelle, who was restrained in her own little car seat in the rear passenger seat, even looked worried.

"Is there something he needs?" Zach asked, alarmed at how little he knew about babies. To date, he had avoided them like the plague. It had been a wise decision at the time, but now, he wished he had a little more experience.

Faith shook her head, all easy maternal grace and confidence. He admired the way she seemed to take everything in stride. "Nope. He has a clean diaper, and he had a bottle of formula right before we left." She reached over and turned on some soft lullaby-like music. "He's just overtired and overstimulated because he didn't get much of an afternoon nap. The combination of the music and the motion of the car should lull him to sleep."

And sure enough, it did.

He was still snoozing when they pulled into her driveway in front of her bungalow.

"Do you think you could give me a hand with Tinkerbelle?" she asked.

"Be happy to."

They eased quietly out of the car. Faith led the way, carrying the infant car seat. Zach followed, with Tink and the diaper bag.

She unlocked the front door and let them inside. Two lamps were glowing softly. She pointed in the direction of the stairs. "I'm going to take Quinn up," she whispered.

He nodded.

Tinkerbelle pulled him toward the kitchen. He saw why. Filled food and water bowls sat on the mat bearing the terrier's name. He unsnapped the leash and let the dog begin to eat.

Faith swept back in. She switched on the overhead lights. "Can I get you anything?"

Surprised she wasn't already showing him out, and even more surprised he was in no hurry to get back to the solitude of his hotel room, he asked, "Coffee?"

"Coming right up." She turned on the single-cup brewer and set a tray containing a selection of different flavors and brands in front of him. He selected a plain coffee from a popular doughnut shop.

"So what do you think of the family?" She popped the pod into the coffee maker.

He watched her close the lid and press Start. "They were all very nice."

As the machine sputtered and dark liquid streamed into the mug, the kitchen filled with the aroma of fresh-brewed coffee. When it finished, she handed him his drink.

"Anyone except my dad give you a hard time?"

Had she seen them together, outside? Or was she just guessing based on past experience with other men? Finding he didn't want to be put in the category of "just another guy," when it came to this woman, he took a sip of his coffee and said, "How do you know he gave me a hard time?"

Faith put another pod in the brewer, this one vanilla-flavored. She added more water and shut the lid with a snap. "Because I know him and how protective he is when it comes to all eight of his children. So...what did he say to you when he was showing you around the ranch?"

"He wants me to give you a clean break if it turns out that Quinn is mine."

Color swept the lovely contours of her face. "Of course, he would," she muttered furiously, slamming both her hands on her delectable hips.

Taken aback by her response, Zach asked, "Why do you say that?"

"Because he—and Harm—were always in agreement that I was too softhearted to foster."

Zach let his gaze drift over her. Although it had been a long day, she still looked every bit as pretty and pulled together as she had when he had arrived nine hours prior. In fact, she was accomplished at everything he'd seen her do thus far.

He reassured her with a smile and said, "Well, then, they're wrong, because you seem great at fostering to me." She was amazing with Quinn, and she hadn't gone all hysterical when he had shown up to share his quandary and request the DNA test.

She shoved a restless hand through her hair; the strawberry-blond waves fluffed out alluringly around her face in a way that made him want to touch the tousled strands and see if they felt as silky-soft as they looked.

Ignoring her coffee for the moment, she toed off her flats and paced back and forth. "You're right, I am great at the caretaking part. That's easy as pie, when you grow up among eight kids. You learn quick how to take care of younger ones." She inhaled deeply, the action lifting and lowering the sumptuous swell of her breasts. Her teeth raked her soft lower lip. "It's the letting go everyone is worried about."

He nodded, beginning to be a little concerned about that, too. The last thing he wanted to do was hurt her in any way. Quinn, either. And Quinn clearly loved and depended on her, as much as she loved the baby boy.

Grimly, he noted, "So your dad said."

She pivoted and gave him a hard-eyed stare. "*Am I* going to have to let go of Quinn?" she demanded, cutting straight to the chase.

He returned her forthright attitude. "Only if you want to. And frankly, I don't see that happening."

A silence fraught with emotion fell between them. This sexy soldier sure was full of surprises, Faith thought.

"What if I wanted to do it all on my own?" she challenged, curious as to just how generous he was prepared to be.

A turbulent sheen darkened his eyes. "Except you wouldn't be. Not with a family of that size standing behind you."

She studied his chiseled features, thick dark brown hair and wide, sensual lips. "So that matters to you?"

"Having a family that is close and loving? Yes. Very much." His gaze drifted over her approvingly. "Especially because of the line of work I am in."

She felt an answering warmth. "You're not close to your family?"

"The only person I ever felt I truly belonged with was my paternal grandfather. I lived with him in Corpus Christi during high school. He was a carpenter. Veteran. Very down-to-earth and compassionate."

So in a sense, Faith realized, Zach had been orphaned, too. Just like she had been, at one point in her life. Aware of the unexpected bond, she asked, "Do you still see him?"

He shook his head sadly and took another long sip of coffee. "My granddad passed a few years ago while I was on a mission. I learned about it when I got back to the States. So I went down there. Paid my respects." Zach held the mug in both hands, then reflected quietly, "He had named me executor, so I settled the estate, except for the personal items he left me, and distributed what was left among remaining family members."

Compassion welled within her. She reached over to touch the back of his hand. "That must have been hard to deal with all that." She released her hold, stepped back and took a sip of her own coffee. "On top of not being able to be there at the time of his death."

Zach's broad shoulders tensed. "We always figured it would happen that way..."

She saw the sorrow he was trying to hide. "But you loved him," she observed softly.

He swallowed. "Very much."

Another beat of silence fell between them. He rose. "Well, I better get going."

She set down her mug. "I'll see you out." Even though walking him to the door after such an intimate conversation suddenly made it feel oddly like a date. Wishing she had left her shoes on, because it would have given her a little more height, she slid her hands in the pockets of her dress. "Do you have plans for tomorrow?"

He turned as they approached the front door. "Actually, yeah. I'm going over to the West Texas Warriors Association to see if anyone there needs help with anything."

Somehow she wasn't surprised he would find a way to spend his time in such a meaningful way. "Have you ever been there?"

"No. But your brother Gabe was telling me about it today, while we were watching football. Apparently, the WTWA helps a lot of older veterans and injured former soldiers. So I thought I would see if there was anything I could do."

She tilted her head back to better see into his face. "That's nice of you."

He shrugged. "Well, you know what they say," he said in a low, husky voice that sent ribbons of awareness tumbling through her. "'All in, all the time.'"

Harm had said that, too. Often. It was that gung ho attitude that had made him such a dedicated special operator.

As she privately cautioned herself against getting too

involved with another military man, Zach flashed another amiable smile. "It will be a good use of my time."

Admiring him even more, she reached past him to open the door. At the same time he moved slightly back, and the inside of her elbow grazed the outside of his forearm. A bolt of sheer electricity moved through her. Stifling a small gasp, she looked up at him. Unable to help herself, she quipped, "You know this would be a whole lot easier if you weren't so likable."

So utterly attractive in that sexy, easygoing way.

So able to make her feel alive…in a way she hadn't been in…well, what felt like *forever.*

She continued sassily, "Then I could just resent you for showing up and putting a wrench in all my plans." Wow, it felt good to admit that. Instead of acting all noble. When generous was the last thing she felt.

Zach seemed as surprised by the words that had slipped out as she was. He chuckled, and with a devilish look in his eyes, moved even closer. "Right back at you, darlin'."

The next thing she knew, his big, strong arms were around her. He was shifting her near. Lowering his head, just as she was raising hers.

That easily, their bodies were aligned, and his lips were on hers. Coaxing, probing, *savoring.* And she was exploring his mouth right back. Tasting the coffee he had just imbibed, and the bolder essence that was all him. Feeling the hardness of his desire pressing against her, even as her middle went all hot and tense, too. Need bubbled up inside her. Along with a wellspring of molten desire.

Shocked, she broke off the kiss and tore her mouth from his. Drew in a quick, shaky breath. She stepped back, but he remained where he was. His gaze sifted over her with the same crazy mix of emotions she felt.

Wonder—that the chemistry between them was so utterly powerful. *Surprise*—that it had happened at all. And an even more remarkable *absence of regret*. At least in that particular moment.

"We'll talk again when we find out the results," he promised gruffly. "Or before, if you need me." And on that note, he turned and headed out.

Mouth dry, her body quivering with unslaked lust, she watched him go. She pressed her fingertips to her still-tingling lips. What had just happened? Could this holiday season get any wilder? Honestly, she couldn't see how!

Chapter Four

"What's on your mind?" Faith asked Tillie Tarrant the next afternoon.

Tillie took a seat in front of Faith's desk. As always, her curly white hair was perfectly coiffed. She wore a crisp white blouse, a pumpkin-colored skirt and matching cardigan flats. "I wanted to speak to you confidentially."

Because the older woman looked hesitant, Faith reassured her, "You know everything about a person's finances here are private."

Tillie winced, looking even more reluctant to go on. "This is about our living quarters."

Faith picked up her pen. "Are you and Ted unhappy with your suite?" The eighty-year-old couple had one of the nicest corner units at Laramie Gardens, with a sitting area, a nice master bedroom and a deluxe bathroom.

Tillie knitted her hands together in her lap. "I was wondering about the price of our suite, actually, when compared with two single rooms. Is the latter less expensive?"

Faith knew the rate schedules by heart. "Yes…but not by a lot."

"How much less, though?" Tillie persisted.

Faith did some quick calculations. "It depends on the

size of the room, and whether or not it has a particular view, but probably ten percent less per month."

Tillie took a deep breath. "Are there any available that are side by side?"

Faith pulled up the chart of vacancies on her computer screen. "Right now? No. There aren't."

"In the same hallway?"

"No," she reported.

Tillie gripped the arms of her chair. "Same wing then?"

"Um… Actually, yes. We've got two residents moving out by year's end to be closer to family elsewhere but those rooms are at opposite ends of that particular hall. So…?" She wasn't sure it would work, given that Ted was now in a wheelchair, and not as mobile as he once had been.

The woman sighed her relief. "Would I need to put a deposit down on those rooms if Ted and I decide to do that?"

"No. Your contract would just transfer to the new accommodations."

"That's good to know," Tillie murmured.

Concerned, Faith prodded gently, "May I ask what is going on that prompted all this?"

Was there a problem with another resident she was unaware about? Noise of some sort? Too much sun in the mornings?

Tillie waved away the inquiry. "I'm just thinking out loud." She rose. "I would prefer you not say anything to Ted about this just yet."

"I won't." Faith walked the older woman to the door. She laid a gentle hand on her arm. "Forgive me, Tillie, but I have to ask. Is everything all right between the two of you?" They had been married over sixty years, and were the most in love of all the couples residing at Laramie Gardens. Or so Faith had thought.

"Of course," Tillie replied, not looking Faith in the eye. She smiled and walked out.

"What a day, huh, buddy?" Faith smiled down at her infant son—and he *was* her son in every way that counted.

Quinn cooed back at her nonsensically. She unlatched his carrier from the car-seat frame and lifted him out of the rear-passenger compartment of her SUV.

Not only had they been at Laramie Gardens longer than usual—a full eight hours that day—but the senior home had also been slightly understaffed, due to the holiday the day before.

"And what was all that with Tillie Tarrant?" Faith asked Quinn as she shifted her diaper bag/carryall over one arm, and carried him up the steps to the front porch that was going to need to be decorated for Christmas soon. "Why in the world is she even thinking about moving to separate quarters?"

Quinn gazed up at her and kicked his feet and waved his arms. He babbled some more.

Faith chuckled. "I wish I knew what you were saying to me, because I feel like you have a lot of wisdom you are eager to impart."

From inside the house, Tinkerbelle barked her greeting. "Coming, Tink!" she yelled to her pet, who was now jumping up to look out the living-room windows.

As Faith hurried to unlock the front door, a vehicle motor sounded behind her.

She turned to see Zach emerging from the rented

white pickup truck he had been driving the day before. His expression serious, he moved toward her, clad in a flannel shirt, sneakers and sturdy work boots. *Uh-oh*, Faith thought, as inside the house Tinkerbelle continued barking even more frantically.

Gallant as ever, Zach moved quickly to assist. "Let me give you a hand with that," he said, reaching out to hold the carrier while she unlocked the door. Tinkerbelle came rushing out. Bypassing Faith altogether and going straight for Zach, she jumped up, putting her little front feet on his shins.

"I am so sorry!" Faith said.

Tinkerbelle's tail wagged even harder.

Zach handed her Quinn, and then hunkered down to give her pet a proper hello. He talked to her terrier in a low, soothing voice and scratched her behind the ears. She settled immediately. Which was no surprise, Faith thought. Had she been tenderly stroked by those big, strong hands, she would be a sudden puddle of relaxation, too. But then she pushed away the unwarranted thought. Given the tenuous situation, and their hot, passionate kiss the night before, she definitely should not be noticing how sexy he was!

Forcing a polite smile, she resurrected the usual barriers around her heart. As their eyes met, she felt another lightning bolt of chemistry arc between them. "I didn't think we were supposed to see each other today."

He rose slowly, towering over her once again. Never once breaking their locked gazes. "I got the test results."

Faith's knees wobbled suddenly.

She had known the DNA results could come in sooner since Gabe had put a rush on them. She just hadn't expected they would come *this* quickly.

And, hence, hadn't bothered to prepare herself emotionally, either way.

Zach slid a hand beneath her elbow and used the other to steady the carrier. "You want to sit out here on the porch or go inside?" he asked kindly. The inscrutable look on his face gave her no clue as to what he had found out.

"Inside," she said briskly, as his eyes continued roving over her, as if measuring her mood.

Reassuring herself she could handle whatever the paternity results were, she drew a deep, enervating breath. Then added matter-of-factly, "It's a little damp and chilly out here for Quinn."

"Right."

They moved through the portal, his big body overshadowing hers. "Do you mind if I get him out of this, and let him stretch his arms and legs a bit?"

"Not at all."

Zach watched as she put the carrier next to the quilt she had spread out on the living-room floor. A multi-arched infant play gym held lots of colorful toys for him to admire and touch.

Faith turned on the music box that went with it, and sat down beside her son, her skirt as far down toward her knees as she could manage, her legs tucked to one side. Her pulse racing with anxiety, she turned her attention back to Zach. "So?" she said.

Zach punched a few buttons on his phone before handing it over. She saw the email notification from the laboratory that had conducted the DNA tests. "Ninety-nine-point-nine percent positive chance of a match."

He moved to sit on an ottoman, opposite them. Then

he leaned forward, his hands clasped between his spread knees. "Yeah." He was looking at her, not Quinn.

Faith's heart was suddenly beating so hard she felt it would fly out of her chest. "So…?" Her voice was dry.

"So—" he paused, treading more carefully now "—I've been thinking all day about what we should do."

Sensing there was something behind that faint glimmer of purposefulness and outward cool, she repeated, even more casually, "We?"

"Yeah. *We*," he affirmed with a brief shake of his handsome head. "'Cause the bottom line is, I'm still in the service. You're still his mom. And you still want to go forward with your adoption, correct?"

What was he getting at? Trying not to think what his deep, masculine voice did to rev up her insides, Faith drew a cautious breath and kept her gaze locked with his. "Yes."

His attention drifted over her son, then returned to her. "So why don't we go with that plan, and raise Quinn together?" he asked.

In his line of work, Zach was used to making decisions on the fly. Improvise, adapt and overcome were his mantras. Faith Lockhart, however, was not in the service, and clearly didn't operate that way.

For a moment, she didn't appear to take a breath or even move a muscle. Slowly, she got to her feet. Glided a slight distance away from Quinn, who was merrily batting at the toys dangling down from the padded crossbars of his play gym.

As if afraid he might understand what was being discussed, she folded her arms. Looked over at Zach, and murmured, "You want me to continue with my plans to foster-adopt?"

Zach nodded. He'd had time to give it a lot of thought. "That way you can be his mom, and I'll be his dad, legally. We don't have to be married to do that. And then he would have two parents who love him and want what's best for him."

She peered at him again, this time beneath a fringe of thick, strawberry-blond lashes. "And you would be okay with me being a permanent part of Quinn's life?" Her eyes glittered, as if she wasn't sure if he was leading her on or not.

He wasn't.

Although his instinct was to take her in his arms and comfort her with a hug, he remained where he was. "I would welcome it." He crossed his arms, too. "That way I wouldn't have to worry about what would happen to Quinn if something happened to me. Because he'd have you, and your entire extended family. So, no matter what, he would be okay."

Finally, she took a breath. He could see her experience as a military spouse coming into play. "That makes sense."

He spread his hands. "This way we all get what we want. Nobody has to lose out."

Faith began to pace. The action drew his attention to what nice legs she had. Slim, sexy.

She came close enough for him to catch a whiff of her sun-drenched wildflower scent. "When you are stateside, are you going to want to have custody of him, or…?" Her tone was soft. Wary. And far too enticing.

"Nope." He caught her palm and gave it a brief, reassuring squeeze. "You are his mother. He lives with you."

She arched a delicate eyebrow.

His palm still imprinted with the soft, silky feel of her skin, he continued like the upstanding man he had been raised to be. "I'll just come and visit whenever I can. You won't ever have to worry about me trying to take him away from you because I won't do that, Faith. Not ever."

To his relief, she seemed to take him at his word.

She squared her shoulders, all business, as she moved away again. "Okay, then. Do you want to go see an attorney together? In advance of the court date Quinn and I already have on Monday? Or would you rather have your own counsel?"

He mirrored her pragmatic tone. "It's probably better if we use the same lawyer, don't you think? Since we've decided to raise him together?"

The corners of her soft lips tilted thoughtfully. "Probably. I'll call my attorney, Liz Cartwright-Anderson. See if maybe she can fit us in tomorrow morning or even later this evening. Depending on what all is involved in terms of paperwork."

Happy this was working out so easily, Zach gave Quinn one last lingering look. Then, doing his best to keep his emotions in check, he said, "Great. And if she can't do it, then we'll find someone else to do my part of the petition over at WTWA." Military always helped other military. No matter the difficulty or time frame.

Her pretty emerald-green eyes widened. "You went there today?"

He nodded. And had felt immediately, completely, at home. "For a while. Then I ended up helping construct a wheelchair ramp for a returning vet, at his residence."

She looked at him approvingly. "Hence the clothes."

He didn't need to think about what it would be like if he ever felt as at home here with her and the baby, as he had at WTWA or with his SEAL team. 'Cause shared child or no, it wasn't likely to ever happen. Not without a great deal of effort, and he wasn't going to be around long enough to try.

And he especially didn't need her looking at him like he was some sort of heaven-sent angel. He ran the flat of his palm across the bottom of his jaw. "Yep. Well, listen, I've got to run." He'd made sure he had concrete plans so this "meeting" wouldn't drag on. "I'm seeing some of the guys there for dinner." Where talk would be about past and future tours of duty. Not emotionally messy matters of the heart.

"Have fun. And, Zach? Thank you for being so decent about all of this."

"No problem." With one last glance at Quinn, he left. Albeit with a heavy heart. But if he hadn't made a hasty exit, there was no guarantee he wouldn't fall victim to the palpable chemistry sparking between them and kiss her again. Now that they knew the facts, this situation was going to be complicated enough as it was, without bringing passion into the mix.

"I understand why you want to join forces, in search of a solution, but I'll be frank. I'm not sure Judge Priscilla Roy is going to go for this," Liz Cartwright-Anderson told them in her office the following afternoon.

Faith glanced at Zach in shared irritation. "Why wouldn't she want them to have two adoptive parents, instead of just one?" she asked.

"Especially now that I can prove I am Quinn's biological father," Zach added, more than happy to take Faith's side.

The attorney tilted her head. "Because I know Judge Roy. She's old-school. She occasionally allows a single parent to adopt a child, if she is convinced it is in the best interest of the minor, but she only grants coguardianship to married couples."

"Well, that's ridiculous!" Faith spouted.

Liz sat back. "It's how she does things."

Zach resisted the urge to reach over and take Faith's hand. But just barely. "Can't we ask for another judge?" he asked.

Another grim shake of Liz's head. "I'm afraid Judge Roy is it for family court in Laramie County."

Improvise. Adapt. Overcome. "What if we were to move our request to another county then?"

"Can't. Quinn and Faith reside here. Plus, Quinn is under the jurisdiction of Laramie County Department of Children and Family Services. So whatever happens, it's going to be decided in her courtroom."

Faith looked at Zach. "Then you and I will just have to make a very strong case."

Although Liz made it clear that she still wasn't sure that would work, she reluctantly agreed with their plan of action. Mitzy Martin-McCabe—the social worker handling Quinn's case—had to be notified of the paternity results, and so did Judge Roy. Liz said it would be best to do that during the hearing already set for Monday morning.

So Zach spent the rest of the weekend putting together character references and his military résumé. Faith did the same for herself. Adding to what she had already accrued. And both of them hoped for the best.

* * *

They all had agreed they would meet outside the courtroom, prior to the hearing. Because Quinn needed another last-minute diaper change, Faith and her son were the last to arrive.

Liz was in her typical gray attorney suit and heels.

Zach was wearing his military uniform. He looked ruggedly handsome. Admirably strong.

Faith had selected an equally serious navy dress with matching blazer. Low-heeled pumps. Between the two of them, Quinn looked adorable in his pram. He had a pacifier clipped to his red holiday sweater-suit, and he kept spitting it out so he could smile. And there was a hanging mobile strapped to the hood, to keep him occupied.

They wheeled him into the courtroom and took a seat at the table next to Liz.

Judge Priscilla Roy listened to their joint request for coguardianship. Then she reviewed their references, along with the DCFS report on Quinn's fostering by Faith, and got caught up to speed on Zach's unexpected entry into their lives.

In her black robe, with her glasses perched on the end of her nose, the dark-haired judge cut an imposing figure as she glared at Zach. "So you only learned you might be Quinn Lantz's father several weeks ago when you discovered your ex-girlfriend was pregnant when she moved out of state."

"Right."

Liz interjected, "Your Honor, with all due respect, it wasn't Lieutenant Callahan's fault that Annette Lantz did not tell him she was pregnant."

Judge Roy drew her glasses down farther on the

bridge of her nose and peered at Zach. "But maybe there was a reason why she didn't want him to have that information?"

If there was, Faith had yet to see it. He had been nothing but kind, courteous and responsible.

"I would have married her immediately, had I known she was carrying my child, Your Honor," Zach said.

"Out of duty?" the judge queried.

Zach squared his shoulders. "Because it is the right thing to do. Every child needs two parents. At least, whenever it's possible. And had I known, it would have been the case."

Judge Roy looked at Faith. "What about you, Mrs. Lockhart-Hewitt? Are you comfortable with Lieutenant Callahan crashing your plans to foster-adopt?"

Faith blinked. While she had been warned this judge was a tough cookie, she hadn't been prepared for her to be this blunt. But maybe it was good they get it all out in the open. "I understand Zach feels it is his duty to take responsibility for his son."

Another eyebrow lift. "So the two of you are on a first-name basis."

"Um..." What was the *right* answer here? She didn't know for sure, but her gut told her it was the one that contained the truth, and nothing but the truth! "Yes..." Faith said, forcing out the affirmation.

"Well..." The judge took her glasses all the way off. "Here's what I think. You just found out how many days ago that Quinn Lantz was actually your son?"

"Three," Zach admitted.

"And in that time you have decided to petition this court to co-adopt said son with a woman you also just met how many days ago...?"

"Five."

"And you think that is a laudable thing to be doing?" Judge Roy pressed.

"Yes. I do."

"Why?" she asked.

"I'm a Navy SEAL."

"So stated earlier."

"I am often deployed overseas for months at a time," Zach explained. "Which means I am going to need someone to help care for Quinn in my absence."

"And you don't have any family willing to do this for you?" the judge asked.

Sadness briefly etched Zach's expression. "No."

Again, the judge looked skeptical. She waved her glasses. "Have you asked?"

Faith watched as Zach tensed again. "No," he said.

This did not sit well, Faith noted.

"Why not?" Judge Roy asked.

Zach's broad shoulders flexed. "Because my parents are divorced and both remarried and busy with their new families and careers. Plus, honestly, I think my folks are both too old to take on a baby, since they are in their early sixties."

His reasoning made sense.

Judge Roy squinted. "So Faith Lockhart-Hewitt is it."

Zach nodded, his expression even more resolute. "She's been caring for Quinn since his mother was killed in an accident. She loves him. He loves her. As far as he knows, she is his mother. And she already was set to adopt him. So it makes perfect sense to me—to us—for the two of us to do this together."

Judge Roy rocked back in her chair. Only partially mollified. "Well, Lieutenant, it might be convenient *now*, but who knows what it will feel like a few months down the road, when one of you falls in love with someone else. And wants to raise Quinn with your new spouse."

Zach's gaze narrowed. "That's not going to happen," he declared flatly.

"I agree," Faith interjected. "Quinn is my number one priority now. And that's not going to change!" she said passionately.

Judge Roy's brow lifted in concern.

"And, of course, I'll be there for Zach," she added. "The way I would for any other deployed serviceman or -woman."

Liz stepped in. "Your Honor, I know this is unconventional, but we've talked to DCFS. They have no objections."

Judge Roy looked at Mitzy Martin-McCabe. One of Laramie County's best social workers. "Is this true?"

Mitzy nodded. "Quinn is doing well. Faith already had plans to adopt. Zach's job keeps him away for long periods of time, yet he wants to be fiscally and morally responsible for his son. So, yes, in our view, it is the best option. Even if it is unconventional."

"I don't agree," Judge Roy said, overruling everyone. "I think this situation bears a lot more consideration before anything permanent is done. So, I am going to require Lieutenant Zach Callahan to take full legal custody of his son for at least one year, before allowing anyone else to join him in the petition."

Zach raised his hand, seeing permission to speak.

The judge nodded.

"Your Honor, I'm going to be deployed again in less than a month. I need someone to help me take care of my son. And I'd like that to be Faith. For her to keep caring for him, exactly as she has been for the last four months."

Judge Roy put her glasses back on and slid them all the way up her nose. "Do you want your son to stay a ward of the court, in foster care?"

"No!" Zach said. "I want to claim full legal custody."

Judge Roy announced flatly, "That's not going to happen. Not today."

"Your Honor," Liz interjected, "he only has until December twenty-sixth..."

"Then be back in my courtroom at 2:00 p.m. on Monday, December twenty-first. And we will revisit the issue. In the meantime, Lieutenant, it's up to you to figure out who is going to take care of your son while you are deployed, and under what conditions. And it is up to social services to make sure that aforementioned plan is acceptable, before they allow Quinn to formally exit the foster-care system."

"What about me, Your Honor?" Faith asked, her voice suddenly sounding very small, even to her own ears. "And *my* petition to foster-adopt?"

Judge Roy frowned. "It's denied."

Faith blinked in shock. Of all the outcomes she had imagined for today, this had not been one of them. "Can I at least continue fostering Quinn while the lieutenant is deployed?"

Judge Roy looked at Mitzy. "That is up to your social worker and DCFS." She paused. "I trust them to delve into this matter and do what is best for all concerned."

Chapter Five

"Is now a good time for us to talk?" Zach asked, at eight thirty that evening.

Actually, Faith couldn't imagine there ever being a good time. Given what had happened in the courtroom that very morning. But Quinn's future was at stake. Plus, she had known after the abrupt way they parted after the hearing that he would eventually seek her out to talk about the baby, so she might as well get it over with. Noting, like her, that he had changed into jeans and a much-washed flannel shirt, she waved him in reluctantly. "It's as good as any other, I guess. But you have to keep it down," she warned grumpily, glaring at him. The emotions she had been suppressing appeared in a burst of maternal protectiveness. "Quinn just went down for the night."

Zach's gaze narrowed at her dark tone. "Oh, that's me, all right," he drawled. "A wild party a minute. A real threat to domestic tranquility and all womankind."

Whoa. Poke the lion and he might poke back. "Sorry," she apologized automatically. Aware that he was the last person she should pick a fight with, she said, "I didn't mean to snap at you, or take Judge Roy's decision out on you. It's not your fault she thought co-guardianship was a bad idea."

Zach followed her over to the dining-room table,

where she had been busy weaving strands of evergreen through a circular metal frame.

Hands jammed on his waist, he looked down at the half-made wreath. "I think her point was that everything has been happening awfully fast."

As if Faith didn't know that! "Well, sometimes that's the way they happen," she blurted before she could stop herself. "Like the death of my husband. That morning, when Harm went off to work, he was alive. That afternoon, he was at the hospital, and he was gone. This morning I was set to foster-adopt Quinn." Hot, angry tears welled behind her eyes. Furiously, she held them back. "But now, this evening, I have to think about the fact that I may only have a few more weeks with him."

Zach sauntered nearer. "And why would that be?"

Faith tried not to focus on how close his big, muscular body was to hers. And instead reminded herself he was actually the source of all her current problems! She eased back into the chair where she had been sitting, and glared up at him, feeling a renewed wave of annoyance as she surveyed his cool, calm demeanor. "Were you not at the hearing?"

He circled the dining-room table and sat opposite her. "Judge Roy didn't deny my claims of paternity." He shifted in his chair, his denim-clad knees accidentally bumping hers, before he pulled away. "She just wanted to see the plan for caring for Quinn, when I am deployed again, before she officially releases him from foster care."

Faith wove more evergreen strands through the wire frame, her fingertips occasionally getting jabbed by the sharp ends of the needles. "Please tell me you're not asking me to be his nanny," she huffed. "After I just lost my chance to be his forever mommy." She tore her eyes away from the neatness of his short dark hair, his clean-shaven jaw.

"Nope."

Okay, that hurt. She really thought he was going to ask her that. "Then…?"

He gave her a contemplative look. "I'd like you to be my wife."

For a moment the entire world stopped. Tilted on its axis. Finally, after several long beats, Faith was able to take a breath. "Could you repeat that?" she asked, aghast.

He rested his forearms on the table. "I'm proposing the two of us get married. Hopefully by the end of the week."

"I know that kiss we shared last week was hot but I'm *not* going to sleep with you."

He shot her a curious look. As if surprised her first thought had gone in that direction. "If we got hitched, I wouldn't expect you to share a bed with me," he told her dryly. "Unless—" he sat all the way back in his chair, the muscles in his broad shoulders stretching the soft flannel of his shirt "—you wanted to…"

Faith sat back, too. She could not believe her out-of-control day felt any more impossible than it previously had, but it did. "You are not making any sense."

His forehead creased. "I went over to the West Texas Warriors office today and talked to the retired JAG lawyer there who helps out current and retired military with all their legal problems. He agreed to finalize the paternity claim for me, and he also went over all the benefits with me, so I can get those in order before I leave, for Quinn, *and* you, if you agree to marry me."

She flushed beneath his quick but potent scrutiny, then went back to working on the wreath. "So we'd be doing this for military benefits?"

He shook his head, his expression grim. "No, that would be illegal and unethical. We would be doing this for the same reason two people who unexpectedly find themselves pregnant often do. We would be setting aside our own needs to focus on the good of the child. Which means providing a secure and stable family environment for Quinn to grow up in. And we would do that by getting married."

His idea was beginning to make sense. Except... "Judge Roy is not going to go for that," she predicted anxiously.

A fierce look of protectiveness washed over his face. "She can't deny my claim of paternity," he growled.

Finished with the evergreen boughs, Faith reached for a silver-edged pinecone, already outfitted with a green twist tie. "Yes, but—"

"All she required from me legally today is that I satisfy DCFS—or the social worker assigned to Quinn's case—that I have an excellent plan for him while I am deployed." He reached across the table and took her hands in his, squeezing them encouragingly. "*You* are that plan. Not as a coguardian as we would have preferred. But as my wife and Quinn's stepmother. And eventually his adoptive mother. Plus, you will be named his guardian in the event anything does happen to me while I am serving overseas. So any way you look at it, it's a win-win situation for the three of us."

Oh, my god—this is too good to be true. The hope that had been eluding her most of the day rose once again. For both their sakes, though, she forced herself to examine the potential pitfalls, just as Judge Roy had. Luxuriating in the warmth and strength of his hands on hers, she asked, "What if you fall in love with someone else?"

He shrugged, telling her that wasn't a problem, at least not in his estimation. He let go of her. "What if you do?"

Not an answer. She picked up a red velvet ribbon and began fashioning it into a big bow. Her fingers trembled slightly as she worked. "I'm done with marriage." She hadn't been any good at it. She didn't want to fail at a relationship again. Or worse, feel incessantly guilty because she couldn't seem to figure out how to make her husband happy. Never mind want to be with her, above all else!

He let out a short, mirthless laugh. "Well, I've never been interested in going there at all."

"Until now," she corrected, with a cool lift of her brow.

Just as matter-of-fact, he countered, "Only as a practical arrangement. For the benefit of *our* son. And he *is* your son, Faith. You are as much a mother to him as Annette was, and I know if she were still with us that she would want you to raise him in her absence as much as I do. So what do you say?" He folded his arms in front of him. "Will you marry me?"

If it meant being able to continue caring for Quinn? In a heartbeat. But leery of doing anything else that could cause her to lose out on the opportunity to be Quinn's mommy, she forced herself to slow down. "We have to talk to Mitzy first."

"And if the social worker okays our solution?"

"Then—" Faith gulped, barely able to believe she

was brave enough to take this leap, yet again, never mind to a military man "—my answer is, indeed, yes!"

"What do you think of our plan?" Faith asked, early the next morning.

Mitzy—who had agreed to meet them in her DCFS office for emergency counseling—sat back in her chair. As the devoted mother of quadruplet sons, and happily married to Chase McCabe, she was known for her huge heart and practical nature.

"Well, it has a lot of the same laudable components your coguardianship petition had, but marriage takes it to a whole new level."

"In a good way or bad?" Zach asked.

"Both," Mitzy admitted.

Knowing her own social-worker mom would agree with her colleague, Faith said fiercely, "It's still the right thing to do."

"We both agree on that," Zach added, reaching over to squeeze her hand.

The gesture did not go unnoticed by either woman in the room.

"You may be right," Mitzy said, her attention then moving to the baby.

Faith offered Quinn—who was starting to get a little restless in his car seat—a new rattle for one hand and a soft toy for the other. Quinn gurgled happily and she smiled, pivoting back to the adults.

"But before I put the DCFS stamp of approval on this union," Mitzy continued, "I'm going to need to see a complete plan on how it's all going to work. Including when Zach is deployed. And especially when he is not."

Faith pulled a notepad and pen from her bag, and began to take notes.

"I also need to see how you intend to handle the finances of the union. Plus, a parenting plan for Quinn."

"What do you mean by that?" Zach asked.

"Basically, how you plan to bring him up. Public school or private. Religion. Bedtimes. What rules you will have up to age five, and what you will do if he breaks said rules."

"Isn't this overkill?" Zach protested. "He's five months old!"

Mitzy nodded. Not backing down in the slightest.

Faith stopped taking notes long enough to turn to Zach. "But we're preparing to do this for a lifetime. So it makes sense we would put ourselves through what is essentially premarital and preparenting counseling."

A soldier's stoicism came into his sea-blue eyes. "All right. I see your point."

"Then when it comes to the actual marriage—" Mitzy continued.

"It's going to be in name only," Faith added quickly.

Zach gave Faith a curious look. Making her wonder if they were indeed in agreement about that.

The social worker lifted a hand. "You don't need to explain to me or the court the private details of your impending marriage. As long as you are both on the same page in regard to whatever the situation is."

Faith wasn't sure what to write down about that, so she wrote *Sex* with a line through the word and a question mark after it.

Mitzy added, "Another home study is also going to be required. This one involving Zach. I'm going to want assurances that he knows how to care for Quinn on his own and that father and son have bonded appropriately. I'll give you two weeks—slightly more if you feel you need it—to get things organized for that."

Zach listened seriously while Mitzy made a few notes of her own.

"When were you planning to get married?" the social worker asked.

"By Friday," he said.

Which was awfully optimistic, Faith thought.

Mitzy made another note, then looked at Zach. "Parents coming into town?"

His demeanor was mystifyingly inscrutable. "We haven't worked that out yet."

"What about yours, Faith? What do they think of all this?"

Oh, Lord. "Um. I haven't run it by them yet. As you know," she said, "my mom and I put up a fire wall between us over every aspect related to me becoming a foster parent." Aware Zach wasn't following, she turned to him and explained, "We didn't want there to be any question of impropriety, since my mom works for the department."

Zach blinked. "She does?"

"Yes. She's a social worker, too."

"And a very good one I might add," Mitzy chimed in with a smile. "But fire wall aside, Faith, you are going to have to talk to your folks about this. Same with you, Zach. And it would be advisable to do so together, even if it's only by FaceTime."

Seeing they both were about to protest the necessity of this—after all, they were both adults, free to do as they pleased!—the social worker held up a hand. "If you want the court and DCFS to take your union seriously, then you-all are going to have to show the appropriate decorum. That means no eloping at the bait-and-tackle shop near Lake Laramie."

Where a number of famous McCabe and Lockhart hasty weddings had taken place.

"Both your families have to know your plan, and have a chance to weigh in," Mitzy concluded soberly. "Plus, you should probably consider sharing space for a few days before you say 'I do.' Just to make sure you are going to be compatible in that sense, as well."

"And if we're not?" Faith asked, not entirely sure what it would be like to have a ruggedly sexy man like Zach living in her cozy abode.

Frowning, the other woman advised, "I think it would be a problem. Perhaps not an insurmountable one, but it would certainly make things a lot more difficult given Judge Roy's dissenting view on coguardianships outside the realm of a normal, traditional marriage."

"But does she really have the right to even weigh in on that?" Faith blurted out before she could stop herself.

Calmly, Mitzy affirmed, "The judge's role in this situation is the same as mine. Our first priority is assuring the safety and well-being of the child."

Which Zach had done, Faith thought.

"Our second priority," she continued, "is to ensure conditions that will support and nurture stable family foundations. For said child..."

Although Faith wanted to argue she had already done all that, and *more*, on her own, Zach accepted the social worker's orders as readily as if she had been one of his commanding officers. "If we do all that, can we count on your support?" he asked.

"We'll have to see what happens in the next few weeks. As well as how the home study goes," Mitzy said.

With a last tender smile at Quinn, Mitzy rose to show them out. Seeming to realize how confused Faith was, Mitzy finished with her trademark practicality. "People get married for the sake of the children all the time." She paused to look both Faith and Zach right in the eye. "Some make it work. Some don't." She opened her office door. "Time will tell which category you-all fall into."

"That went better and worse than expected," Faith said as they walked out to the parking lot. It had seemed silly to use both their vehicles for such a short distance, so they had taken her SUV.

"Better how?" Zach held the infant carrier between them while they walked.

"Mitzy didn't say 'no how, no way' to our marriage plan."

Zach must have read the despair in her voice because his eyes softened as they searched her face. "And worse?" he prodded.

"Because of all the things we are now going to be required to do," she admitted ruefully, liking the way it felt to have him next to her, "to prove this isn't just a lark on our part."

"Like...?"

"Living together!" She shot him an exasperated look. "Can you believe she suggested we share space?"

He was so close she could feel the warmth emanating from his large body. Even with a baby carrier in hand, he had a sexy don't-mess-with-me look. "It's not such a big deal."

To her it was. After she'd ventured out on her own, she had never lived with a man except her husband. She and Harm had even waited until they were formally hitched to share a bed. Not that she and Zach were ever going to be doing that…

He shrugged, looking as relaxed and capable as ever. "I bunk with people I just met all the time. Most of us become lifelong friends."

Somehow she didn't think this was the same thing. "You're talking about your SEAL teammates?"

He regarded her with utter certainty. "And my roommates, back when I was in college. The two of us living in the same house from time to time doesn't have to be a big deal, Faith, unless we want it to be. And I *don't*."

Okay, that came out wrong, Zach thought. He could tell by the shocked look on Faith's face that he had hurt her feelings. Probably made her think that she—not the situation they found themselves in—was inconsequential. He cleared his throat. Tried again. "What I meant was…"

She brushed by him, her head held high. "I get what you meant, Zach."

"Actually, I don't think you do," he countered, as the tension between them rose.

Soft lips twisting into a pretty glower, she folded her arms in front of her. "We may be Quinn's coparents, and husband and wife in the eyes of the law, but as far as you and I are concerned, all we will ever be is casual friends. If that."

He moved nearer despite himself. Aware he was suddenly wanting to kiss her again, *badly*, he rasped, "Or… increasingly good ones."

"Whatever," Faith huffed, pushing a hand through her strawberry-blond waves, tousling them even more. "We just have to find a way to make all this go smoothly. But right now, I am late for work…so we have to get a move on." She picked up her pace as they threaded through the cars in the parking lot.

"Got it." He moved more swiftly with her, being careful not to jostle the infant he was carrying.

Faith opened up the back passenger door of her SUV. She set her carryall and diaper bag on the floor, then turned back to catch Zach gazing raptly down at Quinn.

"You want to put him in the vehicle?" she asked.

Zach hesitated.

"You have to learn. Now is as good a time as any."

Nodding stiffly, he settled the carrier into the base of the safety seat. After showing him how to latch it properly, she gave Quinn his pacifier and a kiss on the temple, as had become custom. Then she shut the door and went around to climb behind the wheel.

Zach climbed into the front passenger seat. He figured he might as well bite the bullet. "How about I go to work with you today? And start learning how to take care of Quinn, while you and people like Miss Mim are there to supervise."

Faith knew it was a good idea. Practical. Especially given the time constraints they were under. Still, she felt an unexpected stab of jealousy at the mention of Miss Mim. She was Quinn's mommy now. She was going to be Zach's wife. Albeit in name only. Shouldn't she be the one who should teach him about caring for his infant son?

On the other hand, maybe it would be easier, less

intimate, this way. And that would be good. Because intimacy made her think about throwing caution to the wind and kissing him again.

"Plus, it would be a good time to start spreading the news about our plans," Zach said as she backed out of the parking space. "Make it common knowledge that we're planning to get hitched ASAP. On account of our mutual love and concern for Quinn."

Faith put the car in Drive and headed out to the stop sign. When they had halted, she turned and sent him a chastising glance. "That makes it sound a little… romantic. Don't you, think, soldier?"

He grinned at her use of the faux endearment. He moved his eyebrows playfully. "Idealistic, maybe. But who says dreams can't come true? Or that we can't go into this situation with the very best of intentions and end up having something completely great happen as a result?"

Something great. Unbidden, the picture of a happy family of three came to mind. Aware there was no one behind her, she kept her foot on the brake and stayed right where they were. "Like…" she prodded, hardly daring to breathe.

"Us becoming a really great family team."

And just like that, her spirits fell like a rock. She should have known in the end it would be all about teams formed out of necessity. SEALs were famous for their attachments to their units. Of course, the soldiers had to be close. Their very lives depended on it. She supposed in a sense, Quinn's future and theirs did, too.

"A team, right," Faith murmured, irritated she had thought, for one really foolish second, that Zach had been going to say something romantic. And completely impractical. Because there wouldn't be love for each other, generated by this union. At least not the typical soul-deep love harbored by a husband and wife. And if she married Zach—or *anyone* again—wouldn't it be true love that she would ultimately want?

Yet, how could she renege on his proposal, knowing that her best chance to continue being Quinn's mother was by getting hitched?

Her emotions in turmoil, she drove the short distance to Laramie Gardens in complete silence, then parked in the staff lot, close to the front entrance.

"So what do you think?" Zach peered at her closely. "You want me to meet up with you later, when we go over to apply for our wedding license? Or stay and help out with Quinn?"

There really wasn't a choice if she wanted this to work. "Stay," Faith said, smiling briskly. "Just be warned, soldier. The residents are all *very* protective of me and Quinn."

Chapter Six

Faith, Zach and Quinn were surrounded the moment they walked through the doors of Laramie Gardens.

"Oh, thank heavens you're back!" Miss Mim said.

"You can say that again." Russell Pierce adjusted his jaunty fedora. "We were all worried when you didn't come to work yesterday."

The elegantly dressed Miss Sadie added, "Oh, my dear, I am so sorry your petition to foster-adopt Quinn was denied!"

Faith blinked. She looked at Quinn, still nestled cozily in his infant seat and being carried inside by his father. "You-all know about that?"

"Of course!" Miss Patricia laid her hand over her heart.

"Word spread through Laramie County like wildfire!" Wilbur Barnes confirmed.

"I don't know what is wrong with you young fellas these days," Kurtis Kelley groused. "Waiting five months to show up to claim your child!"

Faith held up a staying hand. "Hey now. Don't blame Zach! He had no idea. He came as soon as he found out there was even the possibility he had sired a son."

"And now you know for sure?" Buck Franklin asserted with a lifted eyebrow.

Zach nodded. He looked down at Quinn tenderly. "This little fella is indeed my son," he said protectively.

"Well," Miss Isabelle huffed, "that's still no reason to just barge right in and take him from Faith!"

Oh, my gosh, Faith thought. She was beginning to get such a headache. "He didn't do that, either. In fact, he's doing everything possible to make sure I remain the mother in Quinn's life."

Silence fell. "So you still plan to adopt Quinn? Despite what Judge Roy decreed?" Darrell Enloe, the resident peacemaker, asked.

Well, that is the plan, she thought hopefully.

"We're taking it one step better," Zach told everyone gathered around him. "We're going to become a family." He laced a hand around her waist, pulling her close. Then smiled broadly. "I've asked Faith to marry me. And she agreed."

It was all Faith could do to hold her tongue until they were out of earshot of others. "Well, I have to hand it to you, Lieutenant, you left an entire room of seniors, who always have a ton to say, completely speechless!"

He shrugged. Watching as she got out of her coat and hung it up on the hook behind her office door.

Lips quirking, he set Quinn's carrier where she directed, on the love seat in her office. "As I mentioned before, we have to start spreading the word. And look on the bright side—nobody said we shouldn't get married."

Another spark lit between them. *"Yet."* Faith unhooked the clasp on Quinn's safety strap and eased him out of his seat. She checked his diaper, found it still dry, then handed him over to Zach. For a moment, he stood there, motionless, looking like he had just been given a live grenade and was supposed to figure out what to do with it.

He swallowed and awkwardly held out his arms. She put Quinn into them.

The first time Zach had held his son, he had been overcome with awe. And it had only been for two or three minutes while she talked on the phone. Now that he was actually going to be caring for Quinn, Zach was acting like he was holding a Fabergé egg! Both males looked incredibly uncomfortable. Her heart going out to him, since it was clear that Zach really was out of his depth here, Faith stepped in. She put her hands on his forearms, guiding them—and Quinn—closer to his body. "He needs to snuggle, feel supported here, in the torso," she explained. "And the quickest way to do that is to hold him close. Just the way you did last week."

After a while, Zach began to get the hang of it. His eyes twinkling, he flashed her that easy grin that she loved. "You mean he won't break?"

Realizing how right it felt to be parenting alongside him, she smiled back. "You're cute when you're inept, you know that?" she teased.

He chuckled.

Gazing up at Zach, Quinn chuckled, too.

And their baby's melodic giggle made all three of them laugh.

"Hey, pipe down in here!" Charge nurse Inez Garcia poked her head in the door. "What are you trying to do? Make everyone happy?"

For some reason, her words struck Quinn as riotously funny, and he giggled harder, gazing up at Zach adoringly all the while.

And that quickly, Faith knew Christmas had come early for her little boy. And maybe her, too.

"How are we doing on our list?" Faith asked Zach, later that evening, after Quinn was in bed for the night.

It had been quite a day.

Faith'd had a full slate of LG business to take care of. Meanwhile, Zach had learned how to give Quinn a bottle, change his diaper and soothe him when he needed to burp. He had also endured nonstop questioning from the seniors, who were eager to decide if he was a suitable mate for Faith or not.

In their quiet moments, during her breaks, they had also identified a string of tasks. Including the decorating of the interior of her house for Christmas. Because Faith knew everyone would question what was really going on with her if she didn't get up to speed on that!

And everything was supposed to look easy-peasy, right?

Which it would be, as long as she stayed in the holiday spirit, she thought, as she wrapped lit garlands and red velvet ribbons on the spindles of the staircase leading to the second floor.

While she worked, Zach pulled out his phone and went over the progress they'd made against the long to-do list they'd compiled. He checked items off one at a time. "We went to town hall and got our license at noon. So that's taken care of. I talked to the chaplain at WTWA, and he's agreed to marry us Friday afternoon. Location to be determined. But we can do it in his office if we want. It doesn't have to be a big deal."

Faith went to the mantel and adorned it with a lit garland, too. "Famous last words."

Zach followed along, inundating her with his brisk, masculine scent. He leaned one shoulder against the brick fireplace. "You think your family is going to object?"

Faith got out the stockings and the sterling silver holders. She hung up Tinkerbelle's on one side of hers, Quinn's on the other. Belatedly, she realized they would need one for Zach, too, and it needed to be up before the next DCFS home inspection.

She turned around to see him gazing at her admiringly. Her body tingled in response. "I'm…not sure. I mean my siblings have all adopted a live-and-let-live attitude for each other. Which is good. Because we're all pretty set in our ideas of what is and isn't right for ourselves."

"The mark of strong individuals." He shifted his gaze to her lips. "Oh, and by the way, what did your parents say when you told them of our plans?"

Faith felt herself floundering. She walked over to set up the Advent calendar on the dining-room buffet. "I, ah, didn't call them yet."

He came closer. "I thought you were going to do that while I walked Tinkerbelle for you a few minutes ago."

Zach seemed serious now, in a way that said he wanted the two of them to get closer. The heck of it was, she wanted that, too.

Not sure why it mattered to her so much that he respect her, just knowing that it *did*, she wet her parched lips with the tip of her tongue. "I decided to let the dust settle a bit. Do it when everyone has had a chance to reflect on the overall situation and emotions aren't so raw."

"Didn't your folks call you about a dozen times today?"

She turned away from the gentle rebuke in his eyes. “Half a dozen. The other seven or so texts and messages were from the sibs.”

His brow lifted. “You didn’t talk to *any* of them?”

She swung back to him, wanting him to understand this much about her, even if it tarnished his overall opinion of her. “No, I haven’t,” she admitted. “Not yet.” She drew in a quavering breath. “But they probably expected that. They all know it’s better for them to let me come to them, in my own way, and my own time. Rather than be pushed into it…”

She paused, then continued, “It goes back to when I was a foster kid,” she explained.

He touched her arm compassionately. “Something traumatic happen then?”

It would be so easy to slide into his arms. To let him cut through the barriers she had erected around her heart. But she shook her head, refusing to let herself lean on him. “You don’t want to hear about that.”

He caught her by the elbow as she glided past, and pivoted her back to face him. “Yeah, I do,” he told her solemnly. “If we’re going to be married, even if in name only, these are the kinds of things I need to know.”

Realizing he was right, Faith flushed. She pulled out a dining-room chair and sank into it. He settled in one next to her. “I was seven when my parents tragically died when the roof collapsed during a house fire. Old enough to sort of understand what happened, but not mature enough to understand the finality of death.”

He pulled up a chair so they were sitting knee-to-knee. “That must have been awful,” he said.

It had been. Faith looked down at her hands. “I kept thinking that my parents would magically appear one day and claim me, and everything would go back to normal."

"I'm sure I would have hoped for the same thing, in your place," Zach said gruffly.

The depth of his empathy helped her to continue. "In the meantime, I ended up with a really wealthy couple who desperately wanted children. Naomi and Ned were young and personable and they gave me everything a little girl could ever want."

Faith closed her eyes briefly, recalling.

"I had a big room of my own with a canopy bed and tons of toys, and a closetful of truly gorgeous dresses. For the first time in my life, I got to eat what I wanted, not what was served. It was like living in a fairy tale," she admitted ruefully, feeling guilty for how much she had enjoyed the pampering. She shook her head sadly. "And I was the princess."

Zach's knees pressed against hers. "Sounds like it." He cupped her hands. "So what was so difficult about that?"

She looked down at their entwined hands. "I think the perfection of it all kept me from grieving. Or maybe I just wasn't ready to grieve." She soaked in the warmth of his touch. "I don't know."

His grip tightened reassuringly. "When did it all catch up with you?" he asked in a low, husky tone.

"When the Lockharts came into the picture. They had already fostered and adopted four of my siblings, and they were trying to get us all back together. The courts weren't sure they could handle eight kids, and my foster parents were adamantly against it. Ned and Naomi wanted to adopt me. Initially, I thought I wanted that, too. But the psychologist and social worker involved in my case said I couldn't do that before being reunited with my siblings, and meeting Carol and Robert, and seeing how that went."

He studied her intently. "How did it go?"

Faith let out a long, careful breath. "I was extremely hostile. Seeing my siblings brought back memories of the storm and the lightning strike, and the resulting fire that led to my parents' death." She gritted her teeth. "I was angry I had to remember because I didn't want to."

Zach squeezed her hands again. "You can't blame yourself for that," he soothed.

Except she still did. And maybe always would…

"Anyway…" Aware Zach needed to hear the rest, Faith pushed on, "Ned and Naomi argued I shouldn't have to do any more family visitations. And I told the judge that was what I wanted, too. But he didn't feel that was in my best interest, and after a few more times with all my brothers and sisters, I really just wanted to go home with them to Carol and Robert's." She released a shuddering breath. "Ned and Naomi fought it. But they lost."

"And then what happened?" Zach asked grimly.

"They were offered visitation with me, but they refused."

"Wow."

"Ned and Naomi thought it would be best for all of us to make a clean break, and I think in retrospect maybe they were right. The problem was, I knew I had broken their hearts with my selfishness. And I felt terribly guilty about that."

Zach stood and wordlessly pulled her into his arms. He held her against him, stroking a hand down her spine. "You were just a kid, Faith, and a confused and traumatized one at that."

It was all she could do not to lay her head on his shoulder. With effort, she held herself slightly aloof, then pushed away altogether. "It didn't make it any easier on anyone involved." She headed for the kitchen, opened up the refrigerator and got out the orange juice.

Holding up the bottle, she sent Zach an inquiring look. He nodded, so she got out two glasses. Poured.

"What happened when you went to live with Carol and Robert?"

She handed him his. "I withdrew. The more they tried to pull me out, the deeper into my shell I went because I was afraid of hurting and disappointing them." She paused to take a small sip, then a few more. "I felt guilty for being happy to be reunited with my siblings. And for liking my new parents. Plus, in the midst of all that secret joy, I also missed Ned and Naomi terribly. I mean, it was a mess. I had to see a child therapist for a couple of years just to get all my feelings out."

He gazed at her over the rim of his glass. "But you recovered."

She released a deep breath. "As much as anyone can, who's been orphaned and through the foster-care system."

He drained his glass and set it aside. "Is that why you wanted to foster-adopt? To rescue someone who was in the same heartbreaking situation you were once in?"

Feeling a little shaky, Faith poured herself another half glass of juice and put the bottle away. "I know what it is to be a child who has been through hell and needs love and security. So, yes." She picked up her glass again, and held it in front of her like a shield. "I wanted to give back, but…" Her reasons had been selfish, too. "I also wanted a permanent family. Although to be perfectly honest, I'm not sure I could go through what Ned and Naomi did with me, and then sign up to do it all over again."

Zach settled opposite her, his back to the island, his hands braced on either side of him. "Is that what they did?"

"No. Last I heard, they permanently shelved plans to adopt. And instead embraced the child-free life."

He studied her. "You still feel remorseful about not choosing them?"

Faith took another enervating sip of the tart liquid before forcing herself to look right at Zach. "I feel bad about my selfishness and what it did to everyone involved," she admitted morosely. "I've tried not to ever be so self-centered again. To always be fair to others, and think about their feelings, wants and needs, too."

A reflective silence fell between them. "Which is why you agreed to marry me so quickly," Zach finally stated.

She nodded, her heart going out to him. "I know how you must feel about doing the right, honorable thing for all three of us. Because I feel the same way. I also know in the deepest recesses of my soul that Quinn needs both of us. So, yes, if you hadn't asked me to marry you, I probably would have put forth a proposal myself."

Zach was happy to hear he and Faith were of the same mind when it came to the future of their "family." Knowing he wasn't pressuring her into anything certainly lessened his own guilt over coming into the situation five months in and messing up her plans, after she had given her heart and soul to his son.

Wishing the situation had been different and he could take her in his arms and kiss her again, he said, "Well, I'm sorry you went through all that."

For a moment, she looked as if she wanted him to hug her, too. "That's life, right?" She pulled herself together and moved away. "Bad stuff happens to everyone. It's just a matter of which bad stuff, when."

He grinned. So true. "Speaking of potentially difficult moments..."

Faith wrinkled her nose. "Uh-oh." She picked up the wreath and its metal holder, complete with jingle bells, and headed for the front hall. Then eased open the door quietly and centered the wreath she'd made on the beautiful Craftsman-style wooden door. "I'm not sure I like the sound of that."

He followed her back inside. "I have two FaceTime calls set up with my folks. The first is going to start in about two minutes."

"What? *Tonight?*" She spun around so quickly her shoulder hit the center of his chest.

He put out a hand to steady her. "Don't worry. I gave them a heads-up earlier on email. So they know about Quinn, and that we've decided to get married ASAP."

There was a long moment of silence. She looked like she didn't know whether to faint or slug him. Finally, she said, "Are they upset?"

Aware he was still holding on to her arm, he dropped his grasp and stepped back so he was no longer invading her personal space. Not that she had seemed to mind, he noted happily. "I'm sure they will tell me if they are. Neither of my parents has ever held back on what they think."

Some of the color left her cheeks.

"Don't worry," he soothed. "If anyone is less than chill, I'll take the phone and go in the other room." No way was he going to let anyone give her a hard time. Not after all she had done to ensure he would have no difficulty in gaining custody of their son.

And Quinn was *theirs*. He was realizing that more and more every minute.

She touched a hand to the tousled strands of her hair, embarrassed. "Zach, I can't meet your parents, even virtually. I'm a mess! My makeup has all worn off, and I haven't brushed my hair since this morning!" Then she looked down at her oversize denim shirt and black leggings. "Plus, I've got spit-up and drool on my shirt!"

And yet he had never seen her look more beautiful. So sweetly maternal and feminine. The phone rang.

Zach handed her a burp cloth from the top of the laundry basket of clean baby clothes, still waiting to be taken upstairs. "Here." He motioned for her to drape it over her shoulder. "You can use that to cover it up."

He hit Accept. His dad's face came on the screen. Ezekiel Callahan was sitting at the desk in the study of his Washington, DC, home, still in his army uniform. Which meant he had just gotten home. "Zachary," the general growled with his usual gruffness.

It was all Zach could do not to salute. "Sir."

Ezekiel's gaze narrowed. "I understand congratulations are in order."

"That's correct." Zach moved so he was standing next to Faith, and they were both on screen.

Sensing she needed reassurance, which was no surprise given his dad's imposing nature, he wrapped his arm around her waist. Pulled her in close, and said, "Dad, I'd like you to meet Faith Lockhart. The woman I told you about in my email. Quinn's foster and adoptive mother. Faith, this is my dad, Brigadier General Callahan."

"No need to stand on ceremony, son. You can call me Ezekiel," he told Faith.

Although Zach could sense her unease, she managed to appear laudably composed. "Hello, sir."

Ezekiel sobered. "So. You are all right with this solution? The situation being more practical than romantic?"

Faith flashed another smile, this one both purposeful and frank. "Absolutely."

The general surveyed her critically. "What about being a military wife? Are you up for the challenge of that? Because Zachary has quite the career ahead of him and I'd hate to see anything derail that."

Zach answered, "She's had experience with that, Dad. Her late husband was a SEAL, too."

"Killed in the line of duty?"

Faith hesitated, then replied, "No, sir. After he got out. In an accident."

Ezekiel nodded, compassionate as ever in the wake of loss. "I'm sorry to hear that, Faith," he told her kindly.

"Thank you."

An awkward silence fell. Ezekiel cleared his throat, then turned his attention to Zach. "Where's the boy?" he demanded without preamble.

"Sleeping, Dad. We'll let you meet him virtually another time."

"Excellent," Ezekiel said crisply. "Looking forward to it. So when are these nuptials taking place?"

"Friday."

"In Arlington, Virginia?" he asked.

"Laramie, Texas."

For the first time since they had started talking, disappointment flashed across his father's face. "Sorry, son. I have to be in DC. I'm not going to be able to make it."

Zach nodded. The military was a jealous mistress. "I understand. We'll send pictures."

"See that you do," Ezekiel ordered gruffly. He offered his congratulations again and signed off.

"Well, I guess that went okay," Faith said.

It actually had, Zach thought in surprise, a little disappointed his dad couldn't make it to the wedding. Even though he had assumed that would be the case. His personal phone dinged again, with another FaceTime call request. "And there is my mom, Rosalyn, some twenty minutes early."

Not surprisingly, his mother was dressed in a beautiful silk dress, and was also wearing diamond earrings, a necklace and a tennis bracelet. The hum of voices and soft music in the background, along with the number of lights spilling out of her Arlington, Virginia, mansion, told him she and her CEO husband were throwing another party. This one, holiday-themed. She was standing outside, talking to him on the stone terrace…

"Hey, Mom," he said, bracing himself for her unhappy reaction. She didn't like being cut out of the loop on anything. When she was, she tended to get very persnickety.

"Zachary."

Man, he had always hated that tone from her. "If this is a bad time…" he began.

Rosalyn arched an elegantly shaped eyebrow. "Don't you dare hang up on me, after making me wait all day!"

Determined to make this as easy as possible on all of them, Zach cut to the chase. He moved in close to Faith and turned the phone toward them, and said amiably, "As promised, Faith Lockhart is here with me."

Polite greetings were exchanged.

"And your son, Quinn? Assuming you stick with that name? Where is he?" Rosalyn pressed.

Zach contained his irritation. "Yes, we're going to stick with that name, Mom. And he's sleeping."

Rosalyn looked hurt. "I'd still like a peek."

"I can send some video after we hang up," Faith promised. "It was just taken a few days ago. We'll text it to Ezekiel, too."

"I'm not sure your father would appreciate it, but..." Rosalyn said stiffly. "Of course, I would love to see our first grandchild. In the meantime, I would like to offer my advice."

Uh-oh, Zach thought.

"While it is good to take responsibility and move quickly and decisively..."

Here it comes...

"And sometimes it's best to simply concentrate on finding someone who is compatible. And forget the passion and romance, which, to be perfectly honest, never lasts, anyway. But..." Rosalyn paused to take a deep breath. "That said, Zachary, I don't think you two need to rush *quite* this much. Certainly, any ceremony could wait until after the holidays. When we have time to plan..."

"I'll be deployed then, Mom."

"That's precisely what I mean!" Rosalyn sputtered.

"Extricating yourself from the military is what you should be working on. Even if you need your father to help smooth the way for your official resignation and honorable discharge."

Of course, his mom, who had hated his service from day one, would use his paternity to go there. "Dad's army. I'm navy, Mom."

"And you're all soldiers cut from the same cloth. So don't tell me he couldn't get help from another branch of the service if he asked for it...especially at his rank!"

Beside him, Zach saw Faith tense. As if wondering what exactly she was getting into, in marrying him. "Second," Zach continued, "I'm not quitting."

Rosalyn shook her head in disapproval. "You really want your son to grow up the way you did?"

Before Zach could answer, his stepdad appeared at his mother's side. Bart was also in evening clothes. He nodded at the phone. Then turned to Rosalyn, and placed a gentle hand on her arm. "Darling. They're asking for you inside..."

His mother nodded, looking immediately calmer now that Bart was at her side. "I have to go. This isn't over, Zachary."

"Yeah, it is," he muttered under his breath as the call ended.

Sensing Zach needed a moment to compose himself, she went upstairs to check on Quinn. While she was up there, she got out more decorations. Zach was waiting for her in the foyer when she brought them downstairs. "Anything else I can do for you?" he asked.

"Yes." Faith let him carry the heavy box into the formal dining room. She showed him where to set it down.

Then swung back to face him, figuring if he had problems with his family relationships, she needed to know about them. “What was Rosalyn talking about, when she asked you if you really wanted Quinn to grow up the way you did?”

“My dad was never around when I was a kid.”

Sympathy flowed. “You mean he worked long hours? Or was always deployed?”

He reached over to help her loosen the tape on the box. “He volunteered for every conflict across the globe. Plus, he was in a leadership position, so he was fully involved with his assignment.” Finished opening it, he stepped back.

“But surely you were able to talk on the phone.”

Faith reached inside and began pulling out the pieces of the Christmas village.

He helped her with that, too. “A couple times a year, maybe. Never for very long, though.”

She found the dark green cloth that served as the base, she spread it over the buffet. “So Ezekiel literally was never there.”

Zach straightened the other end, where the cloth was slightly askew. Lips compressed grimly, he admitted, “Dad missed pretty much everything. Every ball game. Awards assembly. Father-son thing. He didn’t even make it to my SEALs graduation.”

“Oh, Zach. That must have been devastating, not to have him there to see you honored.”

Indecipherable emotion flickered in his eyes. Zach exhaled. “Well, that I understood. He was in Syria at the time.”

She put the ceramic post office next to the chapel. Added a tree. “It still must have hurt.”

"A little." He lifted more buildings out of the box, then handed them to her, one by one. "Mostly because my mom refused to come, on principle. She didn't want me in the military—period—and she really didn't want me doing what she considered a dangerous job."

Their fingers brushed as he gave her the beautifully detailed red schoolhouse. Faith felt a spark of electricity at the contact.

Grimly, Zach continued, "She was furious with me for becoming a special operator."

Faith could see that. It was hard to be happy about any service-oriented accomplishment when you blamed the military for the ruination of your family.

She shook her head at Zach. Knowing that even though he wasn't technically orphaned the way she had been, in her early life, that he had also suffered greatly.

She reached over to touch his arm. "Still. Given what you had to go through to graduate the BUD/S program..."

He briefly covered her hand with his own, then stepped back. Shrugged. "I had friends there to cheer me on."

She tried to imagine it. "Annette Lantz? Quinn's mom?"

Zach shook his head. "We had just started dating then and she was a bridesmaid in a friend's wedding." He paused. "Were you at Harm's induction into the SEALs?"

She nodded, recalling how proud she had been of her late husband that day, how much it had meant to both of them. She was sad both of Zach's parents had missed the ceremony. "Yes. I did whatever I could to see him wherever, whenever I could."

"A true military wife," he said softly.

Guilt reared its ugly head. "I don't know about that," she admitted ruefully.

"Do you still miss him?"

"Sometimes." Faith paused. Aware her grief was fading, being replaced by happy memories more and more every day. She gazed at Zach. The understanding in his eyes prompted her to continue, "Mostly, though, I wished I had lived more in the present when Harm and I were together. Appreciated every day, every moment. Instead of worrying about the future or the children we didn't have." She sighed, trusting Zach enough to admit, "I think all the time about how I could have done better."

But she couldn't exactly turn back the clock and ask for a do-over. So… His eyes began to twinkle the way they did when he was about to coax her out of a worrisome mood. "Hey." He mimed a playful shove to her shoulder. "We can all do better, all the time," he chided gently, his deep voice a balm to her soul. "No reason to beat ourselves up over it."

She could see he meant it. That he didn't think less of her because she wasn't perfect. Gratitude flared inside her. "You know, I might just like having you around…" Feeling ridiculously close to kissing him again, she went back to rummage through the box to see if anything had been left behind. She pulled out the next tissue-wrapped item. And gasped.

Chapter Seven

Zach's brow quirked. "What is it?" he asked.

Faith quickly tried to stuff the offending item back in the box and hide it from view.

"Well, now I'm curious," Zach drawled.

"It's nothing. Really."

"Uh-huh," Zach replied, a sexy rumble emanating from his broad chest.

He was making her feel ridiculous. And even more embarrassed. "If you must know," she began self-consciously, pulling the offending item back out of the box to show him, "it's mistletoe."

His glance sifted slowly over her face, lingering on her bare lips, before returning to her eyes. "What's so alarming about that? Isn't it kind of traditional?"

It had been when she and Harm had been married. And he'd been lucky enough to be home on leave during the holidays, which hadn't been all that often.

As their gazes locked, he rubbed a strand of her hair between his fingers. The corners of his lips curved upward. "Or do people not kiss under the mistletoe here in Texas?"

Tingling all over for no reason she could figure, Faith scoffed at him. "Of course, they do."

"Then...?"

Insides quivering, she took a moment to consider.

"I just wasn't expecting to see it. And then… I didn't want you to think I intended to put it up."

He grinned. "Why not?" His voice dropped another notch, in a way that sent unexpected need surging through her. He winked at her. "I think we ought to have some mistletoe hanging. We can use it to embarrass your married siblings when they come over to visit."

He was just having fun. Trying to help her do so, too. She admitted she could use a little relaxation. "You're really getting into the spirit." She surveyed him, her own mood lifting.

He ambled closer. "No surprise there. I've got a lot to celebrate. I've got a son who is cute as can be. And will soon have an incredibly sweet and gorgeous wife."

Her heart fluttered in her chest. Was that how he saw her? And if so, how did that bode for their "platonic" future?

Figuring she could decide what to do with it later, when Zach wasn't around, Faith put aside the mistletoe. "Speaking of family," she said seriously. "We talked to both your parents. I was going to wait, but maybe we should talk to mine tonight, too. That is, if you're up to it?"

Zach thought about the conversation he'd had with Robert Lockhart at the Circle L.

If you think there is a chance you will want to raise this child on your own or with the help of another family member, the older man had said, *let Faith know that immediately after paternity is confirmed.*

The assumption being that he would then give Faith

a clean break. In order to avoid hurting her. Which he had not done.

"Sure," he said now to Faith. If Robert and Carol wanted to read him the riot act for the solution he'd found, one that would benefit Quinn, Faith and him, the Lockharts might as well get it over with.

She motioned him over to the sofa, where they sat down, then held up her phone and inhaled deeply. "Here goes..."

Her FaceTime request was accepted immediately. Her mom appeared on the screen. Seconds later, her dad came into view.

"Finally," Carol said, censure in her low tone.

Faith winced. "I guess that means you heard?"

Her mother huffed. "That your petition to foster-adopt was denied? And now you and Zach have taken out a license to marry by the end of the week? Oh, yes," she affirmed emotionally. "We heard. *Numerous* times."

"You probably should have called us, honey," her dad chided gently.

Faith sighed. "Well. We had that fire wall, remember...?"

Carol retorted, "The fire wall only extends to my position as a social worker with Laramie County DCFS and the process of foster-adopting. It doesn't affect my ability to be your mother. Or offer you parental advice."

Zach felt Faith's whole body tense beside him. He remembered what she said about hating to disappoint or hurt her family. Even inadvertently.

"It wasn't her fault," he said, shifting closer to her. "The marriage was my idea because it seemed the surest way to secure Faith's role as Quinn's mother. And we had to act fast because of my deployment, which will be at the end of the month."

Her parents considered that fact.

"Still," Robert said eventually, "it's *marriage* we're talking about. A lifetime commitment."

Faith argued in return, "No one knows what the future is going to hold. All Zach and I do know for certain is that we *both* want what is best for Quinn. And that's for him to have his father and me in his life."

Carol's expression softened. "Clearly, your hearts are in the right place. But there are other ways you could do the same thing. For instance," she continued, "I happen to know that the military requires all single parents to name a legal guardian who has agreed to care for their child or children in the event they are training or deployed. Zach can still name you as guardian, and if the military accepts you-all's plan, then the likelihood is that family court would accept it, too. Then, Faith could continue parenting Quinn while Zach resumes his military service, and you could use the time apart to really think about what you want to do." She concluded on a heavy exhale, "In fact, Zach, I'm surprised you didn't think of this."

His future mother-in-law had a point. "Actually, I did consider that," he admitted. But he hadn't discussed it with Faith. "But you know how it is in the military. Hurry up and wait. So, yes, I can do this, but it could be weeks, even months, before they get around to officially approving it. I didn't want to chance anything going wrong and put Quinn at risk of being stuck in foster care indefinitely."

"I understand the depth of your concern." Frowning, Carol persisted, "But...surely there is someone you could call on, like your commanding officer, to try to speed things up for you? Especially since you've already said you will be leaving in a few weeks and you want your child out of the foster-care system before you deploy."

Faith leaned forward and intervened. "Like Zach said, Mom, this is the surest way to do what is right for all three of us. And it's what we're doing. We're getting married on Friday. So we'd like your blessing, but if you can't give it, then I understand."

Her parents exchanged a long look. Obviously, Zach noted, Carol and Robert had talked about this eventuality, too. "We will always love you and be here for you," her dad promised.

"And, of course, we will be at your wedding!" Carol said, her love for her daughter shining through her worry. "Just tell us when and where..."

Faith's hand was shaking as she ended the call. She hadn't been this stressed out since the day of her husband's funeral.

"Are you okay?" Zach asked gently.

Pretending an inner serenity she couldn't begin to feel, she stood and forced herself to walk to the kitchen. "Of course."

"You don't look all right. You look like you're going to burst into tears at any second," he said as he followed her.

Except she wouldn't. Not in front of him, anyway. "I hate disappointing people."

He cupped her shoulders between his big, warm palms, encouraging her to look at him. "Realistically, there was no way they could approve," he soothed.

Was he right?

"I'm sure they want you to have some big epic love again. A union they could feel confident would last a lifetime."

She leaned into his body, loving the strength his touch imbued. Their eyes held a long moment. "There is no happily-ever-after. At least not in this situation. We both know that Zach. You lost Annette. I lost Harm."

Aware she couldn't afford to rely on his comfort any longer, not without risking further emotional involvement, she eased out of his consoling hold and moved away. Turning her back to him, she walked over to the sink and gazed out the window, into the dark backyard. It looked in that moment as lonely as she felt.

She swung back to him. "Yeah, in some perfect world, we could both find our heart's desire. Again. Maybe have some really wild, passionate affair. But what are we going to do about Quinn in the meantime? Don't we owe him everything a child should have? Love. Stability. Family."

Her lower lip quivered as much as her voice. "I mean, I was prepared to give him that on my own, and I know you want the best for him, too."

"I do," he confirmed soberly.

Another silence ensued.

"So that puts us on the same team," she said. Needing the mood between them to lighten before she found herself all the way in his arms. "And, as a Navy SEAL, I am sure that you understand all there is to know about teams," she reminded him, forcing herself to be the sturdy military wife they both needed her to be.

Zach began to grin, as she added in a light, humorous tone, "What's that saying in the military? 'All in, all the time.'"

He nodded, pleased. "That would be the slogan for us right now, yes."

"Okay, then. So we're getting married. Friday. Like we planned. Naysayers ignored."

He flashed a smile she felt all the way to her soul. "Sounds good."

"And, in the meantime, we have to figure out when you are going to move in."

He ran a hand through his hair, considering. "Tomorrow night?"

Wednesday? Suddenly she felt rattled again. Like events were moving way too quickly for comfort.

Stepping closer, he searched her face. "Or do you want to wait until *after* the vows are said?"

Marveling at his ability to read her mind, she pursed her lips, contemplating. Finally, she sighed. "I think, since we're ignoring a lot of other advice, we should follow Mitzy's suggestion and try to work out any kinks in our living arrangement before our wedding."

He nodded. "Plus, it will make my getting up to speed on baby wrangling all the easier."

She thought about the way he and Quinn had already started to bond. "I don't think you're going to have any problem with it, soldier. You're a natural."

Pleasure gleamed in his blue eyes. "High praise, considering the source." He started to exit the kitchen, then paused, surveying her again. "You sure you're all right?"

She nodded slowly but probably not convincingly. Because, in truth, she was feeling shaky again. This time for a completely different reason. It was right here that he had kissed her for the first time. And more than anything, she wanted him to kiss her *again*. So what the heck was she going to do about that? It wasn't part of their deal.

His gaze drifted tenderly over her. "Hey," he said, closing the distance between them in two strides. "I know a lot has been going on…"

"You're right." She lifted her hands, curving them around his biceps, not sure whether she was holding him at bay or pulling him close. "Talking to all four of our parents in one evening—" and not getting the kind of support it would have been nice to get from any of them…

"Was a lot," he said, finishing for her.

Exactly! Those tension-fraught phone calls had conjured up a wellspring of confused feelings—past, present and future. For her, and judging by the turbulent sheen in his eyes, for him, too. And while she might not know what she wanted out of this arrangement, other than to remain a part of their child's life, right now, he apparently had no such qualms.

Zach's arms surrounded her, pulling her close. And as he engulfed her in a long, strong hug that ignited her from head to toe, a sense of rightness washed over her. "It'll get better once we get married on Friday," he promised gruffly.

She could almost believe that, as his head lowered and he delivered another kiss that was by turns passionate and reverent, sweet and hot. And once again she was swept up into the kind of life that came with every special operator. One that focused primarily on whatever moment the SEAL and his love were in. Because there was no telling what the future held, or even if there *would* be a future together, the time they did have was often intense. Complicated. Emotional. And this was all that and more.

So much more, she thought as his hard body pressed against hers, filling her with aching desire, given the fact that now there was a child they both fiercely wanted to protect at the center of their relationship…

Zach hadn't meant to kiss her again. Their first embrace had shown him how hot their chemistry was. And sex was definitely *not* part of the bargain they had made! Yet here she was, surging against him wildly, her lips opening softly, drinking him in as readily as he was savoring the taste and touch and warmth of her.

The loneliness in him eased. Even as the fierce physical yearning increased. Of all the times to find the one woman made just for him, of all the times to need things to be clear and simple, when they were about as far from that as could get. Still, as she continued to rock restlessly against him, he couldn't resist returning kiss after tempestuous kiss, until it was either stop, or take things to dangerous new heights.

She sighed again, drew back and looked up into his eyes. Smiling dazedly, she said, even more softly, "Oh, Zach. We're in trouble, aren't we?"

For a moment, Zach didn't answer her. He just continued looking at her in that inscrutable, yet rawly honest way. Silently conveying that while his work as a special operator required a certain amount of subterfuge and obfuscation, he didn't hold anything back in his private life. No matter how uncomfortable or revealing it might turn out to be.

So Faith did what she always did when caught in a web of feelings she wasn't sure how to handle. She made light of it. Smiling, she stepped back even farther. "Unless that was another dress rehearsal for our postceremony kiss?"

Another pause. Then her joke got the expected response. He took the pass she gave them both, grinned and held up both palms in surrender. "You caught me, darlin'."

"Well, I think we've got it down pat now, soldier." She sashayed past him, as if hot torrid kisses happened to her all the time.

Zach gave a brief, chivalrous bow. "It would seem so." He grabbed his jacket, and she accompanied him to the front door. Once he stepped onto the porch, he was all business once again. "So, about tomorrow?" he asked. "Do you want me to go to Laramie Gardens with you in the morning and lend a hand with Quinn?"

"That would be great." She did her best to disguise the way her heart was still pounding, her limbs still tingling, from their kiss. She did not know how many more times they could kiss and not get involved in something a lot more heated than a simple embrace.

But then again, he was only going to be here a few more weeks. Then, like her late husband, he'd be gone for months on end.

The reminder gave her the expected dose of cold water. "Eight forty-five okay with you?" she inquired, folding her arms in front of her, to ward off the sudden chill of the December air.

Zach gave her another slow, sultry smile that turned her inside out and devastated her even more. "Perfect," he said in the low, gravelly voice she was quickly coming to love. "I'll see you then."

Chapter Eight

Faith and Zach had barely walked in the door at Laramie Gardens on Wednesday morning when they were surrounded. Everyone, it seemed, had lots to tell her. There was a new resident/patient, Nessie Rogers, coming in from the hospital. She would reside in the skilled-nursing section of the facility.

Tillie Tarrant wanted to meet with Faith as soon as she was settled in her office.

A Christmas tree for the community room was being delivered later that morning, and she was asked to weigh in with her opinion on the dispute over decorations.

And, last but not least, Miss Mim seemed surprised that Zach was there to babysit her son...*again.*

"Well, first of all," Faith said, "it's called parenting, not babysitting."

The normally agreeable Miss Mim seemed somehow bothered by this distinction.

"They have a lot of catching up to do," she added. And a short amount of time in which to do it! "But," she continued, speaking to all the ladies gathered around, "the lieutenant is still on a pretty steep learning curve, so he is going to need lots of help from you-all."

Everyone relaxed.

Still, something remained unsaid.

Beginning to feel a little warm—Laramie Gardens

was kept at a cozy seventy-two degrees at all times in the winter—Faith unbuttoned her coat. "Is there a problem?" she asked the group.

Everyone exchanged telltale looks.

Finally, Miss Mim gestured for Zach and Faith to come a little farther into the big community room, with its big windows, abundance of comfy seating and cathedral ceiling. "Well, yes, there is." As usual, the former librarian acted as spokesperson for the group. "We heard you are planning to get married in the chaplain's office at WTWA on Friday."

"And that is just *not* acceptable," Miss Sadie chimed in.

"Frankly, we're all a little hurt," Miss Patricia remarked. "That we weren't invited to attend."

So this was the real reason for the dour expressions! "Well, there's not really room for everyone over at the WTWA. I mean, I'm not sure anyone except my parents will be there to witness..." Faith explained.

Disapproving scowls appeared all around.

Obviously seeing this was going to go on for a while, Zach set down the infant carrier, took off his own coat and lifted Quinn out.

Quinn gurgled happily up at his daddy, and everyone "a-a-w-w-wed." Beaming in approval, too, Faith eased off her little boy's cap and jacket while Zach continued holding him.

"But we appreciate everyone wanting to support us in this," she murmured.

"That's the thing." Tillie Tarrant squeezed the hand of her longtime husband, Ted, then stepped behind his wheelchair so she wouldn't obstruct his view. "You two should have come to all of us if you needed a place to get married. Laramie Gardens has everything you need for the ceremony, and a very nice dining hall in which to hold a reception! Plus, the entire place will be fully decorated for the holiday by then."

Russell Pierce added, "Everyone here who loves you could witness it and show our support for this noble thing you are doing."

Faith had to admit she was surprisingly touched as she looked at the faces of the people gathered around. Their collective life experiences gave them a compassion and understanding that never failed to put things in perspective. Suddenly, the coil of tension that had been wound up inside her since this all began started to dissipate. "You-all approve of what Zach and I are doing, in getting hitched?"

Nods all around.

Ted reached behind him to grasp his wife's hand. "Tillie and I had a marriage arranged by our families, but we went into it for all the right reasons, and it's lasted sixty years..."

Except Tillie was now thinking about moving out of their shared suite, Faith thought worriedly.

Or *was* she?

Was that the reason Tillie wanted to talk privately? Faith wondered. Because she had changed her mind about all that?

Only time would tell...

One thing was certain. No one knew what really went on in a relationship except the couple involved. Her marriage to Harm had taught her that...

"So what do you say?" Buck Franklin asked.

"Can we have the wedding here?" Kurtis Kelley inquired hopefully.

Zach shrugged, his own feelings in the matter hidden. "I'll talk to the chaplain, but it's fine with me." He looked over at Faith. Seeming to know, as did she, that if they turned down the seniors' very kind and generous suggestion it would break their hearts.

After all the love and acceptance they had shown her and Quinn, and now Zach, she couldn't let that happen. "It would be great, actually."

Miss Mim clapped her hands. "What time Friday?"

Zach said, "Well, it was set for three o'clock."

"Splendid," Miss Sadie said. "I'll talk to the dining hall and arrange a reception for after."

Excited chatter followed. "The women will do the flowers!" Miss Patricia declared.

Wilbur Barnes added, "The fellas will call the Sugar Love bakery in town and manage the cake, if you trust us to do it!"

"When it comes to food, of course!" Miss Mim countered wryly.

"Hear that, guys?" Buck Franklin joked. "We get to do a taste testing!"

Everyone laughed.

Miss Patricia, a former executive secretary, was already taking copious notes. "So, Faith, you said your parents will be attending?"

"Yes."

"What about the rest of your family?"

Now that it was turning into a big event? "Probably."

"Zach?" Miss Patricia prompted.

If he was feeling disappointed, he hid it well. "Not likely. My folks are both on the East Coast, and it's such short notice. They'll probably visit with us later."

Miss Mim said, "You'll let them know the time and

date and details in any case? We don't want them feeling left out."

"Sure," Zach conceded.

"What about music?" widower Ian Baker, a relatively new resident, asked.

"We didn't have plans for that," Zach admitted.

Ian continued, "We should at least get a pianist or string quartet."

Faith did a mental calculation of the costs. "This is getting very elaborate..." she protested nervously. *Especially for a marriage of convenience.* "Zach and I really wanted something simple."

"Then a pianist it is," Ian said with a cordial wink.

Tillie smiled over at the sophisticated former investment banker and financial advisor. Her husband, Ted Tarrant, glared.

And suddenly Faith wondered, Was *that* what was going on? Could sweet Tillie Tarrant, who had been happily married to her doting husband for six decades, now find herself being interested in someone else?

And, if that was the case, how did things bode for her and Zach, long-term?

"Is every day at Laramie Gardens like that?" Zach asked her that evening, when he arrived on her doorstep, ready to move in. "Because I feel like I just went through BUD/S training all over again. Except this time, I didn't get to ring the bell."

"Very funny." She warily eyed the duffel he'd brought in with him. As much as she would like to let him charm his way into her bed, her instincts warned her against it. Which meant the sooner they got down to business, the better. "Ready for a tour of your guest quarters and the rest of the house?"

He flashed a smile. "Sure." His phone buzzed. He pulled it from his pocket, looked at the screen. "It's my mom. Mind if I take it?"

"I think you probably better." Otherwise, from what she had seen thus far, Rosalyn would just keep calling.

Zach stepped out onto the front porch, and to make sure she was completely out of earshot, she retired to the kitchen. Still, she could see him pacing back and forth, cell pressed to his ear. Across the street, holiday lights twinkled, reminding her she needed to get her outdoor decorations up by this weekend.

Not that this would be a problem, with Zach there to help. She could always get a family member to help watch Quinn. And it wasn't like the two of them were taking a honeymoon or anything.

Finally, Zach came back in. He looked as stressed out as she had felt before the seniors had taken over all the details of their wedding, absolving them of any responsibility.

"What's up?"

"My mom has arranged for a military wedding."

Faith blinked, sure she could not have heard right. "I thought you said your mom was against you being in the military from day one."

"This is the one aspect of military life she likes," he explained.

Faith supposed she could see why; military nuptials could be quite dazzling.

"I'm guessing you had a military ceremony with Harm?" he countered.

Faith's heartbeat quickened. "No. We eloped to Vegas

while I was still in college." His surprised look prompted her to go on. "I went to San Diego for spring break, which is where I met him. It's a long story."

He edged closer. "Don't tell me you eloped that same weekend."

"Okay." She glowered at him. "I won't tell you."

"Wow." He gave her a thorough once-over that had her insides fluttering. "When you make up your mind, you really go for it."

Refusing to let him get under her skin, she lifted her brow in concession. "Sometimes. But, in any case, I was young." And foolish and overly romantic. And very, very selfish. But she didn't need to think about that. "So, back to this military wedding." The tension between them ratcheted up another notch. "What does she want us to do?"

"Nothing." He lounged against the counter, looking sexy as hell in a navy blue sweater that clung to his muscular shoulders and broad chest, and a pair of worn jeans that did equally tantalizing things to his lower half. "She's taken care of everything. Even going so far as to foot the bill to send six of my SEAL teammates to Laramie tomorrow afternoon, via private jet, to stand up for us and do the sword canopy send-off at the end."

Pretending she wasn't turned on by the sight of all that hard muscle and abundant masculinity, she breathed, "You're kidding."

He folded his arms. "Nope. She's not happy about the venue, of course. She would rather it be in a church, but apparently Miss Mim sold her on the overall beauty of the Laramie Gardens, so they're going to make it all work."

He ambled closer. "Which brings me to the next

issue. My mother is sending my dress whites. Which is what the guys will be wearing, too. So you may want to think about what kind of dress goes with that. Assuming that you care about that kind of thing, and I sense you do."

He sensed right. Beginning to wonder if they had made a gigantic mistake in not keeping the details of their nuptials private, she warned, "Quinn is going to see these pictures one day, you know."

He stepped close enough that she could feel his body heat and inhale the brisk masculine fragrance of his cologne and asked, "Is there time to get a dress?"

Determined not to let him see how much his nearness was affecting her, she allowed, "Luckily, for you, there is a bridal shop in town, and they sometimes sell their sample dresses off the rack, so you don't have to special order."

He shrugged. "Sounds good."

Except today was Wednesday and the wedding was on Friday. That was cutting it awfully close. "But I will have to do it tomorrow afternoon since they aren't open in the evenings."

He was looking like he wanted to kiss her again, even as he chipped away at her resistance to this increasingly ambitious wedding ceremony. "Can you get off work?" he asked.

Not sure when she had felt so off-kilter and aroused all at once, Faith let out a breath and reluctantly confessed, "They're already pushing me to take the entire day off to get ready for the ceremony and my sister-in-law Susannah wants to watch Quinn, so..."

Zach flashed a wide grin. "Well, that will work out great because I am responsible for picking up the guys coming in for the wedding, as well as entertaining them tomorrow evening."

Another twist she had not been prepared for. "You mean you're having a bachelor party?" She wasn't sure how she felt about that…

He caught her unease. Raised his hands in surrender. "Don't worry," he said, chuckling, "there won't be any strippers."

"Hey." She raised her hands right back, squaring off with him. Pretending not to care when, to her surprise, she did. "Even if there were…" It wasn't any of her business, given the strictly platonic, we're-just-in-this-to-do-right-by-our-son relationship they had.

Zach nodded. From the look in his eyes, she could tell he was not quite buying it, but he went on matter-of-factly, "I thought we might go out to the search-and-rescue training facility on the No Name Ranch. It's run by an ex–Special Forces guy."

Who just so happened to be the love of her LG co-worker's life. "Ah, yes, Zane Lockhart." She warded off the question she got all the time. "No relation to me. Well, not that we know of. Probably if we went back far enough we'd eventually find something."

Zach nodded. "Anyway, I met him today when he stopped by to have lunch with Nora, and he's already invited me out to try out a few of his training courses and tell him what I think of them. So I'll see if he can rustle up a challenge or two for a team of SEALs."

"Actually, that does sound exciting."

Zach waggled his eyebrows. "Maybe for a bunch of adrenaline junkies," he said lazily. "Somehow I don't see you enjoying it," he drawled.

"That's because I wouldn't." She laughed despite herself. "So when are your mom and stepdad coming in?"

"Friday morning. They have to leave Friday evening. But they're coming via private jet, and landing at the Laramie airstrip, so it will be on their schedule."

"You happy about that?"

Zach shrugged. For a second, she saw a glimmer of emotion in his eyes. Afraid she might get all misty, too—what was it about this wedding that was starting to get to her?—she turned away from him. "So, soldier, ready for that tour…?" Because she certainly was!

Faith wanted to start upstairs, but warned they had to be quiet because Quinn was already asleep. "No problem," Zach whispered. Duffel in hand, he followed her up the wide front staircase.

Upstairs and down, the walls were painted a pale sage green. To the right, in the upstairs hall, there was a closed door. "That's the master bedroom and bath," she said. Curious as to why she didn't want him to see it, he glanced again at the door. "It's really messy right now," she murmured, averting her eyes. "I've just been too busy this week to clean it."

And if he bought that, she probably also had some swamp land in east Texas to sell him, too. Not that he blamed her for wanting her privacy. That room had to be her sanctuary.

The next door was open. Inside, a night-light illuminated the nursery. It held a crib, changing table, a comfy-looking rocker-glider and an abundance of infant toys and books. The walls were painted blue. When Faith tiptoed inside, Zach set down his bag and followed soundlessly. Quinn was lying on his back, his cherubic face turned upward, as if he had fallen asleep looking at the mobile above him. He was wearing the kind of sleeper that covered him from neck to toe. The little guy had a pint-size stuffed cow clutched to his chest with one hand, and the other arm was flung out at his side. His breathing was deep and even, his tiny lips moving every now and then, as if he was dreaming. He looked so sweet and innocent, so utterly perfect, Zach felt his heart lurch.

His son...

This was his *son...*

And Quinn was thriving, because of Faith and the love and tenderness she had bestowed upon him, after Annette's passing…

Zach's heart swelled again, as he thought about all he and Quinn both owed the gorgeous woman beside him.

Oblivious to his thoughts, Faith gave Quinn one last loving look and tiptoed out, motioning for Zach to follow. Which he reluctantly did.

She pointed to the hall bathroom. It looked as if it had been recently updated, with white tile and slate-gray floor. Towels, washcloths, soap and shampoo had all been set out for him. "You can use that," she whispered. "I'll use mine."

Down at the other end of the hall, the bedroom door was also open. Inside was a queen-size bed, a bureau and a small writing desk. An upholstered wing chair sat in one corner. "The guest room. I emptied out the closet for you."

"Thanks." He set down his duffel.

She smiled at him, then backed out of the room. "And now for the rest of the house," she said.

Back down the stairs they went. He had seen the living room, which held large cozy furniture, wood floors and a pastel antique rug. The dining room was adjacent, where there was a formal table and chairs, and a buffet.

Behind that was the kitchen that functioned like the heart of her home. Previously, when he had been in there, he had been focused on her. Now he concentrated on the amenities as she showed him where everything was. In addition to the walk-in pantry, there was a lot of nice white cabinetry and a big farmhouse-style sink. New stainless appliances. Dark gray quartz countertops and hardwood floors. A six-foot island provided cooking space on one side, stools and an eating area on the other. Plus, a round table for four filled the breakfast nook. Quinn's high chair sat beside that. Throughout there were little touches that spoke of Faith's femininity and grace. Fresh flowers. Bowls of fruit. Luscious bakery muffins under glass. A coffee station.

"Obviously, make yourself at home. Back here..." She led the way past a half bath, to the laundry mudroom. It held a washer and dryer. More cabinets above them. Plus a countertop for folding clothes. "You're welcome to utilize this room, too."

"You mean you won't be doing my laundry?" he teased, sensing she was beginning to get a little tense.

She turned, with a pretty scowl.

He sent her a flirtatious glance. "Kidding!" he said.

"I hope so!"

They walked back out into the rear hallway. A back door led to a deck overlooking the landscaped backyard. To the left of that was another door. Also closed. He gestured at it. "What's in there?" He knew it wasn't the garage. That was detached and sat at the end of the driveway behind the house.

"Um." She waved disparagingly. "Just a room where I used to work when I was freelancing as an accountant."

She was being awfully mysterious. Which made him immediately curious. "Can I see it?"

She opened her mouth as if to speak. Shut it again.

Really wondering now, he teased, "You're not hiding an illegal bootlegging operation in there, are you?"

She inclined her head. "Of course not!"

"Then?" What was the big secret? He'd see it eventually, wouldn't he, if they were married and he was living here for at least a few weeks every year?

"Fine!" She pushed open the door while speaking over her shoulder. "But it, too, is a mess!"

She was right about that, Zach thought.

Chapter Nine

Faith could only imagine what Zach thought as he looked around her study. Her former sanctuary looked like a disaster zone. There was a single crookedly hung shelf, as well as a broken one that had landed on the floor, creating a gaping hole in the drywall that had yet to be repaired, months after it had happened.

Zach stood there, arms folded, surveying the damage. "Well, either you're a very bad do-it-yourselfer, or you are using this space to take out your aggressions." His eyes twinkling, he pivoted back to her. "So, which is it?"

"Neither." She really regretted showing him this. But if he was going to be living here…

"My late husband wanted to build me some shelves for all my books and install some cabinets for my files."

"And he passed before he could finish the job," Zach stated, taking a guess.

Faith only wished it had been that simple. Not sure how to answer that, she wrung her hands. "Yes and no."

Zach edged closer, waiting.

"He had actually promised me he would do this for me for years. Four years ago, I gave him a plan, and he went to the lumberyard and specced out the materials he would need. The next time he was home on leave, he bought everything. It's stored in the garage, along with the books I have no place for. Then, year before last, he finally tried to start the project. Obviously, as you can see, it didn't go well."

Zach nodded, serious now. "You have to line up with the studs. Otherwise, you're just going through drywall, which won't hold the weight."

"Right. By the time he had figured that out, it was too late. Anyway, I wanted to just hire a professional to do it…but he was adamant he was going to finish it."

"And then he didn't."

"In the meantime, it bothered me like crazy, so I just stopped coming in here and I kept the door shut."

Zach stuck his hands in his pockets. "Even after he died."

Faith dipped her head in acknowledgment. "It bothered me more then."

Zach moved closer.

"Because he was never going to be able to do it?"

Faith wondered if Zach could ever be that stubborn. Somehow, she couldn't imagine it.

She sighed, then answered, "Because I spent a lot of time resenting him for his egotistical approach to the situation. Time we could have simply spent appreciating each other. Instead, the built-ins became a sore spot between us…sort of a symbol of all that was wrong in our marriage. Me, wanting things done quickly and efficiently…and him, wanting to follow his own timetable for things. He said he spent all his time in the military following orders, and didn't want to have to follow them at home."

Faith paused to let that sink in.

Zach winced. "Ouch."

"Yeah, it hurt. But it also made sense." Faith swallowed around the tightness in her throat. "I suppose you feel that way, too?"

Zach's smile came, slow and sexy. His gaze drifted over her yet again. "Depends on the kind of order I'm getting, and from whom, I guess." This time he paused to let his words sink in. Then, sobering, he asked, "Do you still have the plans for what you wanted?"

"Yes."

"Will you show them to me?" he asked.

"If you want."

He did.

Faith stepped around some tools that had been left on the floor, just where Harm had left them, and opened a desk drawer. She brought out a folder. Inside were pictures from magazines, of beautiful custom built-in cabinetry and shelving. A crude drawing she'd done herself, along with measurements of what she wanted. And paint sample cards, with a particular shade of creamy ivory circled.

Zach studied it all very carefully. "You want your cabinets and shelves painted?" he asked finally.

Appreciating his attention to detail, Faith nodded. "I thought it would be a nice contrast to my antique desk, and match all the trim and the crown moldings in the house, which would give it a really custom look."

He nodded. "Very nice."

A little embarrassed at all she had just revealed about herself, she put the folder back in the desk. "Anyway, I would appreciate it if we just kept this door closed for now. It's embarrassing to me and I would rather others not see."

"Sure," he said.

She consulted her watch and saw it was already after

ten thirty. Where had the time gone? "Do you need anything else?" she asked.

"No. I'm good."

"Okay then, I'm going up to…" *Bed*, she almost said. "My quarters," she said instead.

Tinkerbelle appeared in the doorway, yawning.

He stepped back to let her pass. "I'll see you tomorrow," he promised.

"See you then," Faith said.

Zach waited until Faith had retired, then stepped outside to make a call. His mom picked up on the third ring. He could tell from the background noise that she was at another social event. Not surprising. Usually this time of year, she and her husband had daily holiday engagements. "Zach? Is everything okay? The wedding isn't called off, is it?"

Zach rubbed his neck. "No, Mom. The wedding is still on. But I need a favor. You know those boxes of stuff Granddad left me? The ones in your garage? Would it be possible for you to bring them with you when you and Bart fly down here on Friday?"

"You don't want me to ship them?"

"No. They're pretty heavy and I think that would take too long. It can be your Christmas present to me this year." And Faith, to whom he owed so much.

His mom replied kindly, "Consider it done, then."

Zach went to sleep that night knowing he had found a way to at least start to repay Faith for all she had done. And he awakened the following morning feeling like he could handle the rest of it.

"So did my mom call every one of you?" Zach asked his teammates, when his friends arrived at the Laramie airstrip shortly after noon. They piled into the large SUV he had rented and headed for the Dairy Barn to grab some lunch before heading out to the No Name Ranch.

"Just me." Sully settled into the passenger seat. "She asked me to round up five other teammates and head down here, to make sure you knew what you were doing. Make sure someone had your six. So here we are." He gestured at Radar, Gil, Hap, Bull and McDill. "All our dress whites and ceremonial swords in tow."

"In case you actually decide to go through with it," Radar said.

"What makes you think I won't?" Zach asked, pulling into the parking lot.

They all got out. Remained talking next to the Suburban.

Half a dozen shrugs followed. "Well, it's a big step," said Gil, who was the only one of them happily married, but just recently so. Prior to that he had been engaged for six years while he and his fiancée worked everything out.

Hap—who swore he would be single for life—nodded. "Sure you actually *have* to get married?"

"I mean, can't you just have an 'arrangement' and raise the kid together?" asked Bull, the most stubbornly practical of them all.

"Initially that was the plan." Zach then explained Judge Roy's rejection of that idea.

"Which is why you proposed?" McDill asked.

Well, that, and other things that were more difficult to explain. Like the way he felt whenever he was with Faith. Happy. At peace. Intrigued. Not to mention hopelessly, wildly aroused…

Aware his buddies were still waiting for an answer, Zach finally allowed, "You'd have to see the way she looks at my kid and the way he looks at her to really understand."

"It would break their hearts to separate them," Sully said.

Break them, period, Zach thought. After all, how much loss could one child be expected to handle? Quinn'd already lost Annette. Bonded fiercely with Faith—to the point he showed no adverse reaction to having been orphaned.

But, like life, that all could change in an instant. Zach deeply regretted that he hadn't been there when Quinn was born. Or after. He couldn't rewrite the past, but he wasn't going to follow his father's path and let down his firstborn son again. "This is the only way I can be sure Faith will end up with Quinn, and continue to be his mother, while I'm deployed." *Or if something should happen to me.* "I also want him out of the foster-care system. This will accomplish that."

He hoped, anyway. Mitzy Martin-McCabe had told them bluntly there was never any way of predicting Judge Priscilla Roy's decisions. Except to know she always did what she thought was in the best interest of the child.

Sully squinted. "You like this Faith Lockhart that much?"

Hell, yeah, he liked her. Admired her. Thought about her. Almost nonstop. But that could have been because of the overall situation they'd found themselves in…

His teammates were surveying him. Waiting for his answer. With a shrug, he sidestepped the question. "Like I said, she's wonderful with Quinn."

Without warning, Radar began to laugh. He put his Ray-Bans back on. "But how is she with you?"

Generous to a fault. "Nice. Polite."

"Mmm-hmm." Hap burst into a wide grin. "She's hot, isn't she?"

Extremely, Zach thought before he could stop himself. He scowled a warning. "Her looks have nothing to do with this."

Guffaws all around. Bull said, "Methinks our teammate doth protest too much."

"We don't have that kind of arrangement," Zach muttered darkly.

"Yeah, but *will* you?" McDill pressed. "That's the fifty-thousand-dollar question..."

And one he did not know how to answer, Zach noted to himself as they headed for the doors to the fast-food restaurant. That said, he knew what part of him wanted. The part that had kissed her. Twice. And spent more time thinking about those kisses than he cared to admit.

But the practical side of him—the disciplined military side—knew it would be a mistake to let things get unnecessarily complicated. For the maximum chance of success, they needed to take care of Quinn. Hopefully become good friends, as well as coparents. Do whatever they needed to do to keep things on an even keel. And leave it at that.

An hour later, Faith entered the bridal salon with her sisters, Mackenzie, Emma and Jillian. Her sisters-in-law, Allison and Susannah, had decided to tag along at the last minute, too, which meant Susannah had to bring Quinn, because she had promised to watch him for Faith.

This turned out to be a good thing, since Luisa, the fitting specialist who was going to be helping them, could not stop oohing and aahing over their "little mascot."

Finally, though, it was time to get down to business.

"So? What kind of wedding dress are you looking for?" Luisa asked.

The bridal consultant was petite and professional, her olive skin perfectly made up, her inky black hair drawn back into a sleek knot at the nape of her neck.

"I don't know." Faith hedged. "Maybe a suit?"

Her support group of five sighed.

"Are you sure you want to do that?" Jillian, who had recently gotten married herself, asked.

"It's my second wedding," Faith explained to Luisa.

"But your first was in Vegas," Emma pointed out. "She didn't even have a white dress! She just had some borrowed tiara on her head."

It wasn't as if she'd had bad photos taken on purpose, Faith thought. "Harm was shipping out in two days! We had to use our time wisely."

This immediately brought forth a round of lusty chuckles.

Recalling her wildly romantic and passionate honeymoon—which had turned out to be the very best thing about her entire marriage—Faith blushed. "You know what I mean!"

"Right," Susannah said kindly, as she walked back and forth, a sleepy Quinn in her arms. "You and Harm didn't give a hoot what you were wearing. Or where the ceremony was performed! You-all just wanted to focus on each other. And the small amount of time you had together before he deployed."

Faith nodded, glad at least someone understood. “That is exactly it.”

Luisa was still on task. Taking measurements of Faith’s chest, waist and hips. “Second wedding or no, there is no reason you can’t wear a beautiful formal dress.” She scribbled a few notes. “What is the groom going to be wearing for the ceremony?”

Faith turned her attention to the gowns on the racks. Silk. Satin. Lace. Formfitting or full-skirted. They really were gorgeous. She touched the fabric. It was as exquisite as it looked. “His military uniform. Dress whites.”

“Oh! Wow!” Luisa sighed. “Then you definitely want to wear something appropriately formal, too.”

Faith forced herself not to get too excited, and turned back, reiterating what she had already told Luisa when she’d made the appointment. “The thing is the wedding is tomorrow afternoon. At Laramie Gardens.”

Luisa waved away any excuses. “We can make that happen. All you have to do is pick one of the dresses available for immediate sale, and the seamstress will make the alterations this evening. Because it’s a military wedding, we will even waive the rush fee.”

“See!” Emma declared happily. “There’s absolutely no reason not to go for it.”

“I’ll pull some gowns in your size now.” Luisa bustled off.

Ensured some momentary privacy, Faith spun back around. Once again, she felt like a fraud. Just the way she had at the end of her marriage to Harm. She didn’t like it.

Determined to keep a firm grasp on the reality of the situation this time, she told her sisters and sisters-in-law sternly, "Except it's not that kind of marriage." It was more like a business deal. So wouldn't a wedding suit be more appropriate? No matter what Zach was wearing?

"You never know," Mackenzie said. "It could end up being the real deal! After all, I married Griff for similarly practical, decidedly unromantic reasons, and we ended up falling madly in love."

"Cade and I were sworn enemies, until we babysat quadruplets and saw each other in a new light," Allison added.

Jillian reflected with a nostalgic smile, "I found out I didn't have a clue what kind of man Cooper truly was until I saw him with his nieces. And realized how big a heart he had. As soon as that happened, I was in love..."

"And a love like that can lead to being a happy married couple," Emma said dreamily.

Faith turned to her youngest sister. The aspiring footwear designer had on some seriously sexy lace-up-to-the-knee suede boots. "How would you know? You haven't been serious about someone since you and Tom Reid broke up!"

"But I want to be someday," Emma declared, stubborn as ever. "Because if I have learned anything since our siblings all started getting happily hitched, it's that marriage, while it may not be perfect, is *always* rife with possibilities."

"How are you doing, darling?" Zach's mom asked, seeing him before the wedding. He was standing just outside the entrance to the Laramie Gardens community room.

He turned to her. Touched she was there, and a little surprised. He pulled her into a hug. "Doing great,

Mom. But I do have one question for you." He drew back. "Why did you go to so much trouble to make this ceremony the real deal, if you were convinced it was a bad idea?"

Rosalyn ran her fingers over the medals pinned to his chest. Suddenly sentimental, she blinked back a few tears. "Well, it occurred to me that you are my firstborn son, and you are also my very first child to get married, and I didn't want to miss out on that."

He sensed there was more. "Was there any other reason?"

Her eyes darkened. "I wanted this day to be special for you, and for Faith, who has already done so very much for my first grandchild. And I wanted this day to be meaningful for Quinn, too. Because one day he will look back on this day and see the pictures, and I want him to have something unforgettable to latch onto."

Even if, as she feared, his marriage to Faith didn't work out, he thought. But this was no time for worry.

"Well, you and the ladies of Laramie Gardens did a beautiful job, Mom," Zach said.

He looked around appreciatively. The community room had been transformed into a beautiful Christmas chapel. An arch of flowers was placed in front of the window, and rows of white chairs were neatly lined up on either side of a satin aisle cloth. A harpist and flutist had been brought in to play the processional, plus a local pianist was going to handle the reception. He wasn't sure what had been done to the tree, but it was even more spectacular than it had been when it had first been put up.

Zach's six SEAL teammates were acting as ushers and groomsmen. As for Faith's attendants, her five sisters and sisters-in-law, along with a friend, had volunteered to serve as bridesmaids. He smiled to himself, noting that the women of Laramie Gardens were dressed in their finest dresses, and the men either wore ties or, in some cases, their military uniforms from their own years of service.

When Miss Mim gave the cue, Zach escorted his mother to her seat in the front row, next to his stepfather. Then he moved to join the chaplain.

The music changed to Pachelbel's Canon.

His heart kicking against his ribs, harder than it had on any mission, he looked toward the entrance. Faith appeared, on her father's arm. The whole world faded away as she glided slowly toward him. She was wearing a beautiful cap-sleeved ivory satin wedding dress, with a bodice that lovingly hugged her midriff and bared the tops of her shoulders. Her strawberry-blond hair had been styled into a sophisticated updo that supported a sparkling tiara and bared the nape of her neck.

The chaplain welcomed everyone as they approached the altar, and asked, "Who giveth this woman in marriage?"

"We do," Faith's mother and dad said.

Her dad lifted her veil and kissed her cheek. After Robert took the seat next to Carol, the chaplain signaled for Zach to join his bride. As he took her soft, delicate hands in his, their gazes met. Zach saw Faith's eyes were glistening. With tears of joy—or regret and tension—he did not know.

Chapter Ten

Faith hadn't ever imagined being one of the stars in a fairy-tale wedding, never mind actually getting married again. But here she was, standing in front of the chaplain, next to Zach, almost able to visualize them falling in love. And how crazy was that?

Lending to the excitement, of course, was how very dashingly handsome he and all his groomsmen looked in their dress white uniforms. The truth was she hadn't been this caught up in the over-the-top romance of the moment the first time she had gotten hitched.

Of course, she hadn't had everyone she loved present then. And the quirky Vegas vows they'd taken, promising to be each other's best pals in fun and adventure, had turned out to have nothing to do with the serious nature of a real marriage.

Which was probably why the chaplain had insisted she and Zach show this moment the solemnity it deserved and stick with the tried and true. And as she stood there, facing him, her hands clasped in his warm, capable palms, looking deeply into his sea-blue eyes, it was impossible not to feel at least a tiny bit swept away.

Maybe it was how utterly masculine he looked, with the white of his uniform contrasting against his suntanned skin. Or how closely he had shaved or the way his short dark hair always looked so thick and silky and touchable. Plus he smelled so damn enticing, like a brisk winter night filled with deep exotic spice… And never mind how enthralled she had felt the two times he had kissed her. How protected and cared for she felt, whenever she was by his side…

All she knew for sure was that this was really happening! And that he was the kind of man who took honor and his duty to his son, and now her, seriously.

His voice was strong and purposeful as they slid the plain gold rings on each other's fingers and recited the vows.

She found herself meaning the words, too, as they gazed into each other's eyes and promised to love each other from this day forward.

To stay together for richer, for poorer…for better, for worse, in sickness and in health…as long as they both shall live…

And yet, even as the words lingered on her tongue, the cautious part of her couldn't help but wonder nervously. Was it wrong to pledge that? In front of God and everyone?

Then again, how did anyone know, when they stood up in front of all their family and friends, how things would ultimately work out?

All she knew for certain was that it felt, in that moment, anyway, like she and Zach were doing the right thing.

And really, given the way things had turned out, what else could they have done to protect and nurture Quinn? Give their little infant son the safe and secure life he deserved?

"I now pronounce you husband and wife," the chaplain said. "What God has joined together, let no man put asunder." He smiled. "Zach, you may kiss your bride!"

Oh, no, Faith thought. She had almost forgotten about that part. One look into her new husband's eyes, and she knew he wasn't going to shortchange anyone with this. Not after they had all gone to so much trouble.

Zach hadn't planned on giving Faith more than a ceremonial buss on the lips. But with everyone sitting there, waiting, including both sets of parents and a half-dozen members of his SEAL team, who were looking on with more than a little skepticism, he decided to give it his all.

He wrapped both arms about her, and bent her backward from the waist. She let out a little gasp—whether from excitement or delight or simply surprise he did not know. Her pretty green eyes widened and her soft lips parted in invitation. Ever so slowly, he lowered his face, his lips hovering over hers. Still clinging to his shoulders, she waited, giving another little gasp at first contact, then made a little sound that was half murmur, half moan.

Desire swept through him as she surrendered completely to him. And he let the embrace take on a life of its own as he continued kissing her with the kind of unrelenting determination he channeled into everything that mattered to him. He brought her closer still, claiming her as his woman, his wife. Beginning to want the kind of hot, intense connection that would blow away all their barriers. Only the fact they had an audience prompted him to put on the brakes.

Slowly, he let the possessive kiss come to a reluctant end. Moments after setting her back on her feet, his teammates sprang into action. Forming the perfect denouement to every military wedding, the canopy of swords. Zach took Faith's hand in his. They swept through. And then the whole place erupted with glee.

"Okay," Zach told the wedding photographer his mother had hired to record the event several hours later. "This is the last shot."

They had arrived at her home, in the limousine his mother had also arranged for. It was barely nine o'clock. Quinn and Tinkerbelle were with her sister Emma and her folks for the night.

"Just carry her across the threshold!" the photographer directed.

Faith gasped. "Don't..." she sputtered.

Too late. Zach had already swept her up in his strong arms and was heading up the steps to her front porch. He turned at the door, still cradling her against his chest, giving the camera guy the opportunity to get several more romantic shots.

"Now a kiss!" he ordered.

Faith opened her mouth again, to protest. Zach's lips found hers, inundating her with warmth and pleasure. She was trembling when he finally lifted his head. He turned toward the photographer. "Okay, that's it!" he said in a commanding voice that brooked no argument. He looked back at her. "Key?"

It was in her hand.

"Do you want to do the honors?" he asked gruffly.

"I don't know. Are you going to put me down?"

He just grinned, ornery as could be.

Faith rolled her eyes and reached over to unlock the

door. He swept on inside. And only when the door was closed behind them did he set her down again.

Somehow, Zach was not surprised to find that caterers had been in, to set up a table in the living room, and lay out a private supper of sumptuous finger foods and a very fine bottle of champagne on ice.

"Who...?" Faith asked in surprise.

Zach read the card that had been left for them. It said, "Make the most of your wonderful night! Rosalyn and Bart."

He turned it so Faith—who still looked breathtaking in her wedding gown, despite the long day—could read it, too. A slow smile spread across her face. "Wow, Rosalyn really thinks of everything, doesn't she?"

He moved close enough to see the pleasure shimmering in his bride's gorgeous green eyes. "She tries. And she knows how to give a great party."

"That she does." Her elegant features tinged a soft pink, Faith winced and bent slightly at the waist.

The tenderness he felt for her doubled. She had been such a trouper through all of this. "Problem?"

She nodded and lifted her skirt. "I have to get out of my shoes!"

He looked at the delicate ivory evening sandals visible beneath the puffy layers of skirt. The sexy high heels were the perfect complement to her long silky legs. A rush of desire coursed through him, even as he gazed at her. "Want some help?"

She uttered a soft sigh of relief. Then sank down on the sofa, lifting the hem of her gown even higher. "Would you mind?"

"Not at all."

In fact, it was his job now, as her husband, wasn't it?

He bent before her, like a knight kneeling before his queen. Undid the thin straps, one by one, and removed her shoes. Immediately she wiggled her stocking-clad toes. He clasped the arch of her foot and massaged away the tenseness. "Better?" he asked.

She nodded, her body relaxing. Eyes closed, she lay her head on the back of the sofa, as he turned his attention to the other. "Heaven..."

With another soft sigh, she opened her eyes and sat up. Smiled gratefully. "Thanks. I think I'm good now."

He wasn't.

In fact, he had never wanted a woman more in his entire life!

To distract himself, he pulled her garter out of his pocket. Dangled the lacy confection in front of her teasingly. "By the way, do you get to keep this, or should I?"

Her cheeks flooded with color at the tangible reminder of that part of the reception. A part that, thanks to the fellas at Laramie Gardens and his SEAL buddies, had briefly been accompanied by stripper music. It was clear from the way she was looking at him that she remembered the erotic moment, too. "Very funny, soldier. I can't believe they put you up to that!"

Zach could. What was a real wedding, after all, without a few high jinks? "Hey, you were wearing one," he said in his own defense, taking off his shoes, too.

Her chin lifted in indignation. "Only because my sisters insisted." She recited, "You know. Something old. Something new. Something borrowed. Something blue..."

He let his glance sift over her, even as he warned the rest of his body to calm down. "Well, your whole ensemble looked very nice on you," he told her sincerely, trying to move the conversation to safer ground.

Her gaze drifted over him, too. "You looked—*look*," she amended self-consciously, "very nice…in that uniform."

Figuring they might as well enjoy the repast, since neither of them had had much chance to enjoy their own dinners, given they had been too busy socializing, he went ahead and opened the champagne. Then poured two glasses. Their fingers brushed as he handed her a flute brimming with bubbly golden liquid. Wordlessly, they clinked glasses, linked arms just for the hell of it and sipped. "So what next?" he asked finally, aware the evening was still incredibly young.

Faith helped herself to a canapé. Munched on it, thinking. "I don't know."

He consulted his watch. "What do you usually do at ten after nine in the evening?"

She chuckled softly, then admitted, "If I've put Quinn to sleep, I go to bed myself."

He gave her a half grin.

"Read a little and fall asleep. But—" she took another sip of champagne, then ate a tea sandwich "—I'm not sleepy."

He got a small plate and helped himself to several miniature crab cakes. "Neither am I."

Deciding they were hungrier than they knew, they both sat down at the elegant table set for two. The fire had been lit in the fireplace, lending a cozy intimacy to the room.

"We could change clothes," Faith suggested.

It was disconcerting, not having the buffer of dog and baby between them. "Go for a six-mile run."

She wrinkled her nose at him. “That’s *your* idea of a good time. Not mine!”

He grinned. “Watch TV?”

Another dissenting expression crossed her face. “A little anticlimactic. Don’t you think?”

“Probably.” He shifted his gaze away from the voluptuous curves of her breasts, which were swelling up out of the ivory satin neckline of her gown. “We could still get you out of that dress. Me out of this uniform.” Thus ending any wedding-night fantasies.

She rose gracefully, tilting her head at him. Her green eyes glittered with mischief, too. “Is it going to take both of us to do that?”

He stood, tamping down his need to haul her into his arms and pick up where their end-of-ceremony kiss left off. “I think I’ve got mine covered, but you, on the other hand…” Squinting at her, he shook his head ruefully. “There are an awful lot of tiny little buttons on the back of that dress.”

Yes, Faith thought, surprised Zach had even noticed that detail, there were. In fact, between the corset, the petticoat and the myriad of tiny pearl fastenings, it had taken what seemed like an army to get her into this beautiful confection.

She also knew Zach was onto something. The sooner the two of them felt less like a new bride and groom, the better. And key to that would be her losing the gorgeous ivory satin gown, and him, his dashing white dress uniform.

She offered her back to him, ready to get on with it. “Do you mind?”

Once the buttons on the back of her gown were undone, she'd be able to go upstairs and change into something comfy. She imagined he'd want to do the same.

What she hadn't counted on, however, was the way it would feel to have him standing behind her, unbuttoning her dress, one inch at a time. The feel of his breath ghosting over her nape, his warm fingers brushing her skin, was more tantalizing than anything she had ever experienced before.

"So what was your favorite part of the night?" he rasped.

Now. This. Your kiss. Oh, that kiss. Faith swallowed, aware the last thing she could do was tell him the truth. "Um..." She waved a hand and felt her knees tremble slightly. "There were so many...!" She drew in a quavering breath, closed her eyes completely as he moved his way down to the middle of her spine.

He went lower still. "Pick one."

"Well, if I have to choose..." Shivering at his touch, she briefly lost her train of thought but then forced herself to focus on all the meaningful sentimental details of their wedding. "I guess it would be all the retired military residents in their uniforms. Army, navy, marine, air force—it seemed like every branch was represented..."

Zach's fingers lingered at her lower back. "I know what you mean," he agreed reverently. "It's nice to know they all served and are still so proud of their contribution to our country."

"What about you?" Faith turned around, without thinking, to see his face. She studied his handsome features, his blue eyes, sensually chiseled lips. Zach was more than just Quinn's daddy or a dedicated soldier—he was masculine perfection come to life. "What was your favorite part?" she asked, just as softly.

He did not even hesitate. He smiled and looked deep into her eyes. "Seeing you come down the aisle, on your dad's arm. Straight for me."

She murmured an "oh" of surprise.

He reached over and began taking the tiara and pins out of her hair. She caught her breath again as he ran his hand through the tousled waves, rubbing the silky strands between his thumb and fingertips.

"I have to admit," she returned, feeling his heartfelt honesty should be rewarded by hers, "that my first sight of you this afternoon was pretty spectacular, too."

His lips curved into a wickedly sexy grin. "Only one thing to do about that, then," he murmured, bringing her all the way into his strong arms. And then he kissed her. The moment his lips fused with hers, sensations swept through her, as potent and fierce as a winter storm. She flattened her palms across the front of his jacket, and in turn, he slid his hands down her spine, resting them on her hips, pressing her lower half to his. Suddenly, everything she had held back came pouring forth, and what she wanted most, Faith conceded, was Zach.

She surged against him, knowing it was impulsive—and worse, shortsighted—yet she wanted to deepen the connection between them so badly. To find something, *anything*, that would make their marriage real.

They kissed endlessly, their hearts hammering in unison, and she couldn't think of any place she would rather be.

And the best part? He wanted her as much as she wanted him.

Loving the way he made the loneliness melt away, the way the world narrowed to just the two of them, when they were alone like this, she whispered, "Upstairs."

Chuckling, he dropped a string of kisses down the nape of her neck, across her cheek and upper jaw, then hovered over her lips. "*Where* upstairs?" he asked.

Faith trembled at the raw tenderness in his gaze. "Guest room."

She didn't have to ask twice. He lifted her in his arms and carried her, still kissing her all the way to his bed. He set her down gently, resting his hands on her shoulders. "You're sure?" he asked huskily.

Tingling from the way he had already laid claim to her, she threw caution to the wind. "Oh, yes."

She had never given much thought to her own needs and desires, but being with Zach, knowing she was his wife, made her want to change all that. He made her want to give in to the moment, just for a little while. Explore the truth of his desire. Allow herself to be held. Touched. Kissed. Loved. Already easing out of her dress, Faith pushed it past her hips, and stepped out of it. Her petticoat followed suit.

Fierce satisfaction and longing glimmered in his deep blue eyes as his gaze roved over her ivory satin-and-lace bridal lingerie. Drinking in the curves of her breasts spilling over the décolletage bra, seeing the imprint of her pink nipples, he inhaled a jerky breath. "That is some sexy getup," he rasped.

Knowing she could handle what could only be a very sporadic physical entanglement, she unhooked her bra, let her panties and garter belt follow. He couldn't break her heart unless she let him. And she *wasn't* going to let him. All they were going to do was lose themselves in a very passionate, very sexual interlude.

Just once.

Determined to satisfy both their curiosities, she

swept back the covers and sat on the edge of the bed. A feeling of femininity swept through her, intensifying the yearning she felt deep inside. "Your turn," she whispered.

Sexy mischief glimmered in his eyes. He kissed the back of her hand. "Your wish is my command, darlin'." He stripped down, kicking his clothes out of the way. She caught his wrist and brought him down beside her. The next thing she knew she was on her back and he was draped on top of her. She pressed against him, savoring the brisk wintry fragrance of his hair and skin.

Murmuring his pleasure, he rolled so they were on their sides. As they kissed, she explored his sculpted chest and flat abs, then went lower still…to the most masculine part of him. For once, she didn't try to hide what she felt. What she desired or yearned to have. Blood rushed, hot and needy, through her veins. She could see and feel how much he wanted her in the hot throbbing length of him, the bunched muscles, the scorching heat of his skin.

To her delight, he didn't try to downplay what he wanted, either. His lips fastened on her breasts, suckling gently, thrilling her, until the friction of his lips and tongue was almost more than Faith could bear. Her back arched, and her thighs fell farther apart. He moved down her body, kissing and caressing, stroking her thighs, finding the most tender part of her, encouraging her to slide inexorably toward the edge. She quivered with unimaginable pleasure and nearly shot off the bed. In turn, Zach released a low moan that was one-hundred-percent male triumph. She was ready then, yet still he persisted. Holding her fast, he stroked upward, moved his fingertips in, out, then in again. Over and over until she cried out, mindless with desire. He kissed her temples, then her cheeks, framed her face with his hands. "Now?" he said.

"Now," she murmured back.

She trembled with anticipation as he drew on a condom, then lifted her hips to his. He penetrated her slowly, cupping her bottom with both hands, filling her with the hot hard length of him, making her most potent fantasy come true. And then they were one. Kissing wildly, passionately. Rocking together, moving toward a single goal, seeking release, climbing ever higher. Unable to hold back a second longer, Faith arched against him and fell apart in his arms. His climax followed as he relinquished control, and joined her at the edge of ecstasy, and then beyond.

Zach held Faith against him, savoring the feel of her in his arms as they clung to each other until the intensity passed. He wasn't shocked when she pulled away. In fact, he was surprised she had allowed them to get that close in the first place…because doing so made their union feel all too real.

Her gaze shielded from his, she wrapped a blanket around her and departed without a word. When she came back, short minutes later, she was ensconced in a thick and fluffy robe. She handed the neatly folded blanket back to him, then said, "I think we are going to need a new agreement."

Chapter Eleven

"I'm listening," Zach said.

Reminding herself that their marriage was supposed to be a way to support Quinn and give him the family he deserved, nothing more, Faith gripped the belt of her plush ivory robe. "If we decide to continue to have sex, we have to be faithful to each other."

He lounged against the pillows, looking incredibly buff. "I'm up for that." He held her gaze as she tried not to look at everything concealed beneath the half-drawn bedsheet. "The question is, are you?"

Was she? Good question. Faith gulped, trying again to assert control. "I admit I have never before had a relationship that was just physical. But, that said," she continued presumptively before jerking in another nervous breath, "we're both young and healthy human beings, who are now legally married to each other and coparenting our baby boy. It's ridiculous to think either of us could go the rest of our lives without physical pleasure, so..."

Zach gave her an indomitable, hungry, blatantly male look. "If we need it or want it, or just have to have it, it has to be with each other. And only each other," Zach declared, finishing her statement for her.

She knew that, like herself, he had been raised never to take advantage. His training in the military had exemplified this. "Yes."

He offered her a lazy smile, shrugged. "Sounds good to me."

It was good that they weren't trying to deceive each other about the depth of their feelings, wasn't it? "I'm glad."

She began to pick up the scattered pieces of her sexy lingerie, her petticoat and wedding dress. "Anything else?" he asked eventually.

She set them all out in the hallway outside his bedroom door, for dispensing later. Came back toward him. Figuring it was best to get everything out in the open, she wet her lips with the tip of her tongue. "I know anything that makes our marriage more traditional will help us prove to the court that we can build a good solid family for Quinn."

The rims of his eyes darkened. "But?"

"I am still going to need my own space, as will you."

He nodded in agreement but did not share whatever else he was thinking.

Determined to keep herself from losing her grasp on reality, she insisted, "Just so we're clear. This is a convenient physical arrangement, nothing else."

He turned a hand, palm up. Let it rest on his bedsheet-covered thigh. "I'm fine with that...if you are."

What did he mean "*if* she was?" she couldn't help wondering. "So...separate bedrooms?" she proposed, resolutely laying out the house rules.

He nodded, still gazing at her in a way that made her feel far too vulnerable for comfort. "Separate bedrooms."

Her heart suddenly pounding, she started to turn away, ready to leave. "Okay, then," she said hurriedly. "Good night."

He caught her wrist before she could exit and guided her back to sit on the edge of his bed. Threading his hands through her hair, he brought her lips to his.

As the intimate moment stretched out, he gave her a slow, sultry smile.

"Good night then," he told her huskily.

And then he kissed her again. One kiss led to two… then three. The next thing Faith knew she was all the way back in his bed, her robe was coming off and they were making slow, sweet, tender love all over again. She didn't want to need him like this. With an all-consuming passion that took her breath away. But she did.

Exhausted, she fell asleep in his arms. But woke alone, just as Zach had promised her that she would.

As Faith made her way back to her own bed, and heard him moving around downstairs, she had to admit she was relieved. Yet also sad and confused. She forced herself to shake it off.

Their marriage made her Quinn's stepmother. She was now another step closer to officially adopting Quinn and becoming his mother, legally. That was indeed something to celebrate. So what if she and Zach weren't in love, and probably never would be? They had the same objectives. They got along. She just needed to keep the faith that everything would work out in the end.

Luckily, Faith discovered, early the following day, Zach had decided on a similar gung-ho attitude. They could do this, she reassured herself boldly. Together, she and Zach could manage anything if they set their minds to it. They had proved that by quickly coming to agreement about Quinn, getting through their first court date and surviving a wedding and wedding night that had fast gotten out of control…

Not that her new husband made reference to their wildly passionate lovemaking the night before. No, this morning he had behaved as casually as if it had never happened. Focusing instead on the minutia of daily life.

"I say we do it now," Zach announced as the clock hit ten.

"Do what?" Faith cuddled Quinn close, while Tinkerbelle curled up on the sofa beside her. Both had been dropped off by Emma a short while earlier, and now they had the whole weekend stretching ahead of them.

With the plain gold band, which matched the one adorning her ring finger, gleaming on his left hand, Zach continued looking at her half-decorated home. The garlands and wreaths, Christmas village and Advent calendars were up, but there was still more to be done.

Thumbs hooked through the loops on either side of his belt, he turned back to her. He shifted, his big body exuding warmth in the closed space, and she shivered despite herself. "We need a tree," he informed her.

She blinked. "Today?"

He flashed that sexy smile that made her weak in the knees, and as he dropped down next to her on the sofa, she found herself leaning closer to catch a whiff of his mint-flavored toothpaste. "Have anything else better to do?" he drawled.

Lord, he was going to be hard to resist. Especially now that she knew how fabulously he made love. Swallowing to ease the parched feeling in her throat, she said, "Um. Well…" She hesitated, watching as Quinn reached out for his daddy with both hands, babbling happily all the while. "I usually do my errands on Saturdays."

Zach held out his hands, and Quinn lurched into them. He chuckled as the little tyke snuggled happily against his broad chest, then turned back to Faith with a grin. “We could work that in, too.”

We.

She savored the word.

He was really working on this married-couple thing.

Something else that would be oh, so easy to get used to, then hard to do without…

Not that she was going to let herself depend on him. The way she had depended on a soldier who wasn’t going to be there most of the time, in the past…only to have it all end in heartbreak when Harm tragically died… She’d had to pick up the pieces once, when her life had all blown apart. She didn’t want to have to do that again. And the way to making sure that she would not have to was by keeping things casual. Not letting herself depend on him too much. Working together and being a team when it came to Quinn… Maybe even hanging out as friends or making love when the time was right… But otherwise making sure she maintained her independence…

Oblivious to the cautious nature of her thoughts, he continued, “Get the tree and whatever else you want to decorate the outside of the house with.”

The truth was, she could use help with both. It was sometimes a lot to manage just going to the grocery store with Quinn in tow. Never mind the tree lot and the hardware store. And she was already behind in her plans for the holidays. She raked her teeth across her lower lip, still feeling a little like this was all too good to be true. “You’d really want to do all that?”

“Sure.” He snuggled closer. “It will all go twice as

fast as if we work together, and we've got to have a tree for Quinn."

"True." She tried not to notice how good this all felt. How *special*. She put on her coparenting hat once again. "It is his very first Christmas, and I think it should be as memorable as we can make it."

His blue eyes were exceptionally cheerful as he looked down at her. "A fresh tree then?"

"Yes. Although because it's Saturday morning and the first full weekend in December, the lot out by the fairgrounds will likely be crowded."

"I think we can handle maneuvering around a few extra people. It'll just add to the excitement. So..." He leaned in closer, then asked, "What do you say? Do you want to go there first?"

Before she could respond, her cell phone vibrated in her pocket. "Actually..." She frowned, looking down at the screen to scan the text message that had just come in. "The new resident's move from the hospital was delayed, which means Nessie Rogers's financial paperwork will need to be redone."

"That can't wait until Monday?"

Faith knew she and Zach were supposed to be honeymooning. Then again, people knew the circumstances behind their marriage, so it wouldn't be a surprise to see them getting on with their lives, as per normal. "It probably could but I would feel better if everything were ready to go when Nessie arrived Monday morning." That way she wouldn't have to worry about it in the meantime, or get into the office extra early to accomplish it, prior to Nessie's transfer by ambulance.

Zach shifted Quinn into a sitting position. Her son beamed up at his daddy. Zach smiled lovingly back at the baby, then looked over at her. Amiable as ever. "You want to go to Laramie Gardens?"

"Just for ten or fifteen minutes. You and Quinn could visit with the guys, while I slip into my office and get this paperwork done."

Zach took Quinn into his arms and stood. "Then let's do it."

Fifteen minutes later, their son had a fresh diaper and a warm jacket and hat on, and Faith had his diaper bag packed. She and Zach grabbed their jackets, too, and they hit the road. When they arrived at the facility, Zach and Quinn went in the front entrance, while she headed to a side, employees-only entrance so she wouldn't get waylaid before she accomplished her task.

Faith was surprised to see Tillie Tarrant and Ian Baker sitting next to each other on one of the benches in one of the interior courtyards, where the staff sometimes took their breaks. Heads bent, talking low. *Intimately.*

Tillie's husband, Ted, was nowhere in sight.

She appeared tearful. Ian put his arm around her shoulders and leaned in closer, seeming to murmur something to reassure her.

After a moment, Tillie nodded and pulled herself together. Still oblivious that Faith was standing a distance behind them, watching, the elegant older woman removed what appeared to be an envelope from the leather-bound notebook in her hand. She gave it to Ian.

He whispered something to her again.

As they started to get up, Faith ducked back out of sight. What was going on? she wondered.

Was this the reason Tillie wanted to move out of her suite with her husband of sixty years?

Why did Tillie look so guilty as she headed off alone?

And if this was all as innocent as Faith hoped it was, why didn't Ian walk alongside Tillie, instead of pocketing the envelope and going off in another direction?

Meanwhile, feeling happier than he could ever remember, Zach carried Quinn through the main lobby to the community room, which had been transformed back to its usual post-wedding state. Not surprisingly, they got a rock-star greeting from the residents enjoying the weekend morning. "Hey!" Buck Franklin teased good-naturedly. "Aren't you supposed to be honeymooning?"

Zach chuckled. "Hey! This is our idea of a good time. Besides, we wanted to thank you-all for everything you did yesterday. We couldn't have had a better wedding if we'd spent years planning it."

Everyone beamed.

To keep from having to field any more personal questions, Zach moved the conversation along, and asked, "Anyone know where is the best place to get a tree?"

"I always drove into San Angelo, to the Kiwanis lot there," Wilbur Barnes said.

Russell Pierce added, "I like the fairgrounds here." Where Faith wanted to go.

Miss Mim said, "If you want to cut down your own, there's a ranch in the next county..." More details and suggestions followed.

Zach nodded, taking it all in. Watching his dad, Quinn mimicked him and nodded soberly, too.

Everyone broke up.

"Speaking of trees...what do you think about the decorations on ours?" Wilbur asked.

That was a loaded question if he had ever heard one.

Zach turned to admire the towering tree that had been stylishly upgraded for the wedding. Likely by some decorator his mother had hired. In the process, it had lost its down-home warmth. But he knew the over-the-top sophistication appealed to a lot of the women residents, because he had heard them raving about it during the reception.

"It's very nice," Zach said, and left it at that.

A throat cleared. "It could be nicer if you-all let me put the battery-driven ones I invented on it." Russell Pierce showed him an angel, lit up from within.

Zach admired the eye-catching ornament. "This is really spectacular. Did you make the whole thing?" Because the detail on the ethereal angel was really fantastic.

The Laramie Gardens resident shook his head. "No. I just used the ones my late wife collected and hollowed out the inside and installed some battery-operated lights."

"Well, it's very nice," Zach repeated sincerely.

"Do you think we should put all of them up?" Russell motioned at the box full of ornaments next to his chair.

"We can't do that, Russell," Miss Patricia explained. "We have a *theme*. This year it is snowflakes with gold and satin ribbons, and the gorgeous ornaments that were added for the wedding. Your decorations, colorful and interesting as they all are, would *clash*."

Buck Franklin came to his friend's defense. "Well, that tree was fine for the wedding—we didn't want to take attention from the bride and groom, after all—but now it is so big, and so similarly decked out, it seems a little boring to me."

Darrell Enloe jumped in to side with the other men. "I think it could use a little livening up, too."

Miss Mim moved to center stage and took command like the head librarian she used to be. "We know everyone's taste is different when it comes to holiday decorating. That's why each resident has an artificial tabletop tree in their room. So they can decorate to their heart's content. Exactly the way they want."

A brief silence fell.

"Sorry, Russell," Darrell said sympathetically, "it looks like you are outvoted."

The elderly man scowled. "Well, it's a shame to let all of these go to waste—" he motioned to his basket of colorful antique ornaments "—because only about a fifth of them will fit on that tabletop tree in my room!"

More sympathetic murmurs, all around.

Before anyone else could pick up the threads of the argument, Faith walked in, looking absolutely gorgeous in her red turtleneck sweater, jeans and boots. She got the same rock-star welcome he and Quinn had received.

She handled the attention graciously, as always.

Zach knew her well enough by now, though, to read the slight stiffness in her body language, and could tell she was ready to go. Preferably before the talk turned to their adjustment to "married life" or something equally awkward and uncomfortable.

He winked at their audience. "Hate to run out on you-all, but we better get going if we're going to get our own Christmas tree up today."

Faith stepped a little closer to him and tucked her hand in the crook of his elbow. "You're right about that, Lieutenant!" she said flirtatiously. The men chuckled and looked on enviously. The women all swooned.

They departed, waving, to a lot of well-wishes.

Yet the moment they were out of sight, Faith's shoulders slumped dejectedly and her expression turned sad and anxious. Which meant something had happened in the brief time they had been apart.

Happy she had decided to let him do the driving whenever possible, Zach helped her get Quinn's carrier snapped into the base of his car seat, waited to assist her with her door, then circled around and got in behind the wheel. Curious, he asked, "What's going on?"

Faith turned, one eyebrow lifted in question. Feeling surprisingly protective of her, given how short a time they had known each other, Zach told her gruffly, "You look like you just got some very bad news and are trying to hide it."

Faith didn't want to discuss it, but she knew she had to talk to someone about what she had seen or she would carry the worry with her all day. And that wasn't fair to Zach. Or Quinn. She swallowed to ease the tension in her throat, and looked over at him, noting how ruggedly handsome he looked, despite her dour mood. "You promise to keep this confidential?"

He slanted her a reassuring glance. "I promise."

"I just saw Tillie Tarrant and Ian Baker sitting on a bench out back having some sort of *really intimate* conversation."

Zach's brow furrowed. "Isn't Tillie married to Ted?"

She sighed. "Exactly."

"And Ian's a widower," he recalled.

Faith nodded and filled in Zach on a little more history. "Yes. Ian lived alone for a few years, after his wife passed, then found it to be too lonely and sold his home here and moved into Laramie Gardens a month or so ago."

"I don't understand what the problem is. I mean, for all you know Ian and Tillie were talking about Ian's late wife or something."

She would have thought that, too. Except… "I've seen the way Ted looks at Ian. Ted is clearly jealous."

Zach's hands gripped the steering wheel. "You think there is something going on between Tillie Tarrant and Ian Baker?" he asked incredulously.

"It never would have crossed my mind, given the fact that Ted and Tillie have been married sixty years and clearly adore each other. Or *did* adore each other. But lately, things have been a little tense," she admitted.

Zach stopped at a red light. He turned to face her. "What haven't you told me?"

Boy, oh, boy, he could read her mind! A feat that would be helpful sometimes. Others, not so much. "Tillie came to me last week to inquire privately about moving out of the suite she shares with Ted, and into a single room close by."

Zach frowned. "What does Ted think about this?"

"I don't know." She lifted her hands, exasperated to have been put in such an impossible situation. But as the financial director of Laramie Gardens Senior Living complex, it was also her job. "She hadn't discussed it with him! We were supposed to talk again late last week, but because you and I were trying to get married in a rush, she put it off until Monday."

"Two days from now."

"Yes." They had an appointment to speak Monday at 9:00 a.m. Now, Faith wondered if that was too long.

Once again, Zach read her mind. "You can't think Tillie wants a divorce?"

Sadness mixed with worry. "I hope not. Ted would

be devastated. Especially now that his illness has confined him to a wheelchair much of the time."

Zach reached over to briefly squeeze her denim-clad knee. "Illness and injury put a definite strain on a marriage and split up a lot of couples," he told her with the experience of a soldier who had seen that a lot in his line of work. "But for some—" he exhaled and put his right hand back on the steering wheel "—adversity only makes them stronger."

Faith shifted so she could see his face. "What are you saying?"

He shrugged his broad shoulders. "That nobody really knows what is going on in a relationship except the two people involved."

She was glad they were talking about this. He was definitely helping her see another point of view. "So the conversation I saw..."

"Could be about a million different things," Zach offered practically. "Let's not jump to conclusions."

Faith shut her eyes briefly, forcing herself to do a mental reset. "You're right," she said resolutely. "Ted and Tillie have a very strong history." Sixty solid-gold years! "And it's Christmas, after all." She was doing her best to reassure herself. "Tillie'd have to be heartless to leave Ted now that his health is in decline. And Tillie is one of the kindest people I've ever met," she concluded as they reached the fairgrounds. Zach found a parking space with some difficultly and they got out. Even from a distance, they could see the Christmas-tree emporium was packed.

Not surprisingly, the three of them received another rock-star welcome from everyone they knew in attendance.

"Congratulations!" Sage and Nick Monroe said.

"We so admire what the two of you are doing for that baby!" Lulu Kirkland praised, while her husband Sam nodded in approval.

"You two are positively glowing!" Merri Armstrong said.

"You-all do look really happy," her physician-husband agreed.

Their caseworker, Mitzy Martin-McCabe, joined the gaggle surrounding them. "I think they're right. You two both are positively radiant!"

It was hard not to blush when receiving so much attention, Faith thought.

"I heard the wedding was spectacular," Mitzy continued.

Was that approval they saw in the veteran social worker's eyes, or reservation?

"Everyone went all in," Zach said.

Mitzy's smile rested on Quinn, who was snuggled happily in the BabyBjörn baby carrier on Faith's chest, and was curiously looking around at all the people and activity. "Well, that's Laramie County for you. Everyone here is very welcoming and neighborly. It's why we all love it so much, and hopefully, so will you, Zach."

"I admit, I'm beginning to see the appeal of a small town," he returned sincerely.

Which meant *what*? Faith wondered. Was he already thinking about settling here when he eventually retired from the Navy SEALs? And, if so, what would he do for work, if and when that happened?

Noting Mitzy was regarding them intently, as if trying to figure how genuine this all was, Faith decided to change the subject. "Are you here to get your tree, too?"

Mitzy waved at her husband, Chase, who was busy herding their four-year-old quadruplets in the search for a perfect evergreen. He waved back at them. "We sure are," she said.

"Listen, as long as we're here," she added, whipping out her phone, "how about I schedule the home inspection for Zach? Do you think you'll have everything in place by next Friday?"

That was less than a week away. Not much time.

Faith and Zach exchanged glances. "It's okay with me," he said, acquiescing.

"Me, too." Faith had no choice but to agree.

"Great. I'll email you a list of things I am going to need to see when we do meet," Mitzy promised, then dashed off to join her family.

Watching the social worker depart, Faith couldn't help but worry that might not be enough time to prepare. Then again, it would give her and Zach something decidedly unromantic to concentrate on, other than their baby and each other… And that would help keep her grounded. Something, she was beginning to realize, that she needed very much…

Chapter Twelve

"What do you think?" Faith asked, two hours later, unsure what to do next. "Should we wait until Quinn wakes before we put up the tree?" Thus far, the bundled-up evergreen was still tied to the top of the SUV. Prior to that, they'd had to bring in the morning purchases, change and feed Quinn, eat lunch, do the dishes and put their son down for his afternoon nap in his crib upstairs. Now that he was sound asleep, they were free to do whatever needed to be done. "Or go ahead and set it up, and surprise him when he wakes up?"

"Bring it in now," Zach said decisively. "But hold off on decorating it so the three of us can do it all together."

"Sounds good," Faith said, aware once again how cozy and domestic this all felt.

They headed outside.

Zach cut the ties and lifted the heavy tree down as easily as if it was a feather. Admiring his strength, Faith walked on ahead and then held the front door open while he carried in the seven-foot tree. The smell of fresh-cut pine inundated the air.

Aware she was really getting into the Christmas spirit after a shaky start to the holiday season, Faith smiled. Her new husband was gaining enthusiasm, too.

Zach's gaze drifted over her. "You really want Quinn to participate in everything, don't you?"

She followed with the metal stand and set it in the front of the living-room windows. Then kneeled down to guide the trunk into the stand. "It is his first Christmas."

"That is true," Zach remarked, relaxed and affable in a way that Harm had never been when he was on military leave.

He motioned for them to switch places, so he could give the bolts in the stand an extra tightening. Acutely aware of how enticingly masculine he smelled, too, she held the tree steady while he worked.

"But it might be a good idea for us to go ahead and put on the lights now." Finished, Zach stood. He moved back to give her room, watching as she used a pair of scissors to cut the mesh that had been securing the branches of the tree.

"Then we can do the rest with his help," Zach said, stepping back to let her work.

His steady regard had her skin heating from head to toe. Doing her best to keep her mind on their task, instead of how well he kissed, she tilted her head to one side and surveyed him right back. Wishing she didn't enjoy spending time with him quite so much. "Are you humoring me?"

Crinkles appeared at the corners of his eyes. "I'm humoring both of us. I want our little guy involved in every aspect of this holiday, too." He took the mesh and put it aside, for disposal later. "Otherwise, I would have gone off and gotten a tree and brought it home and set it up myself."

Faith opened up the shopping bag that held their new lights, toddler-friendly decorations and a tree-topper. She wasn't sure why she had purchased everything new this year, she just knew she wanted everything to be fresh and different. "I'm sure that would have taken a whole lot less time."

"True." He winked. "And also been a whole lot less fun..."

"Mmm-hmm." She reflected on their tree-selection adventure. How they'd let their baby boy touch the needles to his heart's content. Then later, how Zach had pushed Quinn and the cart around, while she filled their shopping basket in the grocery store. "You seemed to be having fun this morning." In fact, he had played the roles of adoring new husband and daddy to the hilt.

He gave her another flirtatious glance. "Hard not to...given the company."

Doing her best to contain a self-conscious laugh, she opened up the first box of multicolored lights. "It doesn't bother you to constantly be under the microscope of small-town life? Having everyone kind of in our business?"

He helped her unwind the strand from the cardboard holder, moving farther away as they worked. "Actually, residing in Laramie County is a lot like living in the military. Everybody sort of knows everybody else's business, to a point, anyway, and watches out for each other."

"Interesting," she murmured. "I never thought of it that way." Finished, they returned to the tree. Zach wound the lights through the uppermost branches, while she moved close behind him and held the strand to keep it from getting tangled, as he worked his way slowly and carefully around the tree.

"Does the close scrutiny bother you?" he asked her eventually. He stopped without warning, and she nearly crashed into him. He stayed where he was, looking patiently over at her. "Or, having grown up here, is small-town life, knowing someone always has your back, what you prefer?"

Good question, she thought, as he went back to draping lights. "My first nine years were spent in Houston." She reached out to help him untangle a portion of the strand when it got caught on a branch. "So I was used to a metropolitan area. And can still recall the traffic and all the people and places. The variety of pretty much everything that you find in a big city definitely had its upside, I won't discount that. But you're right—this is cozier in a lot of respects."

Finished, they went to get a second strand from the bag. "I'm glad Quinn is going to grow up here."

Faith smiled. "Me, too." As she reached into the hardware-store bag, she accidentally brought out a sprig of mistletoe, with Congratulations Newlyweds! written on the tag. The clerk had pressed it into her hand as they were leaving. She waved the sprig and set it aside. "Although maybe we could do with a little less of this," she muttered.

He chuckled, unlike her, not the least bit dismayed. "It bothers you to have people speculating about our love life?" He seemed surprised.

She blinked back at him, wishing she had his level of confidence. "Doesn't it bother you?"

His broad shoulders lifted and fell in a careless shrug. "I don't dwell on it." He reached out to tuck an errant strand of hair behind her ear. "You do?"

Her skin tingled from his light, warm touch. Doing her best to tamp down her growing desire, she gazed into his eyes. "It just sort of makes me feel guilty. That everyone I know here is so invested in this situation."

She sighed, then continued, "I mean, I know they are wildly optimistic about this all working out, the way it would if we'd had traditional reasons for getting hitched. And I don't want to disappoint anyone."

He cupped her shoulders, urging her to look up at him. "You won't."

The warmth of his palms transmitted through her sweater, to her skin. Aware her knees were suddenly wobbly, she shook her head at him. "You don't know that," she whispered.

He traced her cheek with the pad of his thumb, looked down at her tenderly. "Yes, Faith, I do. Because I know you," he told her. "And you aren't the kind of person who disappoints *anyone* deliberately."

Faith hated being seen as a saint, when in reality she was far from it. Guilt flooding her, she stepped back and moved away. "As much as I'd like to claim otherwise," she said regretfully, jerking in a shaky breath, "that's simply not true, Zach. I disappointed my late husband. *All the time.*"

For a second, Zach thought Faith must have been joking. But the increasingly miserable look on her face told him she was not. Which meant this definitely had to be discussed.

He took her by the hand and led her over to the sofa. As she settled next to him, he looked her in the eye. "You think you made your husband unhappy?"

She knit her hands together in her lap. "I know I did. I was a terrible military wife. I worried all the time, and missed him terribly when he was gone, and worse, wasn't shy about letting him know it. I not only kept asking him not to reenlist, but I also nagged him about starting a family, when I knew he didn't want to do that until he could be here to enjoy it, too."

Zach studied her. "What was his response?"

"Harm just pointed out that I knew he was headed for BUD/S and SEAL qualification training when I met him. And that after that he'd be deployed, most likely to the Middle East, and would be expected to stay in until the eight-to-ten-year mark."

"He quit at eight."

"Yes. And regretted it every day after. Being a special operator was what he knew, what he *loved.* He didn't know what he was going to do after that, but he knew it had to be outdoors. And it had to be physical. No sitting behind a desk for him. So he took a job with a barn-building business here in Laramie County."

"How did that go?"

"Badly. The owner was big on safety and wanted Harm to wear all sorts of bulky equipment that my husband didn't think he needed. They quarreled about it constantly. And he even threatened to fire Harm if he didn't start following protocol. But he never got a chance because Harm slipped and fell off the pitch of a thirty-foot-tall roofline." She released a quavering breath. "So instead of being killed in action when he was off on some combat mission, the way I always feared, he died from a fall that could have been avoided had he only been using all the safety equipment his boss required him to wear."

"And you blame yourself for that."

Unfairly, it seemed to Zach.

But she knew better.

She swallowed around the ache in her throat. "I think if Harm hadn't been so unhappy about prematurely giving up the career he loved, then he wouldn't have been so reckless and difficult. And made the mistake that ultimately cost him his life. And our future. So, yes." She sighed tremulously. "I blame myself."

For a moment, Zach said nothing.

Leaving Faith to wonder if he would eventually resent her, too.

Then he got up and walked away from her. For a moment, he just stood there, looking out the window, at the street beyond. He seemed to be wrestling with some inner demon. The way Harm always had when he'd been home with her, instead of out on some incredibly exciting and dangerous mission.

Finally, Zach pivoted back, appearing to have made some kind of difficult decision. "What if I told you," he said quietly, "that whatever you did or didn't do as Harm's wife had nothing to do with what ultimately happened to him?"

She got to her feet and walked toward him. Maybe it would be better if they got this all out in the open. And who would understand her shortcomings as a military wife better than another SEAL? Guilt flooding through her, she lifted her chin. "I would tell you that you didn't know what you were talking about," she returned soberly.

"Except in this case," Zach said, "I do."

Their gazes locked. "Go on," Faith urged hoarsely.

He folded his arms, biceps bulging beneath his cashmere sweater. "Harm had a reputation for being fearless."

Faith nodded. She knew that, too.

"He was also really good at thinking on his feet, and he never stopped pushing himself and inspiring everyone else around him to do the same. Combined, that made him a very good Navy SEAL. And had him deployed in pretty much every hot spot there was."

Faith sighed, recalling the unending worry that had gone along with every one of her late husband's missions. "Don't I know that," she murmured.

"Stress like that can wear on a soldier." Zach ambled closer. "It can leave you feeling numb or anxious. Or, in Harm's case, invincible."

A taut silence fell. "Are you saying he was in some kind of trouble?" Faith gasped.

He dipped his head in grave acknowledgment. "On Harm's last mission, he took too many chances, and put his team in danger. It all worked out in the end, but it could easily have gone south. When he went to reenlist last fall, his officer in charge suggested he take some time off. Maybe see somebody. Get himself together." Zach's lips compressed in regret. "Harm refused."

That, she could believe. Harm had never allowed himself to show any sign of weakness, and to him, asking for help would have been a shortcoming. "Why wouldn't he have told me all this?" So she could have been there as his wife!

"Maybe he was embarrassed. Or waiting for the right time."

"Or he never intended to tell me at all," she replied heavily, noting with surprise that Zach didn't seem to think less of her, for her lack of knowledge.

Shrugging, he shoved a hand through his hair. "Maybe Harm didn't think you needed to know."

"Except I did!" Faith cried, feeling hurt and angry.

Zach squinted. "Why?"

She lifted her hands, her frustration rising anew. "Because if I had known, I would have pushed him to go see someone and then go back to active duty if that was what he needed to be happy." She wouldn't have insisted he stay in Laramie, and make them both quietly miserable, the way he had been at the time of his passing.

Zach studied her. "What about your plans to have a family?"

What about them?

Sadly, she was used to not getting everything she wanted. To only living half the life she had dreamed of. So Harm leaving again, she realized in frustration, would have been no different than anything that had happened previously.

With effort, once again, she forced herself to be grateful for what she *did* have, and not let herself yearn for more. "I guess that would have had to wait," she said finally.

Quinn awakened shortly after that. Faith was relieved at the interruption, since the last thing she wanted to continue talking about was the mistakes of her past.

Fortunately, Quinn was every bit as excited by the tree decorating as they had hoped. He grinned and babbled, as she and Zach took turns holding him, letting him touch and explore each ornament before they put it on the tree. All the while, Tinkerbelle lounged on her cushion nearby, wanting to be part of the family scene.

"Hey, this is cute," Zach remarked.

He removed a dark-haired terrier that looked a lot like Tinkerbelle from the package of brand-new kid-friendly ornaments. The dog had a red knit scarf and cap on, and was seated on a sled.

He brought it over to show Quinn.

Their son looked down at it, tilting his head, then let out a belly laugh that went on and on and soon had them both chuckling.

"What's so funny?" Zach asked.

Quinn's laugh was so infectious, Faith continued to giggle, too. "I don't know," she admitted, wiping her eyes. "But something about this ornament is sure tickling his funny bone!"

She let the baby hold the plastic decoration, until he pushed it toward the tree. Getting her son's suggestion, she put it on a branch, next to a cocoa-sipping duck.

Satisfied, Quinn nodded down at the package and waved his arms, trying to reach it himself. Zach brought out a red-nosed reindeer.

He gave it to his son.

Quinn held it. Put it to his mouth. Then pulled it away and looked at it, hard and long, before abruptly bursting into another round of delighted giggles.

And so it went.

They chuckled through the Santa, and the elves, and Mrs. Claus. The decorative candy cane. Snow globe. And gingerbread man.

When they were finally done, Quinn lurched for Zach. Wanting to be held in his strong arms.

"So what's next?" he asked.

Trying not to think what an endearing sight father and son were, or how much Quinn was likely to miss Zach when he deployed again in a few weeks, Faith smiled and headed for the kitchen to throw something together for them to eat. "Dinner, bath, bedtime bottle..."

Zach helped out through it all. Asking the questions about Quinn's routine that he was going to need for his own home-study evaluation by social services, and pitching in as they went. Usually by the time Quinn had finished his formula, he was yawning, or half-asleep.

Not this evening.

After he burped, he put his fists on Zach's chest, and pushed far enough away to be able to see into his face. He babbled nonsensically.

Brow furrowed, Zach asked, "What's he saying?"

"No clue."

Quinn continued to do vertical baby push-ups against his daddy's chest. Zach grinned and kissed the tuft of dark hair on the top of his head. Then slanted her a glance. "Does he talk to you this way?"

"Ah, no," Faith answered reluctantly. Which, admittedly, kind of hurt. The most she had ever gotten out of him was a long sigh that sounded a little like "hi," but probably wasn't.

"When will he start talking?" Zach turned to her, his mood as cheerful as her son's.

Although usually Quinn reached for her, wanting his mommy to hold him, whenever she was around, Faith noted her son seemed remarkably content where he was. Snug against Zach's warm, strong chest. "Usually when they are around a year old."

"Do you think his first word will be *Mommy*?"

That would be nice. Trying not to wonder what would happen if Zach continued being this good with Quinn, this sexy and appealing, this enthralled with them both. "I don't know."

"Should we read him a story or walk him around or something?" Zach looked at the clock, realizing Quinn's normal bedtime had passed. "What would make him drowsy?"

Feeling the clip sliding out of her messily upswept hair, Faith reached up to remove it. "Rocking, probably, up in the nursery." She ran a hand through the tousled strawberry-blond strands, doing her best to tidy them without a mirror or hairbrush. "Do you want to do it?" Even though that was her and Quinn's special time together, she forced herself to be generous. "See if you can put him to sleep tonight?"

A pause. The kind that told her he wanted to, but also did not want to fail. "Yeah."

Her heart went out to him. There had been a time, when she had first brought Quinn home, that she had been that uncertain, too. She smiled. "Then let's go."

Faith led the way. Once in the nursery, she lowered the side of the crib, to make putting Quinn in easier, then gathered up his satin-trimmed blue baby blanket and his favorite stuffed animal, Moo Cow.

She held Quinn while Zach got settled in the rocker-glider, then handed over their baby, so he was once again snuggled against his daddy's broad chest. Although Quinn settled against Zach immediately, he was still wide-awake. "Want some music?"

He flashed her a grateful look. "Please."

She walked over to turn on the compilation of favorite soothing lullabies. And while she was at it, dimmed the light substantially. "I'll be nearby if you need me," she murmured. Bending over, she kissed Quinn on the top of his head, then eased from the room.

She half expected the baby boy to protest her departure. But he was so enthralled with Zach's calming presence, he didn't.

With a heavy heart, she went down the hall to her bedroom, and busied herself tidying up. For a while, she heard Zach murmuring nonsensically to Quinn, and occasionally the five-month-old babbled something in return. Eventually that stopped. Leaving only the occasional brief bursts of silence between songs.

She had just hung up the last of her clothes, when Zach appeared in the doorway. He looked impossibly tall and strong. Quinn's head was nestled on his shoulder. Their son had one arm wrapped around his daddy's neck, holding him close, the other clasped Moo Cow and his blue blankie. The sight of them together was so sweet and sentimental her heart filled to bursting. Emotion clogged her throat.

Oblivious to the tenderness wafting through her, Zach whispered, "Can you help me?"

Faith nodded, glad to be needed once again. She tiptoed past him and went down the hall, motioning wordlessly for Zach to follow her. When they were standing next to the crib, she eased the blanket and stuffed animal out of her son's arms. Laid them in the crib. Then gestured for Zach to put Quinn down, so he was lying flat on his back.

Zach did. Wincing slightly as Quinn's brow furrowed and his cherubic little lips worked, as if he was dreaming about drinking from his favorite bottle. Faith took the moment to ease his lovies in next to him, within easy reach should he wake. Then he sighed and lapsed back into sleep.

Soundlessly, she lifted the side of the crib and latched it carefully into place.

Quinn slept on.

She and Zach eased out into the hallway.

"How was it?" she whispered, thinking back to the first time she had held Quinn in her arms and rocked him to sleep. The sweetness had nearly undone her. Still did.

She loved having a baby to parent so much. As much as Zach did, too?

"It was awesome," Zach said, an almost unbearable tenderness creasing his handsome face. For a second, he looked happier and more content than she had ever seen him. He cleared his throat and continued gruffly, "Thanks for letting me do that tonight." He put a light hand on her shoulder.

"Thanks for letting me continue to be part of Quinn's life," Faith whispered back. She took his hand and squeezed it.

Affection gleamed in his blue eyes. He seemed in no hurry to let her go. "Don't you know by now?" he rumbled, his eyes holding hers for a long, palpable moment. "I wouldn't have it any other way."

The next thing Faith knew, she was all the way in his arms. She saw the cool, purposeful intent in his expression, and caught her breath. Tingles surged through her, pooling in her lower abdomen, tightening her nipples. She wanted him so very much. If she was honest with herself, she had since the first day they met.

Zach brought her closer still and his mouth found hers once again. He tasted like mint and man, and Faith felt herself surge to life. Maybe it was the season. Maybe it was everything she had just discovered about her prior life. All she knew was that Zach felt safe. Like the kind of man who wouldn't deliberately shut her out.

And when she was with Zach like this, she wanted

to make him hers, and hers alone. He seemed to want that, too, as he increased the pressure of his lips on hers.

Their kiss was a melding of heat and need. Yearning spiraled through her as he moved his hands tenderly over her spine, across her shoulders, to her waist and hips. And still he kissed her, the feel of his mouth on hers filling her with the kind of love she had wanted all her life. Was it possible, she wondered wistfully, that theirs would soon be a real marriage in every way? Or was this simply the result of them both being alone for too long?

"I want to do this right," he murmured, framing her face with his hands. "So…where?"

Her excitement escalated. "My room this time," she said.

"Whatever my lady wants." Surveying her with distinctly masculine satisfaction, he tucked one arm beneath her knees the other behind her shoulders and swung her off her feet, just as he had on their wedding night, when he had carried her across the threshold.

Her heart pounding with anticipation, Faith held on to his broad shoulders. "I'm not sure this is necessary," she whispered, being careful to keep her voice down so as not to wake the sleeping babe in the nursery.

A devilishly sexy smile slashed across his handsome face. "Why not let me be the judge of that?" he murmured back, already heading soundlessly down the upstairs hall. Not stopping until he set her down beside her bed.

The way he looked at her then thrilled her even more.

"Oh, Zach." She sighed. She went up on tiptoe, wreathing her arms about his shoulders.

"I hear you. I feel the same way," he rasped, cupping

her face between his warm palms and capturing her lips with his. She kissed him back with all her heart, loving the way he tasted, and his tongue stroked hers. And all the while, he never stopped touching her, making her feel as if their coming together like this had been inevitable from the first. "These clothes have to come off!" she said.

He chuckled softly, pressing his lips against her throat. "Ladies first." Off came her red sweater. Her boots. Jeans. His eyes darkened with pleasure as he gazed at her breasts spilling out of her red satin demi-bra and matching bikini panties. He traced the exposed slopes and valleys of her breasts before pushing aside one strap and the other. As he peeled the fabric away, he smiled tenderly. "You are so beautiful…"

Faith felt beautiful when he looked at her and kissed her like this.

Maybe love wasn't involved here, she admitted as they continued to kiss each other with abandon, but it still felt as if their coming together like this was a step toward something unexpectedly wonderful.

The perfect gift for each other in this holiday season…

She clung to him and surrendered completely. Sensations built. Emotions soared. Pressing his lower half against her, hot and hard, Zach groaned his pleasure. Her senses spun as he finished undressing them both and drew her down to lie between the sheets on her bed. He stretched out on his back and pulled her on top of him, his manhood pressing against her. A thrill swept through her.

This time, she took the lead. Tracing his hot satiny skin, learning the mysteries of him as thoroughly and deliberately as he had learned hers the night before. Excitement built inside her and she savored the sensation of enjoying someone without restraint. Until he could bear it no more.

"My turn," he growled, shifting her beneath him. His lips forged a burning trail across her skin, and she cried out as he moved lower still, engaging every sense, fulfilling every fantasy. Trembling at the sensual strokes of his tongue and the soothing feel of his lips and hands, she caught his head in her hands, tangling her fingers in his hair. She moaned, knowing she wanted Zach as she had never wanted anyone before. Her head fell back. Her entire body quivered with pleasure. Need blossomed deep inside her and then she came apart in his hands.

He held her through the aftershocks, and then there was no holding back for either of them. He found a condom. Anticipation building, her heart full, Faith accepted the warm tantalizing weight of him. As he entered her, the ecstasy she'd felt earlier came roaring back. She moaned as Zach buried himself in her, making it an all-or-nothing proposition with each slow, incredibly sensual, deliberate, possessive stroke. Until the rising passion and tenderness quickly turned to fierce abandon and stunning need.

She gave herself over to him, moving her hips to the commanding rhythm of his, until the cry of triumph rose in her throat. She trembled and clenched around him as she climaxed, holding him close. He dove deep. And then all was lost in the wild, reckless turn their marriage of convenience had taken.

Afterward, the only sound in the room was the harsh meter of their breathing. When they finally recovered,

Faith sighed and looked over at the bedside clock. It was nearly 9:00 p.m. "Problem…?" Zach asked.

Only that she was going to have to leave the cozy confines of this bed before she got too comfortable and fell asleep. Wishing she did not have to extricate herself from the warm, strong cradle of his body, Faith started to sit up. "I need to take Tinkerbelle out one more time."

"Why don't you let me do it?" He was already reaching for his clothes. Springing into action.

Damn but he looked sexy in only a pair of black boxer briefs. Much more of this, plus his unending gallantry, and she might be tempted to fall in love with him. She studied the rasp of evening beard on his face. "You don't mind?"

"Not at all." He shrugged on his sweater and jeans. Zipped up his fly. His gaze drifting over her tenderly, he smiled. "Besides, I'm not tired, and you look ready for sleep."

Faith yawned. "I am, actually." It had been a very long couple of days.

He leaned over to brush his lips across her temple. "I'll see you in the morning then." He turned off her bedside lamp, and with one last lingering glance, left the room.

Chapter Thirteen

"Quinn go down okay?" Faith asked the next afternoon.

It was the quintessential rainy December afternoon. Perfect, she thought, for baking.

"Like a champ." Zach took a seat at the island. He glanced fondly down at Tinkerbelle, who was curled up on her cushion. Then turned back to Faith. "I've got to admit, I love rocking the little guy to sleep."

Noting that the charcoal plaid flannel shirt he wore made his eyes look more gray than blue, Faith admitted, just as happily, "I love it, too."

His gaze drifted over her lazily. She hadn't been baking when he'd gone upstairs. "What are you making?"

Recalling how nice it had been to make love with him the night before, she let her eyes drift over him, too. She pointed at the cookbook propped open on the island. "Thumbprint cookies for the seniors."

"I'm not sure what that is."

She put the butter in the microwave to soften, and then took the book over to him, and showed him the photo of the old-school holiday confection. As he leaned in for a better look, his rock-hard body brushed hers. Neither of them pulled away.

He shook his head. "Nope. Never ate them."

Tingles of awareness shimmered through her. Aware

she'd never stay on task if she stayed that close to him, she smiled and moved back to the other side of the work island. "You'll like them," she predicted confidently.

He chuckled. Mischief tugged at the corners of his sensual lips. "How do you know?"

She wrinkled her nose at him playfully. "How could you *not* like a butter cookie, rolled in crushed almonds, with a center 'thumbprint' filled with jam?"

He sat back in his chair, arms folded. Pretending to be a tough customer, when she knew he was anything but a picky eater, he tilted his head. "Hmm."

Hmm?

His sexy grin widened in a way that let her know he was enjoying being the sole beneficiary of her attention and getting under her skin.

"What kind of jam?"

She added the softened butter and sugar to the bowl on her stand mixer. Turned it on, then went into the pantry to get the flour, baking powder and salt. "Any kind you want." She also pulled a carton of eggs from the fridge. "I'm using cherry, blueberry, blackberry and peach-mango, but—" she paused when he jumped up to help her get her armload of ingredients onto the counter, without mishap "—if there is a special kind you want, I'd be glad to make a few of those, too."

He stayed long enough to steady her, his touch as tantalizing as ever. He gazed down at her, as if it was taking every ounce of willpower not to haul her against him and kiss her again.

She knew, because she was feeling the same impulse.

He untangled the collar of her shirt from the neck of her Mrs. Santa Cooks apron. Stepping back, he admitted, "Actually, what you already have sounds amazing."

It would be.

She nodded at the laptop he'd brought in with him. "What are you up to?"

"I'm going to work on the requirements for the additional home study for DCFS. Which means—" he inhaled, sitting down again opposite her "—we have to talk about finances."

What was it she had read? Married couples fought about three main things. Money, sex and in-laws.

Did they really want to go there, when things were going so well, thus far?

Faith focused on adding the eggs and vanilla to the mixing bowl. "I thought it was settled. You weren't going to provide for anything more than half of Quinn's expenses."

"That was *before* we were married. And were trying to demonstrate to social services and the court how serious we are about becoming a family, for Quinn, while remaining independent adults. Now, we're married. That changes things."

It sure did.

He turned his computer around, and showed her the email Mitzy had sent him, detailing the information needed to complete the home evaluation. He pointed at a bullet point midway down the page. "She wants to know how we are going to manage our personal finances."

Faith sifted flour, baking powder and salt into another large mixing bowl, grateful for the purposeful activity. Avoiding looking him directly in the eye, even though she knew he was looking right at her, she shrugged and suggested with a great deal more casualness than she really felt, "Why don't we each pay for what we normally pay for and leave it at that?"

Finally, she dared to look at him. She realized with relief that he understood where she was coming from.

"I agree, it would be simpler," he said matter-of-factly. "But it would also look like we each have one foot out the door. And after the way we already struck out with Judge Roy… I don't want anything to go wrong with the upcoming evaluation with Mitzy. Since she is going to be reporting to the judge and the judge is going to base her decision on that report."

She studied his frown, aware that much made sense, on a practical level. But… "It's more than that," she mused.

He nodded, blue eyes darkening. "I think, as your husband and Quinn's father and the head of the household…that I should be paying the mortgage and the utilities from here on out."

Whoa! Talk about complicating things! Her shoulders stiffened. "Except that would give you a financial stake in my property," she said stonily.

His gaze narrowed as he dismissed her concern, just as categorically. "We're legally married. Technically, we have a stake in each other's property." He lifted a hand. "I mean, if it would make you feel better, we could have Liz draw up a postnup."

She added the dry ingredients, too. "And how is that going to look to Judge Roy and DCFS? If we rush to get a postnup now?" She paused to wipe her flour-smudged hands on a cloth. "Because they would know, Zach. There is no way we could keep something like that from them in good faith. It would be a terrible mistake to even try!"

"Agreed." He exhaled. Stood and began to pace. "But why don't you want me to help pay, or pay the bulk of, your expenses?"

Because, Faith thought, it would just add another layer of comfort to a situation that was already way too cozy! She walked over to stand next to the window, facing him. Outside the rain kept on pouring down. "Because," she reiterated calmly, "I don't need you to do that for me, Zach."

It was his turn to see past her surface remarks. "And?"

Faith inhaled sharply. Figuring if they didn't want to fight about money in the future, they would have to at least talk about it now. "What you are suggesting could cause me to start depending on you in a way I don't want to depend on anyone ever again." Aware the dough would be ruined if she let it mix any longer, she swiveled away from him and went back to switch it off.

Zach edged closer, his arms folded in front of him. He leaned against the end of the island, facing her. Careful to continue to give her room to work, he asked, "Did you and Harm fight about money?"

Heat filled her face as she got out baking sheets and parchment paper. "All couples argue about finances from time to time."

He watched her roll balls of dough in chopped almonds, then press her thumb in the middle of it, to form a well for the fruit. "Not an answer to my question," he said.

She supposed she owed him an explanation. Finding it too difficult to bake and continue to explain a very complicated situation, she went over to the sink to rinse the sticky dough from her hands.

Finished, she turned back to Zach. "When we were married, Harm wanted me to live near my family, and that made sense, given how long some of his deployments were."

Zach nodded his understanding.

"So we bought this house in Laramie. I only took temporary accounting or finance jobs because I wanted to be free to go and be with my husband on a moment's notice."

She sighed, recalling how ridiculously romantic and impractical she had been as a newlywed.

"As you can imagine, living that way can be feast or famine, and I always felt guilty about utilizing the bulk of Harm's military income for fixing up our house—which was pretty much a disaster when we moved in, which was how we could afford it. I mean, I paid for my own food and clothes and things, but he covered all the big-ticket items."

"That's the way it is in most military marriages, Faith. Mainly because it's hard for the nonservice spouse to build a career of their own if they are constantly moving around from one base assignment to another."

Faith returned urgently, "But it comes with a price, Zach. Because I didn't actually earn the money that I was spending, I always felt a little guilty about it, or like I had to ask Harm's permission to do things, even when I knew at the outset that he wasn't going to understand why I wanted a really nice stove, when he felt a bargain-basement appliance would still get the job done."

Zach looked at the offending appliance. "Did he ask you not to buy it?"

"No. But I saw the look on his face when he came home and found out what it cost." She winced ruefully, recalling. "It was one of the few times I ever saw him speechless."

"Well, it's a good thing he never met my mother

then." Zach laughed, the sexy rumble filling up the space. "Because you want to talk about expensive tastes..." He shook his head.

Faith sent him a withering glare and propped both her hands on her hips. "I'm serious here, Zach!" She was trying to tell him what she did not want again!

He straightened to his full six-foot-four-inch height. "So am I," he told her soberly. Their gazes clashed as surely as their wills. "I grew up listening to my parents argue about money. It's not anything I will *ever* do in my own life. You are not going to have to ask me for permission to buy anything, Faith. I don't plan to ask you, either. What I would like to do, however, is provide for you and Quinn the way a normal husband and father would."

Oh, my god, why did he have to be so nice and reasonable? Faith shoved her fingers through her hair. "That sort of makes sense when you're here, but when you're deployed...you really shouldn't have to pay for food and utilities or a share of the mortgage..."

He frowned. "Do you really want to count pennies that way?" He searched her face. "Put us on a per diem basis?"

Put that way, it did sound ridiculous. She twisted her hands in front of her and let out a long, slow breath. "No."

"Well, neither do I. So..." He came close enough to cup her shoulders between his big, warm palms. "Are we agreed?" he demanded resolutely. "I'll take over the household expenses?"

Aware she was as strong-willed as he was, Faith dug in, too. "I still want to personally pay all the bills, if for no other reason than you could be deployed when they're due. But, if you really want to reimburse me, every month…" she conceded finally.

"I do."

"…that would be fine."

"Great." He gave her a huge grin. Stepped back. "One more thing."

It was all Faith could do not to roll her eyes at him. *Hadn't he won enough?* "Yes?" she prodded coolly.

"Your home office has got to be fixed before the home study on Friday."

Zach knew he'd hit a sore spot the moment the words were out. Which was a shame, given how careful he had been not to get in the way of her and Quinn's regular routine or impose on them in any way.

The last thing he wanted to do was end up feeling as unwelcome as he had after his parents' divorce. Or the way he had with Annette. It had been okay in the short term, as long as there were good times and hot sex. But it hadn't worked long-term. No matter how useful and unobtrusive he made himself, when he was around.

Faith went back to baking, her mouth set in an uncooperative line. "We don't have to touch that."

Yeah, Zach thought, they *did*. "Quinn will be walking by summer, if not before."

She finished filling one baking sheet, then reached for another. "So, I'll put a lock on the door." Turning, she saw his growing exasperation. "Listen, I know it's sort of an eyesore, but it wasn't a problem before, when I passed my own home study."

Maybe it hadn't been an issue. Then. "And when was that?" he asked mildly.

"When I signed up to foster-adopt, a couple of

months after Harm passed. Mitzy knew I couldn't deal with that room just yet. She told me to take my time. I'm sure that still goes."

Zach edged closer. Forcing her to meet his gaze. "And if it doesn't?" he challenged, starting to lose his patience. "I don't want to lose my chance to gain legal custody of Quinn in two weeks, because that's still not done. And for all they know, might never get done. Do you?"

"No." Lips set, she continued making cookies.

He waited for permission to proceed. This was her home, after all.

It never came.

He moved closer still. Inhaling the lemon-and-vanilla fragrance clinging to her hands, he pushed on, seeing this as just another mission. "I can get the building supplies out of there, and patch the drywall, and paint the cabinets, if that's what you want. Or I can build the bookcases for you."

Finally, she stopped what she was doing and looked at him skeptically. The fact she still doubted him stung.

"My granddad was a master carpenter who specialized in custom built-ins, remember?" he informed her, wishing she would trust him a little more. "I spent four years helping him out, weekends and summers. And I've got his tools."

Faith paused in shock. "Here?"

Zach nodded. "He left them to me, in his will. I had my mother bring them when she and Bart came down for the wedding."

Her expression thoughtful, she slid the first batch of cookies in to bake. "Where are they?"

He watched her set the timer. "Still at the Laramie airport. But I can pick them up anytime."

He could see she was tempted. But still, her gaze narrowed warily. "Would you really have time to do that?"

He understood she didn't want to be left with another barely started job on her hands, when he deployed after Christmas. "I looked at the materials in the garage last night. The cabinets Harm bought just need to be assembled. The shelves built and put on above that. If you still want what was in that picture on your desk."

Her teeth raked her plump lower lip. "All that work will probably get pretty noisy, though, won't it?"

He could see her beginning to surrender. Just like she had when they'd gone from making out to making love. He nodded, satisfaction roaring through him. "Which is why I'd have to do it when you and Quinn are at Laramie Gardens this week."

She came close enough to gaze up at him. "How long do you think it would take?"

He took her hand and led her around to the other side of the island, to sit on the stools there. "If I got started tomorrow, I'd be painting it by Wednesday." Their knees bumped as they settled side by side, facing each other. Eager to reassure her, he took her hand in his. He wanted her comfortable with the plan.

Tracing the delicate inside of her wrist with his fingertips, he murmured, "Naturally, I'd stop all the sawing and drilling and hammering before you got home with Quinn. And, of course, I'd still find plenty of time to be a good dad and help care for Quinn before and after your workday."

Finally, she began to relax. "Well, actually, that might help me out in other ways, too." She brushed a spot of flour from the knee of her yoga pants.

Trying not to notice how well the black knit clung

to her spectacular legs and hips, he asked, "What do you mean?"

She made a face. "I heard the LG ladies talking at the reception. As much as they have loved seeing you with Quinn, they have missed taking turns, caring for him." Faith's breasts rose and fell seductively as she released a long breath. "Miss Mim wasn't even sure she should continue managing the sign-up sheet."

Zach paused. "She does that?"

Faith grinned. "Oh, yeah. You have to be fair. All the ladies there love babies, and enjoy being around them. Helping out. It keeps them feeling young, they say, and the babies thrive with all the attention. Which is why I'm allowed to bring Quinn with me to work, and Nora was able to bring Liam, when he was an infant, and so on. If I hadn't been allowed to take Quinn to work with me, I never would have accepted the job. I would have found something else."

"You and Quinn are really lucky to have that option."

"I know. Believe me, I don't take it for granted."

A contemplative silence fell. Zach realized they had just avoided their first argument. "So it's settled?" he asked with relief, studying her face. "You'll let me finish this for you?"

Faith nodded. "If you think you can get that study fixed up once and for all, I say go for it."

He smiled back at her. "All right, I will."

Hopefully, when it was finished, she would see not only was he handy to have around, but she would also never need to doubt him or his intentions again.

"I don't understand what the problem is," Faith's sister Mackenzie said later that evening, when Zach went out for a long run after Quinn had been put down for the night.

Faith curled up on the sofa in front of the fire, watching the licking flames and listening to the rain tapping against the windows. Tinkerbelle, who didn't like wet weather, had declined Zach's offer to go out, and was sleeping on the sofa next to Faith.

"I thought you wanted to get that done," Mackenzie continued from Fort Worth, as the two of them Face-Timed with each other.

She did! Faith stroked Tinkerbelle's silky head. Tink snoozed on. "It just seems wrong for Zach to succeed where Harm failed."

"As a husband or a carpenter?"

Both. She swallowed. "He's so wonderful."

"Well," Mackenzie countered, "you kind of are on your honeymoon."

"I know."

"But…?" her sister prodded gently.

Faith traced the holly-and-ivy pattern on Tinkerbelle's collar. "It's only been a little more than forty-eight hours and I already find myself wanting to depend on him."

"And you don't want to do that, because he's going to be deployed again."

Right! She admired the beautiful tree they had put up together. The memory of that warmed her soul. Even as she worried about the chilly aftermath to come, when he left. "I thought it was going to be different this time." A mixture of sorrow and anxiety filled her gut. "Because I didn't love Zach the way I loved Harm."

"Wait…what? Are you saying you're falling in love with him?" Mackenzie demanded.

She definitely had a royal crush. "I love the way he is with Quinn."

"Well, that's good," her sister responded, relaxing, "since he is Quinn's daddy. And the two of you want to raise him together."

"That's the problem." Faith rushed on honestly. "Quinn's starting to depend on him, too. I mean, I see him looking around for Zach whenever he wakes up from a nap. Or hasn't seen him for a while and enters a different room."

Mackenzie was silent. "I imagine it will be hard on Quinn when Zach leaves. But he'll still have you. And the rest of the Lockharts. And he won't know anything else. Except having a military parent. So he'll get used to the absences. To him, that will be normal."

But did she really want it to be normal for her son? Belatedly, Faith realized she had been thinking of herself up to now. Worried about how she could stay a part of Quinn's life. Not about how her son would feel when his daddy departed for months at a time.

Another silence fell.

"So what else is bothering you?" her sister asked eventually.

Faith told her about the finances.

"He's right. Better to be safe than sorry when it comes to preparing for court."

True. Faith sighed again. "I just worry the money thing will change things between us."

"Oh, honey," Mackenzie soothed with a sympathetic chuckle, "*marriage* changes everything. So it's best not to waste time worrying about what will or will not happen, and just buckle up and go along for the ride."

"I know it made a huge difference for you and Griff."

They had gone from being longtime platonic friends who tied the knot for a whole host of unlikely reasons, to being wildly in love, and contented parents of twins.

Could that happen to her and Zach, too? Faith could only wish.

Chapter Fourteen

"Are you sure you don't want me to go with you to Laramie Gardens? See you and Quinn get settled in for the day?" Zach asked at seven thirty Monday morning.

Funny, Faith thought, not sure whether to be touched or amused that her husband seemed to be having as much trouble saying goodbye to her and Quinn this morning as she was to him. Maybe that wasn't such a surprise, though. The weekend of togetherness had brought forth a feeling of cozy security.

To the point it was beginning to privately worry her about her growing attachment to him. So last night she'd made sure she was in bed, with the baby monitor on and her door shut, when he returned from his evening run. And when he'd gotten back she'd heard him stop briefly in the kitchen—probably for some water—and then head straight for his room, too. So they'd both had a night of solitude.

Luckily for the two of them, Quinn had slept well and woken up in a very good mood. Which had been infectious…

Trying hard not to notice how good Zach looked this morning in a cotton shirt, jeans and work boots, a day's scruff of beard on his handsome face, Faith packed up her stuff and Quinn's diaper bag. "I won't say no to helping get him in the car, but after that I've got it covered."

"You sure?" Zach snuggled Quinn closer to his chest, while their son gazed happily up at his daddy.

"Yes. We'll be fine. You go on out to the airport and pick up your boxes of tools so you can get started here."

He walked with them. Kissed Quinn gently before putting him into his car seat, fastening the safety harness and shutting the door.

Faith had been hovering nearby, in case Zach needed help with anything. Which, of course, he didn't. For a second, he stared down at her, as if tempted to haul her close and kiss her goodbye, too.

A thrill shot through Faith.

Followed swiftly by an equally potent warning to herself.

They were coparents, friends and lovers, only! This was *not* a traditional marriage. Merely a family in the making, for Quinn's sake. If she didn't want her heart broken, she needed to remember that.

"I'm glad you were able to come in a little early. We have a full slate this morning," the LG director said, minutes later, when Faith walked in.

She set down the infant carrier first, then eased the bags off her shoulders. Quinn gurgled up at her happily and kicked his feet. She smiled back at him, as she shrugged out of her coat. Then turned back to her boss. "Did Nessie Rogers come in yet?"

Diane shook her head. "The transport ambulance from the hospital should be here any minute."

Faith picked up the folder she had prepared on Saturday. "Her paperwork is all ready to go."

"I know." The other woman smiled her relief. "I saw.

Thank you for coming in to do that over the weekend, even if it was your honeymoon."

"No problem," Faith said. "It's my job."

Miss Mim approached, with her posse of fellow baby-minders. The six seniors crowded into her office, eager for an update. "How is Zach?" Miss Sadie asked.

"Great." Faith unstrapped Quinn, and began easing him out of his snowsuit.

"Is he coming in today?" Miss Patricia asked.

"No."

Faces fell. Although they all wanted plenty of time with the baby, they clearly enjoyed flirting with her handsome soldier-husband, too. She explained to the group, "He's taking care of some things around the house. Putting together the built-in for my home office."

"Are you sure he knows how to do that?" Miss Isabelle queried in a worried tone.

Everyone had heard what had happened to the wall when Harm had tried. Faith lifted a hand. "He says he does."

Faces turned anxious, all around. But she let them know there was nothing to dread. At least she didn't think there was. Time would tell. "His granddad was an ex-marine and a master carpenter. Zach worked for him all through high school."

"Oh," the women said in unison.

When the transport vehicle arrived, Miss Mim and the ladies took Quinn to the community room. Faith went and got the paperwork. As expected, Nessie Rogers was anxious to get everything signed right away. The ninety-year-old widow was as scrappy now as she had been all her life. "I shouldn't be here at all," the retired lady rancher fumed.

"You just had surgery for a broken hip," Nurse Inez Garcia said.

"You're going to need physical therapy to get back on your feet," Nora Caldwell-Lockhart agreed.

The two nurses worked as a team to transfer Nessie from the stretcher to her hospital bed. As gentle as they were, it was easy to see Nessie was still in tremendous pain.

"Fine, but I'm going to be back home in time for Christmas. I haven't missed Christmas at the ranch my entire life. I'm not missing this one, either!" Nessie turned to Faith with a glare. "No matter what social services says!"

Uh-oh.

Nessie harrumphed. "So you tell your momma and her friends over at Laramie DCFS that!"

Figuring it was better she not get in the middle of a quarrel over what was going to be necessary for the older woman's recovery, Faith nodded. "I'll relay your message. In the meantime, I want you to know all your expenses here are going to be paid by your combined Medicare and supplemental insurance plans. So you don't need to worry about that."

"I'm not worried! I'm not going to be here long enough for that!" Nessie proclaimed.

Papers signed, Faith eased out of the room.

Tillie Tarrant was waiting for her in her office. "I've decided I want to make the change to separate rooms," she informed her. "And I want you to help me convince Ted that we should do it."

Oh, dear, Faith thought. "He's not on board?"

"I haven't told him yet."

Whoo boy. She slipped behind her desk and turned

nputer. "Don't you think you-all might want ..nis conversation privately?" she asked kindly.

..iie shook her head. "My husband will be calmer if you are present."

A decisive knock sounded on the door. Ted wheeled his chair in, looking baffled. "What is going on?"

Suddenly feeling like a principal who had the task of counseling unruly students, Faith explained Tillie's desire to cut their expenses.

The usually mild-mannered gentleman blew up. He glared at his wife. "You do what you want. Move out. I'm staying put!"

"But—but…that will increase our expenses dramatically!" Tillie countered.

"Tell it to your new boyfriend!" Ted snapped at her. Then abruptly wheeled his chair out of the office.

Faith and Tillie sat in stunned silence. Finally, tearing up, Tillie asked, "What is he talking about?"

Ian Baker. Figuring the less she said at this juncture, the better, Faith shrugged. She studied the genuinely hurt look on the elderly woman's face. "I think you should ask Ted."

"I don't have a boyfriend!"

Always good to hear.

"And I am certainly not cheating on my husband."

Even more wonderful to know. "Then are you having money problems?" Faith asked calmly, doing her best to make sense of the building calamity. "Ones maybe your husband doesn't know about?"

Tillie flushed. "I can't talk about this," she said. Regally, she rose and left the room.

Faith stared after her, mystified. Ted and Tillie had always enjoyed an enviably solid marriage up till now.

In fact, they'd been the lovebirds of Laramie Gardens. But if they couldn't make it work forever, after sixty happy years together, she had to wonder. What kind of chance did she and Zach have for a lasting union?

Zach was surprised at how lonely the house seemed without Faith and Quinn. Of course, he had Tinkerbelle to keep him company. She followed him around, staying out of the way, while making sure she didn't miss a single thing he did. He stayed as busy as possible, too.

Still, it was a relief when he heard Faith's SUV in the drive shortly after five o'clock.

He shut the door to the study and headed out to give her a hand. The clothes that had been pristine when she left that morning were now rumpled, and stained with what looked like a little formula and spit-up. Her hair was tousled. Her lips bare. Slender shoulders slumped.

"You look beat."

Straightening, she tossed him a wry look. "Thanks, soldier."

He reached over to give her a brief, companionable hug. "I wasn't trying to insult you," he told her gently. "Just empathizing for what looks like a very arduous day."

"It was that, all right." She kneeled down to pet her dog, then stood. He hugged her shoulders briefly. "C'mon. Let's get you-all inside."

She leaned against him briefly, then stepped back with a small sigh of relief. "Sounds good."

He opened the rear passenger door. Quinn gurgled happily. "Hey, little guy," Zach said. When he eased his son out of his car seat, Quinn cuddled against his chest and gazed up at him adoringly. Faith and Tinkerbelle remained close. Zach's heart swelled until it felt too big for his chest.

"How was your day?" she asked, carrying the diaper and shoulder bags up the front steps. Zach followed behind her as she led the way into the house.

"Busy," he said.

She eased off her coat. "Something sure smells good." She whirled to face him, surprise and delight shining in her eyes. "Did you make dinner for us?"

Glad he'd taken the initiative, he grinned. "I did."

She hung up her coat, while he laid Quinn on the sofa and eased him out of his snowsuit.

Beaming, she headed for the kitchen. Went straight to the stove and peered inside. "Spatchcock chicken and roasted veggies!"

"Sounds good?"

"Oh, yeah." He observed that she was wincing the way she always did when her feet ached, so she toed off her heels. "When will it be ready?"

He consulted the clock. "Another fifteen or twenty minutes."

"Do you mind if I run up and change clothes?"

"Not at all."

She returned short minutes later in an oversize red denim shirt, sleek black leggings and ballet slippers. He noticed she had run a brush through her hair and put on some lipstick. Maybe a little of the perfume he liked, too. He studied the energetic color in her face. "Feel better?"

"Starting to, yeah."

So was he. Although he'd just been a little lonely, not fatigued. Noting how cozy this all was, he watched as Faith prepared rice cereal mixed with formula and mashed banana, which constituted Quinn's evening meal. Together, they put on his bib and settled him in his high chair. While she fed their son, Zach put the last touches on dinner. By the time Quinn had finished, they were ready to eat, too.

They sat at the small table in the breakfast nook, the baby's high chair between them. "Where did you learn to cook like this?" she asked.

"My grandfather. Although I have to warn you, my repertoire is all hearty traditional food. Granddad was a meat-and-potatoes man."

"No sushi?" she teased.

He laughed at the thought. "No. Although my mom and stepdad are rather fond of it." He studied her warmly, realizing he was really going to miss times like these when he deployed. It felt good knowing he was an integral part of a close and loving family. Not a third wheel. "You?"

"No-o-o," she said, wrinkling her nose in distaste.

He chuckled. "Well, another problem solved, when it comes to the home study! We're on the same page, menu-wise, when it comes to consuming raw fish."

She gave him a sobering look that said, "If only it were so easy."

Their knees touched beneath the small table. "So why was your day so difficult?" he asked her, surprised at how eager he was to hear about her day.

Faith cut into her chicken. "The new resident isn't happy to be there. So that's hard to deal with."

Zach could imagine.

With a sigh, Faith went on, "I want everyone to be happy, especially this time of year."

He could see that, too. Although she took far too much upon herself, responsibility-wise.

"Oh, and Tillie told Ted her plans for separate spaces. With me as witness."

He squeezed her hand. "I'm guessing that didn't go well?"

Briefly, she leaned in to his grasp. "You guessed right. Ted exploded and wheeled himself out of my office. Went straight to all the guys, and complained to them, which alerted the female residents to the situation. Before you knew it," she lamented in exasperation, "*everyone* was getting involved."

"Which made it worse?" Zach asked.

"Initially, yes. I mean," Faith continued with a heartfelt sigh, "who really wants advice on their relationship, especially when you have been married sixty years?"

"No one," he said.

"*Exactly.* Anyway, all the chatter had both of them taking refuge in the privacy of their suite. I don't know what was said *there*, but when they came out, Tillie told me they wouldn't be doing anything until after the holidays, if then."

"How did Ted react to that?"

Her soft lips compressed into a frown. "He was slightly mollified, but still pretty hurt and confused."

Zach tried to make sense of the situation, too. "And no one knows what is really behind Tillie's request?"

"Correct. Which is why I touched base with their son in San Antonio."

"You told him what happened?"

"No. I couldn't do that for privacy reasons. But I could ask him if he had any questions or concerns about his parents' residence at Laramie Gardens."

"And?" he asked.

Another heartfelt sigh. "He didn't have any."

"So the son knows nothing about his parents' distress."

She looked perplexed. "Apparently not. However, he did say he was going to be coming up in person to see them the week after next. So maybe one or both of them will confide in him then."

Wishing he could take her in his arms and make love to her until her tension eased, he said, "It really upsets you to see Tillie and Ted quarreling, huh?"

"It's just so out of character!" Her lips tightened. "I always thought they had a love story for the ages!"

Zach shrugged. The holidays could be hard on people for all sorts of reasons. "Maybe they still do."

The yearning was in her emerald eyes, even if she remained conflicted. "Maybe." But she didn't sound convinced.

The two of them shared bath duty that evening, with Faith doing most of the instructing and Zach doing much of the actual work. They sat together while Quinn had his last bottle of the day and read him a Christmas story together. Then they split up. With Faith taking the dog out and Zach heading off to rock Quinn to sleep.

The house was silent as she and Tinkerbelle came in the back door. Wondering just how much progress Zach had actually made on her study, she reached for the doorknob.

"Please don't open that door," a low voice said behind her.

She swung around. A little surprised and a lot frustrated. "I don't even get to peek?" She unsnapped Tinkerbelle's leash and watched as her terrier headed off to her water bowl.

"No." Zach put his big body between her and the portal, about as movable as a two-ton pickup truck. "Let me finish," he said gruffly. "Or at least get further along. I really want to surprise you..."

That was the problem. She had been surprised before. With a huge gaping hole in the drywall. But Zach wasn't Harm. She had to remember that.

She turned to face him. "Do you think it will be finished by the home study on Friday?"

"Yes, definitely. I'll be painting it on Wednesday."

She hoped he was right, even as the evening yawned ahead. By eight thirty, Quinn was fast asleep. Tinkerbelle had been walked and was ready for bed. And they couldn't continue to remodel the study, for noise reasons. Plus, they'd both already spent the entire day working. With Christmas looming, and all the extra things they had to do for that, they really didn't need to wear themselves out unnecessarily.

Still unsure what to do next, she started through the hallway from the mudroom and study, to the kitchen. Stopped at what she saw out of her peripheral vision, and looked up. Mistletoe, fastened to the light fixture in the hall. "Did you put this up?"

He shrugged his broad shoulders, ambling closer. "Well, it was me. Or Quinn," Zach drawled. "And I am not sure he can reach that far yet."

"Why would you do that?" When she was trying to put the brakes on the two of them, emotionally, anyway.

"Because nice people gifted us with it, and hence we should put it to good use."

Faith drew a long, steadying breath. "But people are going to think..."

"What?" Quirking an eyebrow, he flashed her a wickedly mischievous grin. "That we're newlyweds?"

Clearly, unlike her, he wasn't one to struggle with his emotions while consequently running hot and then cold. He only had one temperature, she noted, as he gently and purposefully invaded her space. *Sizzling hot!* "Zach..."

He wrapped his arms around her, pulling her close. Until they were touching in one long, electric line. He lowered his head and delivered a breath-stealing kiss. "I missed you last night."

She moaned, then admitted hoarsely, "I missed you, too..."

He chuckled, kissing her again, shattering what little caution she had left. Her lips parted beneath the pressure of his as his tongue swept her mouth with long, sensuous strokes over and over, until her whole body was alive, quivering, completely engulfed in flames.

She kept trying to deny it, she realized as their kiss went on and on. But the truth was it felt so good to be wanted and needed, to be held possessively against him like this. To have the barriers between them start coming down. Desire tumbled inside her, making her tummy feel weightless. Her spirits soaring, she surged helplessly against him, chest-to-chest, thigh-to-thigh, sex-to-sex. She could feel his erection pressing against her, hot and urgent, his heart pounding in his chest.

"Let's not waste time." Zach rained kisses down her throat, across her cheek, her lips. Framing her face with his large hands, he forced her mouth up to his. "Not when we could be together like this..."

He shifted her back so she was against the wall and kissed her again, this time with surprising tenderness. Lifting his head from hers, he continued to watch her in that unsettling way, and asked in a low, raspy voice, "Tell me you want this, too..."

"Yes," Faith breathed, savoring the tightening of his muscles beneath her fingertips, and the heat emanating from every part of him. She had never experienced this kind of sweet, rapturous need before. And she didn't care if she was behaving selfishly once again. Because she had to see where this astounding passion would lead them. Would it bring her as close as she wanted to be to Zach? Would making their coparenting arrangement also an ongoing sexual one, truly link them forever as husband and wife?

She had no answers now. All she knew was she felt white-hot. And that feeling this way was the best unexpected Christmas present she could ever get.

His body pinning hers to the wall, he bent his head and kissed her again, slowly, thoroughly, and she surged against him. His palms slid beneath her clothes, loosening the clasp of her bra. Claiming and molding and caressing her breasts.

The next thing she knew, both their pants were coming off. He slid down her body, kissing the hollow of her stomach, stroking the silky insides of her thighs. He traced her navel with his tongue, then dropped lower still to deliver the most intimate of kisses, until she was awash in desire, shuddering. He was on the brink, too.

"Now," she whispered.

He grabbed a condom from his jeans. Together, they sheathed him. And then she was lifting her hips, pleading wordlessly for more. He shifted her higher on the wall, his manner all the more possessive. Their tongues twined urgently and he slid home in a way that was wonderfully sensual, hot and wild. Their bodies took up a primitive rhythm all their own, until there was no doubting how much they needed each other, needed *this*. What few boundaries that still existed between them dissolved. He pressed into her as deeply as he could go, withdrew and filled her again. And then they were lost in a soul-searing pleasure that surpassed anything Faith had ever known.

Eventually, they made their way upstairs, fell back into her bed and made love all over again. She drifted off to sleep wrapped in his arms, and awakened that way, too.

Chapter Fifteen

"You're serious?" Miss Patricia said, Thursday afternoon, as Faith and half a dozen other women carried out the platters of Christmas cookies from the walk-in freezer-refrigerator at the assisted-living center. "Zach spent all day building bookshelves for your study and then made you dinner three nights in a row?"

Faith blushed. She didn't know why she had ever told Miss Sadie that. The news had hit the Laramie Gardens grapevine with the speed of light. Yet it was hard not to brag about her new husband; he was just so perfect!

She was not used to perfect.

"Well..." Faith shrugged off the idyllic memories suffusing her, and also ignored the fact that she and Zach had bypassed their initial boundaries and had begun sleeping together in her bed every night. She went on as casually as she could, "As Zach said, 'he has to eat, too,' and his granddad taught him how to cook. So..."

"Is he a talented chef?" Miss Isabelle queried.

"Amazing actually. Last night he made this shepherd's pie. And let's just say it was melt-in-your-mouth delicious."

As the women contemplated the idea of coming home to a hot man waiting for them, delicious dinner at the ready, there were envious sighs all around.

Miss Mim arranged the platters of cookies on the

cloth-covered tables. "If they had made men like that in my day, even I might have married," Miss Mim declared.

Everyone laughed.

Miss Patricia turned to her. "You never even got close, Mim?"

"Actually, I did," Miss Mim said regretfully. "But he was in the military and I was afraid I would miss him too much so I told him I would marry him when he got back from the war. And then," she choked out, "he didn't come back."

Everyone sobered. "Oh, Mim." Faith was closest, so she was the first to hug the retired town librarian, who had been a guardian angel to every one of the children who had come through the library doors.

Patricia, Sadie and Isabelle followed suit.

As they broke up, Miss Mim fanned herself comically and said, "And speaking of our handsome hero..."

Zach strolled in, Quinn ensconced in his arms. He had kept their son at home that day, so she could focus on work and setting up the party. The sight of them together made her heart sing.

All the women were similarly affected.

"The lieutenant certainly has taken to fatherhood quickly," Miss Isabelle declared.

He certainly had.

Zach joined them. "Hello, ladies!" he said with a huge grin.

Nurse Nora came in with her ex-special-operator husband Zane. Their three-year-old son, Liam, was walking between them, holding on to both their hands.

Another chorus of greetings followed.

Diane, the LG director, appeared soon after. "Any

luck getting Nessie to join us this afternoon?" she asked the assembled group.

The ladies shook their heads. "She just wants to go back to her ranch."

But, Faith knew, that wasn't going to be possible. The ninety-year-old widow would need at least six weeks to recover from her hip surgery; she had only been at Laramie Gardens less than a week.

"I'll try!" she volunteered.

"We'll go with you." Zach fell into step beside her. He gazed fondly down at Quinn. "After all, who can say no to this charming little fella?"

"No one who has come into his orbit thus far..." Faith smiled, basking in the feeling of family.

As they passed Russell Pierce's room, he stepped out into the hall. In a safari shirt, khaki cargo pants and a worn leather jacket, he bore a striking resemblance to Harrison Ford. With a vigor belying his eighty-eight years, he held up his mug of green tea in salute and greeted them warmly, "Howdy, y'all." He grinned at Quinn and tenderly chucked him under the chin before turning back to the adults. "Why don't you come in and see my tree?"

The tabletop decoration was lit up beautifully with the ornaments he had enhanced. Faith beamed. "Gorgeous!"

"Stunning," Zach agreed.

Russell, who'd had his own problems adjusting to life at Laramie Gardens, several years prior, after the death of his wife, added, "The community-room tree could look like this, too, if only they'd agree to let me put my ornaments up." He inclined his head at the basket of extra decorations. "A shame to let them go to waste..."

Yet, Faith noted, the tabletop tree would not take any more without toppling over. She brainstormed a solution.

"You don't want to alternate them?"

Russell shook his head. "I've tried that. It just..."

She understood. It was hard having your masterpiece ignored. But there had to be a place for the beautiful holiday ornaments... Then lightning struck.

"I have an idea." She smiled. "Grab that basket and come with us!"

Together, they all trooped down to Nessie Rogers's room. The door was open. Nessie was seated in her lift chair, gazing dejectedly out the window, her walker within reach. She, too, had a cup of tea in hand.

Faith smiled. "Hello, Miss Nessie!" she said enthusiastically. "We are just checking in!"

Nessie sighed grimly. She did not so much as turn and look at them. "I already said I didn't feel up to a party," she grumbled.

"I understand," Faith said. "But we thought maybe you would like some help decorating your tabletop tree." Which sat on a table, opposite her bed, unadorned except for the clear prelit light bulbs that had come already on it.

Nessie scowled. "I already said no..."

Russell shuffled forward, wicker basket in hand. He had never forgotten his own adjustment difficulties, a fact that made him a particularly compassionate and understanding resident.

Russell pulled up a chair opposite Nessie, although Faith was fairly certain that had he been able to manage it, he simply would have kneeled in front of her.

"Here's the thing, Miss Nessie," he said gently. "Maybe it's growing up with parents who lived through the Great Depression, but I can't stand to see anything go to waste."

The elderly woman straightened. "I can't, either!"

Russell showed her the wicker basket filled with treasures and explained sentimentally, "These belonged to my wife, Esther. They were on our tree every year she was alive. But for the last couple of years, ever since I came to Laramie Gardens, they have remained in the box. Mostly because—" he teared up "—I couldn't bear looking at them. It reminded me of my beloved and it hurt too much."

Nessie nodded, her eyes glistening.

Faith and Zach's eyes filled, too.

Russell pulled himself together and cleared his throat. "Anyway, this year I decided things needed to change, that I needed to spend the season celebrating, rather than mourning my loss. So," Russell continued thickly, "I spent most of the summer and fall rigging these beautiful decorations so they would light up inside, via battery, but they won't let me put them on the community-room tree and there are too many for my own tabletop tree."

Nessie nodded. She had apparently heard.

"It breaks my heart seeing them go unused."

Nessie sat up even straighter. A little color came into her face. "You want me to put some up?" she asked compassionately.

"Would you?"

The woman nodded.

Russell rose. Nellie reached for her walker and brought it close.

"Need some help?" Zach asked.

"We got it," Russell and Nessie said in unison. In fact, Russell was already moving over to steady Nessie's walker while she rose.

Realizing the older couple did indeed have things handled, Faith grasped Zach's elbow and nudged him toward the door. "Don't forget the cookie swap!" she said over her shoulder on the way out. "And we'll send some down to the room if you don't want to pick them out yourselves!"

"We'll be down in a few minutes," Russell promised. This time, Nessie did not demur.

"Wow. That worked better than I thought it would," Faith murmured as she and Zach headed down the hall.

He snuggled Quinn even closer to his chest. "Sometimes a person just needs to be needed."

She sighed. Truer words had never been spoken. Because she—and Quinn—both needed Zach.

Would it be enough to keep him coming back, at the end of every tour of duty? Time would tell. But right now, Faith admitted, she felt hopeful. Very hopeful.

"I should probably tell you," Zach drawled, several hours later, as they walked up her front porch. He slanted Faith a glance, hoping this wasn't going to be a problem. "I did *not* make dinner for us tonight."

Smiling, she laid a hand over her tummy. "And a good thing, too." She unlocked the door and swung it wide. "I don't think I could eat a thing after all those cookies we sampled at the LG cookie extravaganza!"

True. He followed her inside, aware for the first time he didn't have to envy others' happiness. "How many different kinds do you think there were?"

"At least one hundred." She took off her own coat, then relieved him of Quinn, so he could get out of his.

He hung up both their jackets, then assisted her in getting their baby boy out of his snowsuit. "Well, it was an incredible spread, I'll give you that."

She handed Quinn over to him, again, picked up her baby carryall and headed for the kitchen. "I'm glad you were there with us," she said over her shoulder.

He tracked the provocative sway of her hips beneath her wool skirt. The sexy strides of her luscious legs. "Me, too."

She took the empty bottles out and put them in the sink, then turned to him. They exchanged glances. The kind that usually presaged lovemaking…

Forcing himself to get back on task, Zach cleared his throat. "Speaking of fine company…" He glanced down at the little one curled up sleepily on his chest. "Do you think he's about ready for bed? Since he did have his dinner and bottle earlier."

"Yes. We can give him a bath tomorrow before Mitzy comes over to do your home evaluation." She gave him a relaxed smile. "I'll just change him and get him in his jammies, if you will take care of Tinkerbelle for me."

"My pleasure." Zach loved having a dog around as much as the rest of his new family.

Their hands brushed as Zach handed Quinn over to her. As she mounted the stairs, he took Tinkerbelle outside. The terrier was just finishing her dinner, tail wagging happily, when Faith joined them again. He noticed she hadn't bothered to change into casual clothes. Then again, it was late. She might prefer to go straight to pajamas. And then bed…

His body stirred.

"So," she said, oblivious to the amorous nature of his thoughts. "When do I finally get to see my study?" she asked.

He had made her wait until it was completely finished, for both their sakes. But he could no longer put it off. He slid his hand around her slender waist. "Right now sounds good."

They moved through the hallway that connected the kitchen to the mudroom, study and back door. Hoping liked hell she was going to like what she saw, he swung open the door.

Faith gasped and splayed her hand over her heart.

"Oh, Zach!" she exclaimed. "It's gorgeous!"

He surveyed the row of built-in cabinets and shelving along the wall behind her desk. All had been painted the same creamy ivory as the trim and crown molding that ran through the entire house. He had taken the pale pink-and-gray-and-blue Aubusson rug that had been rolled up in the corner of the room out of harm's way, and spread it beneath her desk. Her reading chair and ottoman stood in the corner. All the books she'd had stored in boxes were now shelved, according to category. Home repair, cookbooks in one area. Finance and accounting guides, another. Fiction a third.

Her antique wooden desk, with the matching swivel chair placed in front of it, was adorned with a counting tabulator, laptop and phone charger. And, last but not least, there was a glass vase filled with a dozen red roses.

She beamed, still looking around. "You really outdid yourself, soldier."

He'd never been so happy to please someone in his life. His heart thundered in his chest. "So you like it?"

"I adore it!" She threw her arms around his shoulders and kissed him on the lips.

"You think it will pass muster with Mitzy, too?"

"Oh, my, yes. Remember, she saw the 'before' situation the last time she was here. She'll be very impressed with the 'after.' I could stay in here all night, just gazing around."

He took her by the hand. "Or..." he said, leading her back out into the hallway, toward the mistletoe, where they spent some time kissing before moving on to the next sprig of mistletoe, and the next. "We could pass the time...in other ways," he proposed.

Amusement sparkled in her eyes as she splayed her hands across his chest, rubbing, stroking. "But first," she purred, "I've got to get out of these clothes."

At her direction, they headed for her bedroom. Once there, she didn't quibble with his desire to dedicate himself to making her as happy and content and fulfilled as she had made him, and somehow that made the culmination of their desire all the hotter.

Loving how much she wanted him, he took her face in his hands and kissed her with deep, abiding hunger. Her lips softened under his, inviting him into her sweet urgent heat. The connection between them intensified, as did their growing need for each other. Impatient now, they helped each other undress, laughing, then groaning at their clumsiness. Naked, they came together again. He loved the way she looked, so beautiful, so ravished.

And still they kissed and touched with the wild abandon that pushed them both toward the edge. She responded just as hungrily as she had before, wrapping her arms around him, crushing her breasts to his chest, molding her soft body to his. Wanting her full surrender, he used the light caress of his thumb to encourage her to part her legs for him again. To his delight, she sighed in pleasure and closed her eyes. Quivering. Swaying. Her breathing shallow and erratic. But not there…yet.

Doing his best to ignore the growing ache in his groin, he guided her down onto the bed. Not about to go without her, until they had both had their fill, he held her wrists in one hand and used his other to touch, stroke, love. She trembled at his erotic domination, and he kissed her again, taking her mouth with his. "Like this?" he growled against her mouth.

As willing to explore as he, she grinned and kissed him back. "Oh, yes…"

Her skin grew hot and flushed and her thighs splayed wide to accommodate his legs. Their kisses turned soft and luxuriant. His sex pressed intimately against her, she surrendered even more fully, and a wave of tenderness swept through him. He hadn't expected her to be so warm and welcoming, so open to loving him. But she made him feel like he was hers, and hers alone.

Realizing, even if she didn't yet, that *she* was the one who was conquering *him*, he kissed her until she was silky wet and trembling. Ready. Wanting. Needing.

"Zach…" she whimpered.

He found a condom. Her hands caught his hips, brought him against her, closed around him and guided him inside. The last of his restraint fell away as she drove him to the brink.

For the first time in his life, Zach learned what it was like to be with a woman, heart and soul, to avail every part of him to every part of her. They were married. They were part of each other. They shared a child and a family and now a life.

He hadn't known he could want like this. Hadn't known he could need. But, oh, how he did, he thought, as the climax inevitably came, crashing over him in wave after exquisite wave.

When the aftershocks subsided, Zach touched his lips to her face, her hair, the nape of her neck. Faith was so sweet. So kind. And so wild. And she was all his.

Christmas had definitely come early this year.

Chapter Sixteen

"Looking good, little fella," Zach told Quinn the next morning, when Faith brought him to the living room, after his bath. She'd been conflicted about how dressed up their baby boy should be and, after a wardrobe crisis that had rivaled her own earlier one, had finally outfitted Quinn in cute engineer stripe overalls, a turtleneck with a Christmas train print and little shearling-lined booties.

Zach's glance roved her emerald sweater and black skirt, tights and shoes. "Mommy looks really nice, too!" he murmured, closing the distance between them.

She gazed up at him, silently absorbing his strength, drinking in the brisk masculine scent of his cologne. He kissed her temple and held out his hands to Quinn, who went into them happily. Looking over at father and son, Faith couldn't help but think how perfect the two of them looked together.

"Thanks." Nervously, Faith glanced at the papers Zach had assembled for the home-study visit. She plumped the pillows on the sofa and bustled around the room, giving it one last appraisal. Not that there was any tidying to do. Zach had even plugged in the Christmas tree! She checked out the folders neatly arranged on the coffee table. "Do we have everything that was requested?" So much was hinging on a good report from Mitzi!

He nodded. Looking devastatingly handsome in his pale blue button-down and dark gray slacks, he edged closer. She had the feeling he was about to tell her to relax, when the phone in his pocket buzzed. She took Quinn so he could answer.

He frowned and put the phone to his ear. "Hi, Mom. Listen, this isn't the best time…Could I…Yes, we got the presents you-all sent. They're already under the tree. Thank you. I'm—*we're*—sending you the usual gift certificates…Mmm-hmm." Zach made a face at Faith and walked into the kitchen.

"Yes, I did get your emails. All fifteen of them… No, I haven't…" With an ever-deepening frown, he scrubbed a hand over his face and moved into the back hallway and then out the back door into the yard, just as the doorbell rang.

Faith went to let in Mitzy. The social worker oohed over Quinn, and then bent to greet the madly wagging Tinkerbelle, too. "Where's Zach?"

Faith smiled. "He had a call from family. I think he's still on the phone. I'm sure he'll be right in."

Mitzy took off her coat. "Everything okay, I hope?"

Was it? There was no doubt he had been stressed, Faith thought, but there was no sense in borrowing trouble. She waved a hand, praying everything would go as well as it needed to go for all of them. She smiled again. "I think it's just the normal holiday stuff."

The back door opened.

Zach strode in, looking calm and in command. And the home evaluation commenced.

"I just have a few more questions, about your employment," Mitzy told Zach when the home tour and parenting interview had concluded.

She had already observed Zach interacting with their son, and quizzed him on everything from Quinn's usual routine and diet. Likes and dislikes. If he had a fussy time of the day. What was the best way to help him through it. And so on. To Faith's delight, her new husband had sailed through it all.

They all settled in the living room. "What would you like to know?" Zach asked, sitting next to Faith.

Mitzy read from a list of prepared questions. "How long have you been a SEAL?"

"Ten years."

She made a note, then looked up, her expression serious. "How much longer do you plan to continue?"

Zach shrugged. "Most special operators conclude that part of their career after fifteen or twenty years."

Mitzy watched him carefully. "Depending on…?"

"Their situation," he replied candidly. "Sometimes soldiers get hurt, and their injuries prevent them from taking on a combat role again. Other times they burn out, or just want to spend time with their family, or discover a new career. It all depends on the person and their situation."

None of which had really answered Mitzy's question, Faith noted nervously.

The social worker made another note. "What do you see yourself doing when your time as a SEAL comes to an end?"

Faith saw another look of telltale hesitation on Zach's part. "Up to now, I haven't really given it a lot of thought," he admitted.

But now, because of Quinn, she knew it was something simmering between them every time they made love, or went somewhere together as a family, or made plans for the rest of the holiday season. Even if she and Zach hadn't actually spoken about it directly.

Mitzy leaned forward. "How long did you originally think you would serve in that capacity?"

"The full twenty years."

"And then…?" Their caseworker pressed on. "Would you take a desk job or a leadership role in the military? Maybe teach…or get involved in some aspect of BUD/S training?"

Zach exhaled, his expression becoming more serious. "Initially, yes, that's the direction I thought my career would go," he answered forthrightly.

Her expression softened sympathetically. "And now?" The social worker continued asking all the questions Faith wished she herself could ask. Without coming off as too nosy and interfering.

Zach reached over, took Faith's hand and gave it a squeeze. "I think when I've concluded my service to my country, I am going to want to come back to Texas and be close to my son."

My son, Faith noted. *Not me.*

"And Faith?" Mitzy prompted.

Zach let go of her hand and offered a wry smile. "They are a package deal, in case you haven't noticed. But, yes," he said sincerely, "I would like to be close to Faith, too."

Well, that was good, since they were *family*.

Mitzy smiled and sat back in her chair. "Would you live here in Laramie, or ask her and Quinn to move to be with you if you got a job elsewhere?"

"I'm not going to ever ask Faith to leave her extended family."

That was a surprise. But a pleasant one, Faith noted, pleased.

"I'd find something here in Laramie County," Zach continued.

Which was, unfortunately, exactly what Harm had said...and tried to do...

"Like search and rescue? Or law enforcement?" Mitzy persisted.

It didn't appear as if Zach was interested in either. A brief silence ensued. Finally, he said cagily, "Again. Not sure. There are a lot of options yet to be explored."

Which was a nice way of not answering.

Mitzy is up a staying palm. "You're right. I shouldn't be asking you to look into a crystal ball to predict the future."

Although right then, Faith would have appreciated having a magical view into the future, so she would know what their upcoming life together held.

"What I can tell you is that my first priority will always be to make sure that Faith and Quinn are well taken care of."

Mitzy jotted something down. Rifled through some pages, then finally looked up. "In the meantime, though, you are slated to go back to your unit after Christmas."

Zach's expression turned grim. It was almost as if he wasn't looking forward to that any more than she was, Faith mused with mixed emotions.

"December twenty-sevenththth," he confirmed, matter-of-fact. "Though I'd be leaving on the twenty-sixth."

The social worker turned to Faith. "And you're okay with taking full responsibility for Quinn in Zach's absence, no matter how long that is?"

She straightened. "Yes. I'll be both mommy and

daddy to our little boy…and a good wife to Zach," she added hastily, turning to smile at him, "until Zach comes home again."

"And I'll do everything I can to keep in touch and support my wife and son, until such time that I can be here with them permanently." Zach squeezed her hand again, firm in his resolve about that.

With her hand encased in his warm, strong grasp, Faith began to relax.

Just because she had struggled with some of Harm's long absences did not mean she would not be able to handle Zach's deployments. For one thing, she had Quinn to care for and love now. Tinkerbelle to help keep them company… During the times when his mission did not force him to "go dark," they would have email. Phone calls. Video chats. Time to catch up and really get to know each other. Or, at the very least, bond further over Quinn.

"Well…" Mitzy shut her notebook, looking satisfied. "I think I have everything I need." She rose gracefully. "I have to congratulate you. You've done an incredible job forming a close and caring family unit."

Faith knew she wasn't supposed to ask. But she couldn't help herself. "Does this mean all will go well in the next hearing with Judge Roy?" she asked anxiously.

That Zach would leave Texas in a few weeks, having secured permanent legal custody of his son? And that she would be able to continue caring for Quinn, in his absence?

Mitzy began to pack up. "I can't make any promises. Judge Roy is a known stickler when it comes to the permanent placement of children. Knowing they are protected to the nth degree." As she drew on her coat, she flashed an encouraging smile. "But what I can tell you is that she's going to get a very positive report about what I've seen here today."

Faith and Zach walked her to the door. Given the speed of their nuptials, along with the fact she and Zach had barely known each other when they'd said "I do," Faith had braced herself to have to do some persuading. A little shocked that hadn't been necessary, she looked over at their social worker. "You don't seem surprised," she observed curiously.

Mitzy—who'd had her own against-all-odds love story with Chase McCabe—didn't even try to pretend to be taken aback by what she had found. "I never bet against love."

It was true, Faith surmised—she and Zach both loved Quinn dearly. They were definitely united in that sense and always would be.

But as for loving *each other*, the way most husbands and wives in successful marriages did...well, that hadn't happened yet, she noted with a surprising depth of disappointment. Even if it felt sometimes like it just might...

"Still worried?" Zach asked, after Mitzy had driven off. Faith was looking oddly pensive, which was never a good sign, in his opinion. "Because," he continued, determined to ease her fears, "no matter what happens at the next court date, we *will prevail* in the end." Just as his SEAL team did.

"Because like Mitzy said," he murmured as he took her—and Quinn—in his arms and gazed tenderly down at them both, "love always wins."

"You think?" she asked, nibbling worriedly on her lip.

"For sure." He flashed a grin. "And besides, we have an awful lot of people supporting us right now, including your family, and mine, and all the seniors at Laramie Gardens."

To his relief, his pep talk seemed to help. She inhaled deeply, the movement lifting the soft swell of her breasts. "You're right." She squared her slender shoulders, then swung back to face him in a drift of wildflower perfume. "We've got this."

Yes, Zach thought, just as determinedly, they did.

She wet her lips. "What we don't have," she said as she eased away, "is Quinn's Christmas taken care of." New worry clouded her irises. "I only have a couple of presents so far, and those are just clothes…which is *not* going to be very exciting to him."

Suddenly, Zach could relate. And time was a-wastin'. "Well, I haven't gotten him anything," he admitted, tucking a strand of hair behind her ear. "Want to go shopping together?"

Her face lit up. "As it happens, I already have the afternoon off from work!"

Zach's spirits lifted. "Sounds good to me." He reached over to let Quinn take his hand. "What do you think, little fella?" he asked softly.

"He can't go!"

Zach swung back to face her. Not sure what the issue was. "You think he'll be fussy in the store?"

Faith rolled her eyes at him, like he was the densest man on earth. "No, silly! He'll see what we're buying! And that will spoil the surprise on Christmas morning. Plus," she continued, her melodic voice taking on a fretful undertone, "I had planned on some of it being from

Santa, unless you have an issue with that…as some people do?"

Zach found it kind of cute, how wound up she was. "No. Santa is fine," he soothed. "But…you really think *he*—" Zach nodded his head at their son "—would understand what we were doing and remember what we bought?" But he also, admittedly, had ulterior motives for wanting the little boy to come along. Zach had missed being with Quinn 24/7 this week, in his rush to get the study done for Faith and prepare for the social-worker evaluation today.

He had been hoping to spend a lot more time with Quinn before he shipped out again. Even if he was sharing his son with the residents of Laramie Garden part of every day…

Faith blew out an exasperated breath. "Well, duh! He remembers you! And me! And everyone else he meets, usually after the very first time, even if it's only for a few minutes… So why *wouldn't* he remember the toys he had seen?"

Put that way… Zach conceded to her maternal wisdom. He took both mother and son in his arms and kissed them both. "Good point," he whispered in Faith's ear. Giving her another kiss while he was at it. "He is pretty smart."

Faith beamed in agreement. "He's very smart. Which is why, if we're going to do this today, and we should, I need a sitter. Pronto."

Chapter Seventeen

"So you're taking the hot one off for an afternoon alone?" Emma said when she came in, half an hour later.

Faith glanced out at the backyard. Zach still had Tinkerbelle out there, while she changed Quinn's diaper up in the nursery.

"Stop!"

Emma laughed. "Can't help it. You look more well-loved than I have ever seen you."

She was. But Faith did not want to talk about that for fear she would jinx it. Her convenient marriage was turning out far better than she ever could have imagined. And she wanted it to stay that way.

She cleared her throat, to try to reset the conversation. "I hope you mean that in the platonic sense."

"Mmm..." Emma grinned mischievously. "I think it's a little more than pillow talk, but we'll just leave that to the imagination..."

Faith fastened the snaps on Quinn's overalls. "Thank you."

"I'm serious." Her younger sister mugged at Quinn and elbowed Faith lightly. "It's good to see you so happy."

It felt good, too. Which was why Faith didn't completely trust her near constant euphoria and contentment.

Finished, she lifted Quinn and shifted him into Emma's

waiting arms. "The diapers are up here, as you can see, and there are more downstairs on the baby-item shelf in the pantry. Plenty of bottles of formula in the fridge. I've written Quinn's schedule out and all the emergency contact numbers on the paper in the kitchen. And, of course, you can call me on my cell."

The other woman winked as they headed downstairs. "Yes, commandant."

Zach ambled in, Tink by his side. He grinned at Emma, correctly reading the situation. "My wife giving you a hard time?"

My wife...

Emma grinned back, suddenly in cahoots with Zach. "She's being *so difficult*, in fact, I think you need to whisk her away *right this very second!*"

Zach's rich laughter filled the foyer. "Sounds good to me," he said.

And off they went.

Zach had never enjoyed shopping. He usually went in, got what he needed and got out. The less time and energy expended, the better. But shopping for his son's very first Christmas with his new wife was an entirely different experience.

He actually liked going from store to store, first in Laramie and then nearby San Angelo, perusing what they had, debating whether or not something was age-appropriate for Quinn.

By the time they had finished five hours later, it was close to dinnertime. Faith called Emma to see how things were going. "Quinn and Tinkerbelle and I are having a great time! Stay there and have a nice dinner," her sister encouraged. She turned the phone so they could see the crew, as they were already sitting down to an early meal in the kitchen. It was true—all looked happy and content as could be, Zach noted.

Faith sighed her relief. "Okay, thanks, sis. I owe you."

Emma grinned. "Don't worry. I'll find a way to collect!" She ended the call. And Zach and Faith turned to the question of where to have their very first meal by themselves.

They settled on an upscale Mexican restaurant, ordering fresh-made guacamole to go with their chips and salsa while they studied the extensive menu.

Trying not to notice how soft and glossy her hair looked, Zach teased, "Having trouble deciding?"

Faith rested her chin on her upturned palm. "Truthfully? I am having trouble accepting that I am actually out for a grown-up dinner without Quinn!"

He knew what she meant. Normally at this point in his R&R, he felt anxious to get back. Ready to be with his SEAL team. Instead, he found himself wishing for more time. With his wife and son.

Zach thought their marriage would be completely platonic. That it would be like having a roommate, albeit one of the opposite sex. So when he had first proposed, he figured they could reside under the same roof whenever he was in Texas. Share care of their baby boy and her dog. And pretty much go their own separate ways the rest of the time.

But he realized now that was going to be impossible. He couldn't be anywhere near Faith without wanting to hold her and kiss her and touch her. His feelings were admittedly territorial. Male. Instinctive. He wanted her to be his woman in *every* way, not just as a friend with benefits he also happened to be legally married to.

Unfortunately, that wasn't the deal they had made. And he wasn't sure she would be amenable to taking things to the next level before he left again.

"Is it a good or bad thing, for us to be out alone?" Zach asked, taking her hand.

She took a deep breath, and her voice took on a rich, husky timbre that revealed the depth of her conflict. "Good. But…unexpected, too, I guess." She went back to looking at the menu.

He knew what she meant. They'd had the near-constant buffer of their infant and their families, co-workers and LG residents since the first moment they had met. Despite the fact they had known each other for a little more than two weeks, and been married for one week, this was the nearest they had ever come to having an actual date. Yes, it was starting out a little awkward, but that could be rectified with practice. He tightened his grasp on her hand, and said casually, "Maybe we should think about having a date night every week." He could see himself getting into that… Quality time alone with his wife where they could relax and unwind and focus solely on each other. Would she want the same with him?

"Sure. When you're here," she said, biting her lip.

But who knew how often that would be, he thought, his spirits falling once again. He was supposed to have thirty days R&R every year. However, depending on what was going on, sometimes he had a little more, sometimes less…

He couldn't waste time worrying about that. He needed to focus on the here and now and the beautiful woman sitting across the table from him.

He smiled, letting her know how much he appreciated her company. She truly was the most amazing woman he had ever met. The fact she was now mother to his son, here with him now, was even better…

"So what do you think?" He went back to looking at the menu, too, realizing he was famished. "Do you want to start with soup or salad…?"

"I don't know," she murmured in the soft, sexy voice he loved.

Everything looked so good—the decision was difficult. They mulled over their choices. Placed their order, ordered two Mexican beers and sat back.

Aware it was really beginning to seem like a first date, he asked, "So who else do we need to shop for?" He shifted. Beneath the table, their knees touched and he savored the feel of her, so close, so feminine.

Faith announced happily, "I've already done my family." She lifted a hand, signaling he didn't have to worry. "The presents I got can be from all of us."

Made sense since they were married.

"What about your folks?" she asked.

Zach admitted reluctantly, "I need to get that done, too."

Her expression gentled. "Need any help?"

If it meant spending time with her, the answer would be "hell yes." Then again, was that really how he wanted to use his remaining time? Trying to figure out the impossible? Having her become just as frustrated? "I'll just do the usual," he said.

She sipped her drink, looking perplexed by what he meant. Her emerald eyes narrowed. "Which is?"

"Gift certificates. That way they are never disappointed."

She leaned close. "Someone hasn't liked your presents in the past?" she asked.

Not sure she would understand, given how close she was with her own family, he took another drink. "My mother is very particular. It was painful, watching her trying not to return something. And my dad just doesn't really care about presents. He thinks it is unnecessary."

She paused. "What did they give you?"

"My mom always gave me clothes. Still does. She wants me to be a well-dressed civilian in the worst way. My dad sends me books on military history."

"Interesting ones?" she asked hopefully.

"Yeah," Zach admitted, aware he had never looked at it quite that way. "Usually, very interesting."

"Where are those books?"

She assumed right that he had kept them. Because they had meant something to him, too. "In a box in one of the storage rooms at my mom's place in Alexandria."

She gave him one of her soft, encouraging smiles. "You could shelve them in my study if you want. Or the living room, if you prefer. In fact, you may want to have a lot of your stuff shipped here."

This, he hadn't expected. "Will you have space for it?" He fought against the emotion welling up inside him.

She kept her gaze locked with his. "We'll make room."

There she went again…making him feel welcome in a way he never had been before. He wanted her to know how much that meant to him. But how to say it without sounding corny, or having her think he was unfairly pressuring her in some way, was the real dilemma.

Aware that was going to require some consideration, he said, "Speaking of presents…" Their waiter put their sizzling-hot entrées before them, then promptly disappeared. He nudged her knees playfully beneath the table, his need to make love to her…soon…intensifying. "What would you like Santa to bring you this year?"

A shy blush lit her cheeks.

"Um…" She ran the tines of her fork through her chili-lime salmon and grilled veggies, then looked up at him again, squinting. "Santa hasn't left any presents for me in a while."

Finding he was as famished as he was after any well-executed mission, he dug into his own grilled steak and diablo shrimp. "Well, that has to change!" he countered, appreciating how pretty and feminine she looked in the muted lighting of the restaurant. "How are we going to explain to Quinn that Santa didn't leave Mommy anything?" He winked. "And don't tell me he won't remember what happened this year because we already went over that."

She laughed softly. "I guess we did."

"So…?"

She started to speak. Stopped. Tried again, then sat back and gave up. "I have no idea!"

"That's not a helpful hint, darlin'," he said teasingly.

"You really don't need to get me anything, Zach."

He thought about all she had done for him—the way she had brought him into her and Quinn's life, and opened up her home and heart to him, so he could go back to work without ever having to worry that Quinn would be without love. Family. Safety and security.

He squeezed her hand again. "Actually, Faith, I really do."

The following day, Laramie Gardens was hosting its annual adopt-a-grandparent holiday luncheon and party.

"How long ago was this program started?" Zach asked, as he drove through the festively decorated streets of Laramie. To Faith's pleasure, he had accepted her invitation to attend the party with her and Quinn, and that made her feel all the more like part of a real family.

Faith, sitting in the passenger seat, looked over at him. The marine blue cashmere sweater he wore brought out the lighter blue of his eyes, and his hands commanded the steering wheel with the same easy expertise he made love. It was hard not to desire him when they were together like this. But she forced her attention back to the lovely wreaths on every streetlamp downtown, and the conversation at hand. "Miss Isabelle was instrumental in getting the program up and running several years ago. The holidays can be very lonely for older adults who don't have family nearby, or sometimes at all."

Zach nodded compassionately. "Like Nessie Rogers."

"Yes." Fortunately, Nessie had agreed to get involved with some of the kindergarteners who came by to color pictures and read books. And the retired lady rancher was still spending time with Russell Pierce, and a few others at mealtime now, so she seemed a little happier. Although Nessie was still adamant she would return to her ranch in time for Christmas, doctor's permission or no.

"And it helps the little ones, too, since many of them don't have the opportunity to see their own grandparents very often," Faith continued.

"That's nice." Zach smiled. He checked out Quinn in the mirror, seeing that their little boy was happily enjoying the SUV ride, as usual. Then reached over and squeezed her knee affectionately, his warm touch lingering briefly. "I know how much it meant to be close to my own grandfather. But I enjoy swapping stories with the guys at Laramie Gardens, too."

His kindness was laudable. "They sure love you, too," she remarked admiringly.

They were both part of the volunteer crew, so once there, Zach helped the other men set up extra folding tables and chairs to accommodate the visiting little ones, and their parents, while she watched over Quinn. He then took over care of their son while she retreated to the kitchen to help put out the luncheon, which included contributions of all kinds of goodies from everyone in attendance, as well as what the dining-hall staff had prepared in advance.

"You've been awfully quiet this morning," Inez Garcia remarked, arranging platters of cookies and tarts on the buffet.

Her fellow nurse, Nora, observed, "Yeah. You look a little tired."

That was because she and Zach had been up half the night making love, after they had returned from their "date night."

"But happy overall," Nora added hastily, setting up the sliced ham and turkey.

Faith knew she was happy. Too happy?

"Something on your mind?" Inez asked.

As Faith arranged the bread in baskets, she focused on what she *could* talk about. "I can't figure out what to get Zach for Christmas."

"Ohhhh..." Both nurses groaned in unison. Together, they went back to get the food in chafing dishes.

"That can be tough, your first year of marriage," Nora sympathized.

"Any year of marriage," the long-hitched Inez said.

Carefully, they set up the hot-foods part of the feast.

"I don't know if I should go with something practical—" which was what Harm had always wanted from her "—since Zach is about to deploy again. Or go for something more, um, meaningful, I guess."

Her heart said go for the sentimental, while the cautious side of her warned her not to overdo it... After all, things were good between them right now.

Nora stepped back to check out the buffet. "What's the dollar limit?" she asked.

"That's just it. He didn't give me one. He just said that he was sure he would be happy with whatever I gifted him."

More groans of sympathy came her way.

"What did you *want* him to get for you?" Inez placed plastic cups, with a holly-and-ivy design, around the punch bowls.

"I have no clue."

Both women laughed. "Well, you better think of something fast—" Inez winked "—because Christmas is only thirteen days away..."

Their court date was just a little more than a week away.

And he was leaving for heaven knew where in fourteen days...

Suddenly, Faith wished she could just stop counting. And live in the moment, the way they had last night, and every night since their wedding night. When things had really begun to change for the better.

* * *

"Why did you give me that look when they asked me to be a judge at the ugly-sweater contest?" Zach asked curiously, hours later, after they had returned home and put Quinn to bed for the night.

Faith set out the bottles for the next day and began filling them with dry formula. "Because you don't want to be a judge," she said, making sure to measure each one just right. "You want to be a *contestant*, with me and Quinn."

Zach went down the line after her, adding water to the bottles. "So you said..."

Thrilled by how well they worked as a team, Faith swung back to face him. Too late, she realized. "I guess I should have asked you what you wanted first." Instead of doing what she had in her previous marriage, and just assuming...

Had she pushed him away, with her presumption?

Zach added the nipples and screwed on the caps, while she went after him, this time, and snapped on the plastic lids. "No need for that." He turned to her with a reassuring smile. "Of course, I want to be part of any family activity, whenever I can be." Together, they shook the bottles, to mix them. Then slid them into the fridge. Finished, he studied her, knowing her well enough to realize there was more. "But...what's so bad about being a judge?"

Because if he was a judge, he couldn't be a contestant, and if he couldn't be a contestant, he couldn't be on her and Quinn's "family team"...

Wanting that for them was probably selfish and self-centered of her.

Then again, this was their son's very first Christmas.

There would be pictures of it, just like there would be pictures of the wedding. She didn't want any one of them to feel like they were missing out.

"Have you ever judged the contest?" Zach asked.

"Um, no, luckily," Faith replied.

He shot her another quizzical look.

Fearing she was going to collapse if she didn't get off her feet soon, she put her hand in his larger, callused palm and guided him into the living room. She didn't mind discussing this, but she wanted to be more comfortable while they did it. She also wanted to listen to some Christmas music. So she selected a soothing orchestral holiday collection and turned it on. Then watched while he lit the fire he had laid earlier, and switched on the Christmas-tree lights. The mood for a relaxing evening set, they settled on the sofa.

"It's very competitive," she told him, snuggling close. "I don't know what it is about the contest, but everyone wants to win."

Understanding lit his blue eyes. "Ahhh." Zach draped his arm along the back of the sofa and guided her even closer to his side.

Cuddling happily against the curve of his tall, strong body, Faith continued, "If we have any judge who knows the LG residents, there are always accusations of favoritism."

"Uh-oh." Zach grinned.

"'Uh-oh' is right! Which is why the last few years, we've had staff from senior homes in nearby counties that don't know a soul here come in to do the honors."

Sobering, he entwined their fingers, squeezed. His gaze never left her face. "Seems fair."

Faith loved hanging out with him like this. She was

definitely going to miss him when he was gone. It already hurt, imagining how lonely her evenings would be. "It absolutely makes the contest more fun," she admitted with a sigh.

Zach rubbed the sensitive skin on the inside of her wrist with his fingertips. Then tilted his head, his expression mischievous. "You know what else is fun?" he drawled.

"I have an idea," Faith murmured back as he kissed her neck. The next thing she knew they were making love again, next to the Christmas tree, with the sounds of sleet hitting the windows, as a winter storm rolled in.

"I wish it was snow," Faith admitted with a yawn as they headed for bed.

Zach climbed in beside her and wrapped her in his arms. He pressed a kiss to her hair. "Me, too."

Determined to enjoy every single second she had with him before he left, Faith put her head on his shoulder and snuggled close. They had just fallen asleep when his phone rang.

Chapter Eighteen

Early the next afternoon, Faith's house was extraordinarily quiet. Quinn and Tinkerbelle were both napping in their beds, and her sister Jillian had come over to decorate ugly sweaters with her. "Zach is still in the woods around Lake Laramie?"

Faith nodded as she continued setting up her portable sewing machine. He had been there since one in the morning, helping Lockhart Search and Rescue and local law enforcement search for a lost hiker.

She had been up most of the night, after he'd left, worrying about him. *Missing* him. Quinn had kept looking around for his daddy when he had woken up, too. A harbinger of the weeks and months to come? If she missed him now, when he was still in Texas, what would it be like when he was thousands of miles away, or worse, on a mission and incommunicado?

Mistaking the reason for her anxiety, Jillian glanced out the dining room. Sheets of ice-cold rain alternated with sleet pounded against the glass. "Terrible weather to be caught out in," she murmured.

"I know. It's been raining steadily since last night, and the temperature hasn't gotten over forty-two degrees, although it has dipped as low as thirty-one."

Her sister pinned the pattern to the fabric. "I hope they don't get hypothermia."

Faith began to cut the multicolored felt shapes with as much precision as possible. "I'm sure the searchers are all in protective gear." She paused as an image of Zach, as he had been when he had left, appeared in her head. His demeanor had been warrior-tough. If anyone was meant for a situation such as this, it was him.

Resolutely, she shook off her persistent worry. "I don't know about the lost teenager, though."

"Well..." Jillian laid out the pieces in the holiday design she had created for her girls' sweaters. "We will hope for the best... So how are you doing? I heard the home evaluation with Mitzy went well."

Faith sat down behind the sewing machine, relieved as she admitted, "It did."

Jillian, who'd had her own share of heartaches with the wrong guy, twice, slanted her another look. "How are you adjusting to married life?"

*Too well for comfort. Shouldn't she and Zach have gotten on each other's nerves by now? Or fought over something...*anything*? Maybe even decided that sleeping together had been a mistake?*

Resolved to keep her problems to herself, Faith threaded the bobbin with the same dark pine-green thread as their matching sweaters. "I'm doing fine."

Jillian scrutinized her with another long gaze, clearly not believing everything could be rosy given the way it had all started, just a few weeks prior.

And yet, Faith thought, it was. She lifted a staying hand. Forced a smile. "It's not my first rodeo, sis."

"I know that." Jillian continued to pin the coordinating reindeers on all five sweaters. "But living together can be tricky. So can marriage."

When she'd finished sewing the pattern on the first

sweater, Faith got up to give her sister a turn at the machine. As she looked toward the living room, she thought about the makeshift bed they had made with throws and pillows, on the floor beside the beautifully lit Christmas tree. "Zach is very easygoing."

Jillian, never one to hold her tongue, snorted. "Come on. Zach *must* have some flaws. Something you want or need to vent about."

"Hmm." Faith tried to come up with something but when she thought about Zach, all she could think about was…perfection. In bed, and out. "We don't really have any issues." Not like the ones she and Harm had had, when their relationship began to fall apart, anyway.

Jillian lifted her brow, wordlessly pushing her to be honest. "None?" she echoed in disbelief.

Faith shrugged. "That I can think of."

Except for the fact it would be very easy for me to see myself falling in love with him. And love isn't in the cards for us at all. Not romantic love, anyway. Because that could not be conjured up on demand. No matter how much I wish otherwise, Faith thought dejectedly. *Because if it could have been, her previous marriage would have worked out a whole lot differently.*

The afternoon passed without word. Dinnertime came and went. So did bath time. Finally, just as Faith put the sleepy Quinn to bed, her phone rang. It was Zane's wife, Nora.

"Hey, Faith. I just wanted to give you an update. They found the kid, but he's at the bottom of a deep ravine, and they're having trouble getting him out without further injury."

Which likely meant everyone helping was in some level of danger, too. "Oh, no."

"Yeah." Nora sighed, sounding both as worried and relieved as Faith felt. "The hiker's lucky to be alive. He probably wouldn't be if he hadn't managed to pull his sleeping bag overtop of him, for shelter. Anyway, there's no cell reception at the accident site, so they have to use radio. Zach wanted me to call you and let you know he should be home in another couple of hours."

"Thanks."

"You can go on to bed if you want." Nora quickly added, "Zach's words, not mine."

Sleep would be impossible if her husband was in any kind of danger, and he *was* her husband, in more ways than she wanted to count. "I'll wait up."

Nora made an approving sound. "Exactly what I plan to do. Anyway, I'll see you at work tomorrow."

"Thanks for calling." Faith ended the call.

The next few hours dragged. She finished laundry, made lunches for the following day, then pulled a hearty chicken-tortilla soup from the freezer and put it on the stovetop to heat.

Restless, she retreated to the study Zach had finished remodeling for her and sat down behind her computer. Deciding to put the time to good for use, she shopped for his gift. She had just found it and placed the order when she heard a vehicle in the driveway.

He came in the back, instead of the front. When she saw him, she knew why. It looked like he had come straight from one hell of a battle. Zach was wet and muddy from head to toe. He had a vicious-looking scrape across his cheek, down his jaw. Another smaller one on his neck. And he was incredibly tired around the eyes. But he appeared as happy to see her as she was to see him.

Her heart kicking against her ribs, she grabbed him and hugged him hard.

He wound his arms around her and buried his face in her hair. For a moment they stayed just like that, holding each other fiercely. Finally, he said gruffly, "Miss me much?"

So much. Blinking back the tears of relief and joy that she refused to let fall, she stepped back to survey him again. "What happened to you?" she asked, aghast. Had Zach fallen down the ravine, too? Or just been hurt rappelling down?

He shrugged in the way that let her know she would not be hearing any of the scarier details from him. Sighing, he rubbed the flat of his hand across the underside of his jaw. "I spent nearly twenty-two hours looking for a lost kid."

Already thinking ahead to what he might need first, Faith helped him out of his coat.

"Is the hiker going to be okay?" she asked.

His broad shoulders sagging with exhaustion, Zach went into the laundry room and began to methodically strip off his wet and dirty clothing. Then kicked off his hiking boots. "They think so, but he's going to need surgery and will be in the hospital for a few days after that."

"His parents must be relieved."

"You have no idea. His mother couldn't stop crying and his dad was so overwrought he couldn't speak."

Faith teared up, imagining. "Listen, we need to get you into something warm and dry…"

"I like the sound of that," he murmured devilishly.

"Seriously. I'll run upstairs and be right back with something for you to put on." She was embarrassed she hadn't already thought to do that! Since she had guessed this would be the situation when he came in.

He caught her arm before she could dash off. "How about I head for the shower to get cleaned up and then have some of that delicious soup you've got on the stove."

Right. He would want to get the mud washed off. She swallowed, aware once again she was presuming too much. Seeing his boxer-brief-clad form, she forced a brisk smile. "Want anything else?"

"A beer…?" He furrowed his brow. "And maybe a hot sandwich of some sort…"

Unable to help herself, she touched his uninjured cheek gently. "Coming right up."

Muttering his thanks, he headed out of the kitchen, up the stairs. He was back five minutes later, smelling of soap and shampoo. A long-sleeved thermal T-shirt, sweatpants and thick wool socks cloaked his frame. Despite the scrape on his face, he had never looked so good to her. She bustled around, setting his meal in front of him. He nodded at the soup. "Don't you want some?"

"I ate earlier." It was all she could do to look at him and drink him in.

"So tell me about your day," he said, chowing down.

She did. Making more of the process than there really was, just to keep him entertained. "Am I going to get a look at these ugly sweaters that are probably anything but ugly?" he teased.

They were pretty in a festive kind of way. At least she hoped that he was going to like his. "On the day of the competition. I don't want you accidentally giving anything away."

He leaned back in his chair, wiping the corners of his lips with his napkin. "Think I can't keep a secret?"

She squinted. "I think you might brag to the other fellas at Laramie Gardens."

"You're probably right about that. I do like to talk about my awesome wife and kid." He winked. Finished, he pushed back from the table.

"Stay right there, soldier."

His mind immediately went to the bedroom. "Why? What do you have planned?"

"Not that." *Yet.* She rose and got the first-aid kit out of the cupboard. "I want to tend to those scrapes..."

He made a face, but remained where he was, shoulders back, long muscular legs stretched out in front of him. "I washed them in the shower. They're fine."

Faith straddled his lap. Hand beneath his chin, she lifted his face to hers. In full caretaker mode. "I want to clean them out again and put some antibiotic cream on them."

His eyes twinkled, even as he humored her, "If you insist..."

While she worked, Zach told her about the search and rescue. How tough it had been to cover so much heavily wooded ground, in bad weather, with only a dozen searchers. She had to admit, she didn't know much about the local capabilities in that regard. "Is Laramie County always that short-handed?"

He nodded grimly. "Yeah. Other rural counties around here are, as well. That's why Zane started Lockhart Search and Rescue."

She soaked in his steady, masculine warmth as she

covered the injured skin with antibiotic cream. "He must have been glad to have you there today."

"He was."

Faith eased off his lap. Washed her hands. Put the kit away. Then asked as cavalierly as she could, "Did he try to recruit you to come to work for him when you eventually get out of the SEALs?" Maybe this would be a good fit, she thought hopefully.

Zach got to his feet and pushed the chair in. He stood with his hands hooked over the back. "He tries to recruit everyone with my experience. Including all the special operators that came down for our wedding."

Oh.

Still, Faith had to look him in the eye as she asked, "Would you consider taking a job there? Eventually? When you're out of the service, whenever that is?"

There was a brief hesitation on Zach's part. For a moment, she thought he was going to sidestep the inquiry altogether, with a quip or an evasion of some sort. Then something changed in his eyes. As if a decision was made. He shook his head. "No. I don't think so."

A mixture of disappointment and despair roiled through her. Similar to what she'd felt when her late husband had struggled to build a new life, outside of the SEALs. "Why not?"

Another shrug. This one less amiable. "It's just not what I see myself doing when I get out," he told her quietly. "Why? Does that disappoint you?" he asked gruffly.

Did it?

The truth was, she wanted him here, in Laramie County, 24/7 when the time was right. Yet at the same time, she couldn't envision him doing anything else but what she knew he felt he'd been born to do.

So, bottom line? She didn't want to tell him how to live his life…any more than she wanted him telling her how to live hers.

Gathering her courage, she shook her head and for both their sakes, fibbed with all her might. "No. It doesn't."

Zach wasn't sure what he had wanted her to say. *Hell, yes, I want you here with me, and Quinn, right here, and right now.*

Or, *I don't care what you do as long as you're happy and you're here.*

Something—anything—along those lines.

But that wasn't their deal, he knew. And he shouldn't be expecting it to change. At least not this soon.

Maybe in time…

Pushing aside his crushed expectations, he carried his dishes to the dishwasher. "Got any dessert?" he asked. Figuring the best thing to do was just move on to something a hell of a lot more pleasurable.

She suddenly looked as on edge as he felt. "White-chocolate peppermint fudge?" she asked cheerfully.

"Sounds great."

She brought out the tin. As they savored the yuletide treat, a smile bloomed on her face. She elbowed him lightly. "You must be wiped out."

"If that's a hint it's time to hit the sheets…" He turned so her back was to the counter, his hands braced on either side of her.

Smiling up at him, she wrapped her arms about his neck. "You can't possibly have the energy."

He kissed her temple, her cheek, then her lips. "I guess we'll see, won't we?"

They made their way through the downstairs, making out all the way. They kissed their way up the staircase, too. And down the hall…into her bedroom.

The scene was already set. Pillows plumped. Covers turned down. Bedside lamp low. Drinking in the sweet wildflower fragrance of her, he lowered his head and kissed her, determined to make this last. He had been thinking about her all day. Wishing he could be with her, having her press intimately against him, kissing him back just as ardently. Just…like…this. Need sprang up inside him as he cupped her breasts in his palms.

Her nipples budded. Sighing softly, she swayed against him. "Zach…"

He knew she wanted to make this fast—for his sake. While he wanted to make it slow—for hers. "Trust me, you're not ready…" he whispered as she took him by the hand and pushed him to sit on the edge of her bed.

She offered him a sexy smile. "I will be…" Her sweater came off, then her jeans. Along with her bra and panties. She helped him dispense with his clothes, too. Then moved between his spread thighs, catching his head in her hands, tangling her fingers in his hair, and promised, "Just watch…"

He cupped her bottom with one hand, ran his fingertips across the warm silky skin of her thighs. She hitched in a ragged breath and he felt her tremble again. Rejoicing in her responsiveness, he stroked the delicate folds. Tucked a finger into her core, found it damp, hot and tight. All the while she gripped his shoulders, hard, and let her head fall back, as he finally gifted her with the ultimate pleasure.

Enjoying how beautiful and utterly ravished she looked, he eased her back onto the pillows and stretched out overtop of her. He kissed her again, sweetly and tenderly this time. “I love it when you tremble for me…” He slid between her knees. “And open for me.”

She rocked against him, and suddenly she wasn’t the only one shivering with pent-up yearning. She stroked him, wrapping her legs around him. He was hard as a rock, throbbing, wildly aroused. Hands low on his hips, she urged him on. He took a deep breath and paused long enough to roll on a condom. Then shifting, arching, he was inside her, filling her, possessing her with a need that only she could satisfy.

Their lips locked in a primal kiss. She tightened her body around him, taking him deep, gifting him with everything he had ever wanted and needed. Showing him what it was to give and take without restraint. What it was to want to be with someone with every part of his soul.

Afterward, they clung together, holding each other as they drifted off to sleep.

All along, he had been telling himself not to rush Faith. To take things one day, one step at a time.

And though that policy had initially worked to keep their convenient marriage on an even keel, it was still less satisfying than he wanted. Maybe because there were still so many things they hadn’t yet been able to talk about. Like what their future was really going to look like.

It was also the season of miracles.

His leave wasn’t over yet. Not nearly.

Maybe if he were patient enough, if he addressed this like any other mission, and worked hard enough to come up with some sort of solution for the long term, all their Christmas dreams would come true after all.

Chapter Nineteen

"You look happy today," the Laramie Gardens director observed cheerfully on Monday, after they had finished their late-afternoon meeting.

"I am." Faith smiled back at Diane.

The truth was there was a lot to be happy about.

Even if new resident Nessie Rogers was still missing her ranch…

And the long-married Ted and Tillie Tarrant were sharing a suite, but barely speaking as they awaited the holiday visit of their only son…

But, those things aside, Quinn had a daddy. She had a husband, who was also quickly becoming her very best friend, in all the world. And Zach was still in Texas!

In fact, he had spent the entire day at Laramie Gardens, alternately helping out with Quinn and letting the ladies all have their turn with their beloved "mascot," and swapping stories with the men.

She had caught bits of conversation here and there, and they'd been talking about everything from the men's experiences in the military, to their return to civilian life, and the jobs they had taken or the businesses they had started. Zach was sincerely interested in every bit of it.

"Are you worried about being too sad again when he leaves?" Diane asked.

Faith steeled herself against the pain of his upcoming departure, the fact it would be months before she and Quinn saw him again. "I think I will handle his deployment okay."

"Because you have Quinn now."

As well as a new attitude, she thought.

Zach's absence for almost all of Sunday had shown her what it would be like when he wasn't around. That had made her more determined to enjoy every minute when he was here. And make sure his son could do the same.

So that night, all three of them went out to dinner after work, and then over to the town square to sip hot chocolate and hear the joint performance of every choir in the area singing Christmas carols.

Tuesday, Zach spent the morning doing mysterious holiday-related errands. Faith got everything else she needed for his present on her lunch hour. That evening, they took a hayride through the Christmas village set up at the fairgrounds.

On Wednesday, Zach decided he wanted to purchase actual presents for his mom and dad that year, so she and Quinn accompanied him on a trip to the San Angelo mall.

Thursday, Zach took her to Laramie Gardens, then returned home to work on building an organizational system in the garage for his grandfather's carpentry tools, that would keep everything neatly stowed and well out of a curious child's reach. That evening, they met some of her siblings and their kids for pizza.

When Friday rolled around, Zach again disappeared for a mysterious errand, returning with a brand-new extended-cab pickup truck. "I've missed having my own vehicle," he admitted, while showing her and Quinn the many features of the luxuriously outfitted truck. "And, I figured I should have something to drive when I'm home..." he added, as if he needed an excuse, which, of course, he didn't.

Home! She loved the sound of that!

"Instead of relying on rentals," he said. Winking, he joked, "Or borrowing yours all the time."

She laughed at his mischievous expression. "I don't mind you driving my SUV." Ever. In fact it was somehow incredibly comforting to have him behind the wheel of her Highlander.

On Saturday, they wrapped and mailed the presents to his folks, then took Quinn to the community center to stand in line and see Santa.

Sunday, they just hung out at home, making *bûche de Noël* cakes to freeze and then take to her parents' ranch for the 4:00 p.m. family celebration on Christmas Day.

They were just finishing frosting them when Zach's government-issued smartphone went off. No question... he had to get it. He walked into the other room as he took the call.

She couldn't hear much except the low rumble of his voice. When he returned, he looked grim. "What is it?" she asked, her nerves already jangling.

"The mission has been moved up. I'm shipping out on the twenty-sixth, not the twenty-seventh." His gaze drifted over her, as always seeing far more of her vulnerability than she preferred. "Which means I have to fly out of Dallas in the afternoon on Christmas Day."

Not about to return to the kind of wife who needed constant reassurance from her man, Faith pushed aside her disappointment. This was all part of the military lifestyle; she *knew* that. "I understand. We will still have Christmas together before you leave."

"I'm sorry." Zach wrapped his arms around her and guided her against him. He pressed a sorrowful kiss in her hair. "I wanted to spend the whole day with you and Quinn."

She drew a breath and tried to get a handle on her churning emotions. "It's your job," she reminded him, calling on all her inner strength.

Just as hers was to be the best military wife possible to him. And military wives did *not* make their spouses feel bad about their service to their country.

"But this does change things," she said, calling on her inner impishness to lighten the suddenly somber mood. She went to the cupboard and got out two plates, a knife and two forks. Directing him onto one of the stools at the counter, she brought one of the freshly baked yule logs over to them. "If you're not going to be here to enjoy them at my parents ranch on Christmas night then… We'll have to do this now…"

To their mutual delight, the cake was as delicious as the tender and passionate lovemaking that followed.

Now, Faith thought, as she continued taking their life together day by day, with the very best, most positive attitude possible, all she and Zach had to do was get through the court hearing that would decide whether or not he would get full legal custody of Quinn.

Early the next afternoon, Zach walked into Judge Roy's courtroom, with Quinn in his arms and Faith at his side. They took a seat at the table, next to their attorney.

He looked at his beautiful wife beside him, who had changed his life in immeasurable ways.

Normally, Faith was so confident. Yet now, she looked so pale.

Thinking it might help her to feel better if she was holding Quinn, he handed the baby to her. Then wound his free arm about her shoulders, pulling her close, and leaned in to whisper in her ear, "We've got this." At least he hoped they did. As both their lawyer and social worker had pointed out, there was never any predicting what Judge Priscilla Roy would rule.

Faith's gaze met his. So sweet and so sincere. "I know you do, Zach."

You.

Not we.

She was talking about the fact that this hearing was about his claiming full immediate legal custody of his child and what plans would be made for his son in his absence, not her wish to co-adopt.

So what she said made sense.

Technically, anyway.

He *did* have this.

Because he wasn't leaving Texas without securing the future for his son, and his wife, and their family.

Fortunately, it wasn't necessary to put forth any more valiant effort. Judge Priscilla Roy was ready to tell them her decision. "I have to admit," she said from the bench, lowering her reading glasses down to the end of the bridge of her nose, "in light of your recent hasty marriage and upcoming deployment, I was prepared to see plenty of reason not to award your son to you just yet, Lieutenant Callahan. Then I read the report from social services. And saw your parenting plan for Quinn had been approved by the military. And I realized how invested both you and Faith are in creating a warm and loving environment for Quinn to grow up in."

The judge paused to smile in approval. "You've gone the extra mile, Lieutenant, and although I would have liked to know more about your future plans for either continuing your military service, or stepping down, because all that was rather vague and indecisive in the report, I still feel that Quinn belongs with you. And your wife."

"Thank you, Your Honor," Zach said, while a teary-eyed Faith cuddled Quinn even closer.

Judge Roy nodded. Seeming to know what their attorney's next question was going to be, she continued, "As far as Faith Callahan's petition to co-adopt goes, it continues to be denied right now, but…if in a year things still look the same, she can resubmit and the court will listen to it at that time." She banged her gavel, signaling their hearing was over.

Overcome with emotion, Faith brought Quinn in for a "family embrace" with Zach. "I am so happy for you," she choked out.

"For *us*," Zach confirmed, gently hugging them back.

They stopped to collect their papers from the clerk, and then walked out into the hallway. From there, they proceeded down the courthouse steps, where Faith's entire family was assembled, waiting. Zach held up the papers. "It's official!" he told everyone. "We're a family!"

Cheers erupted. Tears flowed. Hugs followed.

"Everyone out to our ranch for dinner," Carol Lockhart said.

Robert winked. "Not to worry, all you lovebirds. We've got plenty of mistletoe."

Everyone laughed and scattered to their cars and trucks. Once again, Zach knew what it was like to be part of the big, loving Lockhart clan. Which made him wonder, how he was going to be able to give this up. Even knowing he would return.

"Well, if you ask me," Mackenzie mused, while the women got the buffet in the kitchen set up, "Zach is nesting."

"I agree." Jillian nodded her head enthusiastically as she put out the salads.

"Buying a pickup truck to drive in Texas, when he's not even going to be here most of the time? Organizing his tools in your garage so they'll be ready to use the next time he comes home?" Allison said. "That is the sign of a man marking his territory."

"Or claiming his woman," the ever-romantic Emma said, and winked.

"Not that Zach needs to buy a truck to convey to everyone in Laramie County how he feels about you," Susannah said.

Jillian smiled and paused to give Faith a sisterly hug. "That soldier is clearly in love with you!"

But was he? Faith wondered. And why was it suddenly bothering her that he might not be? Zach had honored the deal they had made. They both had. Wanting it to be more... Well, that was probably just her getting caught up in spirit of the holidays. Where she'd been raised to believe that even the most far-fetched dreams and wishes could come true...

Luckily, with dinner ready, the women in the family had no more chance to tease her about her love life, or lack thereof. They all sat down, a mix of families, incorporated into one big group. Food was enjoyed. Stories flowed. At the end, during cleanup, everyone took on appropriate tasks.

Zach's was taking care of Quinn while helping her brother-in-law Griff watch over the littlest ones.

They made quite the sight, those two big, handsome, masculine men. Standing side by side, talking, with all the easy calm of parents at the playground.

It was funny, Faith thought, as she approached Zach to tell him it was time to go, how fatherhood could change a man. Make him sexier and tenderer all at the same time.

As she neared, she caught the end of their conversation. "Yeah, of course I'd be glad to help clarify things… But you know your bride is an accountant as well as a financial director so she can explain all that…"

Zach opened his mouth, as if he was about to say he didn't *want* to ask her whatever it was his question was, when he saw her approaching, snowsuit and coats in hand. "Hey." He smiled, his conversation with Griff abruptly over. "Ready to go?"

Faith told herself she had nothing to worry about. Zach was not like Harm. He was not hiding things from her that she had every right to know.

She smiled. "I am. And I know our little fella has to be exhausted."

Together they walked out to his new extended-cab pickup truck. They settled a sleepy Quinn in his car seat, then climbed in.

Faith waited until they were on the way back to town, then unable to wait a second longer, she ignored her best instincts and asked, "What were you and Griff talking about back there?"

* * *

Zach tensed. He didn't like hiding things, but until he knew what the situation was...he didn't want to confide, either. So he told her what he could. Without saying anything that would upset or worry her.

"When I was talking with the guys at Laramie Gardens last week, they were arguing the merits of LLCs versus S corps versus C corps. It was all pretty convoluted, at least to me because I never studied business setup in college. And, of course," he continued on, sticking firmly to the facts he could reveal at the moment, "they all wanted me to weigh in. When I said I really didn't know enough to comment, they all tried to explain the differences between those three types of small businesses, anyway, and have me make a decision on the spot."

Zach saw the tension leave her body as quickly as it had appeared. Faith let out a soft musical laugh, sharing his exasperation. "That sounds like those guys!" She reached over to squeeze his biceps lovingly.

Relieved he had dodged a bullet—again—he covered her hand with his left, gave it an affectionate squeeze back. "Yeah, well, I am sure I haven't heard the last of that subject," he lamented. "So I was trying to get Griff's opinion, him being a lawyer and all, and then I could just impart *his* wisdom the next time the subject comes up. Instead of giving an unschooled opinion of my own."

"Ah." Faith gave him another admiring glance, which made him feel all the guiltier. "Nice dodge, soldier," she said.

Zach inhaled. He kept his eyes on the road. "Yeah,

well, sometimes it pays to keep the peace." Or wait until things were settled to tell your wife what you really had on your mind, he thought.

"Well, what do you think?" Faith asked the next afternoon, as they all got dressed to go to Laramie Gardens. She twirled around, showing off her—and Quinn's—holiday garb. Which also connected thematically with his.

Zach shook his head in comically exaggerated disapproval. "I hate to tell you this, darlin'," he drawled. "But these are definitely *not* ugly sweaters. In fact, if I had to describe them, I'd say they were downright cute."

She blushed. Guilty as charged. Leave it to her new husband to call her on it! "Well, it *is* Quinn's first Christmas," she said, defending herself self-consciously. "And I tried—I really did—but at the end of the day, I just couldn't make him look anything but adorable."

Zach tickled Quinn's belly and was rewarded with a delighted baby-laugh. "He is that in his little elf sweater, which looks *suspiciously* a lot like him."

"It does, doesn't it?" She sashayed closer, eyeing him up and down, her gaze lingering on his broad chest. She wrinkled her nose playfully. "I like the way your Santa looks, too, soldier."

"With his military haircut, clean-shaven face, and aviator glasses…and the Trident pinned to his red suit?"

"Well," she began, aware she'd had a little help from the artistic Emma, in making the profile of St. Nick very Zach-esque, "I had to have *a little* fun."

"Looks like you did that with your sweater, too, since your Mrs. Claus closely resembles you, too."

Faith shrugged. Aware that, too, just seemed like the

right thing to do. "I kind of feel like Mrs. Santa Claus this year. Like I'm in charge of making sure everyone gets exactly what they want..."

"I think we've all managed that." Zach reeled her in. Their lips met in a sweet and tender kiss.

"Bah-bah!" Quinn yelled. His new word for bye-bye.

Reluctantly, they drew apart.

Zach winked. "Guess that's our cue."

The party was in full swing when they arrived. The twenty-second of December, everyone was in a great mood. Except for Ted and Tillie Tarrant, who had stationed themselves at opposite ends of the community room, and Nessie Rogers, who was suddenly looking a little blue again. Faith left Quinn with Zach and made her way over to Nessie.

"I love your sweater," she remarked.

Nessie shrugged, not in the spirit at all. "It's not ugly." She peered at Faith closely. "Unless you think Christmas cardinals are ugly."

Aware that the still-recovering ex-rancher was just looking for a reason to quarrel with someone, Faith sat down next to her. "Not at all," she returned gently. "As you can see, I had a hard time going for the unattractive, too."

Nessie nodded. Appreciating the kindness.

They chatted a little more. When Russell Pierce came over to talk to her, Faith eased away.

As she made her way over to talk to Tillie, she saw Zach had handed Quinn off to Miss Mim and the other women. They were all taking turns holding and having their pictures taken with him, and their handsome baby boy was merrily eating up all the attention.

Zach was standing off to one side, talking intently

to former investment banker Ian Baker. Wondering what was so serious, she joined Tillie at the windows. Last Christmas, the eighty-year-old and her husband had worn matching ugly sweaters. This year, neither sported one.

"How are you doing?" Faith asked.

Tillie forced a smile. "Fine."

"When is your son coming to see you again?"

Some of the tension left Tillie's slender frame. "Tomorrow. I know you're probably awfully busy with the holiday coming up and Zach leaving, but I was hoping you could sit in on a meeting with Ted, our son and me."

As referee?

"We have some financial things we are all going to need to go over and I was going to try to wait until after Christmas, but with Ted still so upset with me, I think we better do it while our son is here."

Made sense. Willing to do her part to ease the tension, Faith pulled out her phone and consulted her calendar. "Is two o'clock okay?"

"Sounds fine. Thanks, Faith."

She gently touched the older woman's arm. "No problem."

Seeing that Ted was now surrounded by the other men, as they laughed and swapped humorous stories, she breathed a sigh of relief. Maybe having their son here with them would end the impasse. And things could get back to normal for the Tarrants and the long-married couple would be reconciled soon after all. She certainly hoped so.

Also noticing that Quinn was still happily occupied, she went to refill one of the punch bowls. She had just cleared the door to the kitchen when she heard a familiar pair of men's voices.

Nora's ex–Special Forces husband, Zane, said incredulously, "So Faith doesn't know *any* of this?"

"No," Zach returned curtly.

A sense of "already been here, done this" swept over Faith. Followed swiftly by hurt at having been shut out of whatever was going on with her new husband.

"Oh, man…" Zane lamented, as if Zach had just made the worst mistake of all time.

A chill going through her, Faith sagged against the edge of the stainless-steel kitchen counter.

"I just haven't found the right time," Zach said, defending himself hotly as the two men came out of the walk-in, big trays of appetizers in hand.

They stopped dead in their tracks when they saw her. And she knew without a shred of doubt that she had been deceived. Again. By the man she should have been able to trust the most.

"Time for what?" Faith demanded.

Chapter Twenty

"Are you ever going to look at me?" Zach asked that evening.

Faith set the newly filled bottles of formula into the fridge, then swung around to face him. "Hey. You have no room to complain, soldier. You could have answered my questions hours ago. When we were still at Laramie Gardens! Instead, you insisted we stay for the rest of the party, then come home and get Tinkerbelle settled and Quinn in bed and—"

He stood in the doorway to the kitchen, about as movable as a two-ton pickup truck. "I wanted us to have our privacy, Faith."

"Oh, I gathered that, Lieutenant." Still bristling with pent-up anger, she leaned against the counter, facing him, her arms folded in front of her.

Then waited.

To her building frustration, nothing was forthcoming.

"Well?" she said finally. She lifted her chin and speared him with a testy glare. "What does Zane know that I don't?"

He inhaled sharply. "I'm quitting the SEALs."

For a second Faith was sure she hadn't heard right. *"What?"*

A muscle ticked in his jaw. "I'm not going back after Christmas."

She threw up her arms, her emotions suddenly as fired up as his. "When did you decide this?" she demanded, suddenly feeling all the more betrayed.

The rims of his eyes darkened. "Monday."

She struggled to try to put everything together that she had missed. "Yesterday?"

His head dipped in a nod of acknowledgment. "Yes," he confirmed gruffly.

How could he possibly do this on the spur of the moment? Worse, without even talking to me about it once! "That's insane."

He went still. "Not exactly the reaction I was looking for."

She watched him come farther into the kitchen, bypassing the stools, to lean against the island, opposite her. Anxiety thrummed inside her. The last thing she wanted to do was be with a man who regretted leaving the military before he really wanted to depart. But that appeared to be exactly what Zach was doing.

Aware her knees were wobbling, she braced her hands on either side of her. "You can't just give up a lifelong career on a moment's notice and not expect to regret it later, Zach."

"It's not a moment's notice."

"Really?" she snorted. "You haven't mentioned anything about wanting to quit. Even when Mitzy was interviewing you. In fact, you were ridiculously cagey to all her military-service-related questions with your answers then."

His sensual lips compressed into an unforgiving line. "I did that because I hadn't made up my mind and I didn't want to lie. Or think out loud. Or appear indecisive." Which was the kiss of death for any Navy SEAL.

"Which, clearly, you were at the time," she countered.

He exhaled. "Let's just say I thought I knew what I was going to do, but I wasn't one hundred percent—"

Faith guessed where this was going. "Until you had the moment everyone talks about, when you just knew in your heart that it was time to hang up your trident for good."

Another brief hesitation. An evasive emotion she didn't want to see flickered in Zach's eyes. "It was kind of like that, yeah."

"When?" she pressed him further, giving him no more chance to obfuscate.

"It was at the hearing, when Judge Roy ruled, and named me Quinn's sole legal guardian—"

And the judge had simultaneously shut me out, at least in a permanent legal sense, for now. And his noblesse oblige had really kicked in.

"—that I knew what the right thing to do was," Zach finished soberly.

Of course, he had known then he had to take charge of his son. But quit the SEALs? Abruptly end what was, or at least had been, the biggest part of his life for years and years? When they had a plan that would have allowed him to continue, without worrying about her or Quinn? And if he really had experienced that moment all the retired SEALs talked about, why hadn't he just said so, flat out? she wondered, noting the way he was still dancing around her questions, carefully parsing all his words, avoiding a simple yes or no. Was he mistaking his duty and sense of personal honor for a real wish for a career change? Was it possible that he hadn't yet really had that life-defining epiphany…? And instead was just hoping he didn't really need an a-ha moment himself, to know?

And if he hadn't really had one, as she suspected, what would that mean for them down the road? Because it only took one unhappy person in a marriage to make the union miserable.

She went back to the overheard snippets of conversation that had started the first and only quarrel of their relationship thus far. "And yet somehow, Zane—who wasn't at our court hearing yesterday—knows all about this?" *And felt you should have told me. A whole hell of a lot sooner!*

"I knew he had wrestled with the same issues before he married Nora and adopted her son, Liam. So, yeah, I talked to him at length the day we were out searching for that hiker."

Hurt filled her heart. That he could confide in someone else instead of his wife. The person who should have been his best friend in all the world. Because he *was* her best friend now! The person she wanted to turn to for everything. So why wasn't she his?

"Why didn't you say anything to me in all that time?" she asked in a low, broken voice.

"Because I knew Harm had promised you he would quit long before he ever did, and how his broken pledges devastated you. I didn't want to put you through that kind of uncertainty and heartache again."

Made sense.

And yet, she couldn't shake the feeling that while she had mistakenly thought everything was super great these past few weeks, that in reality she had been living her marriage half in the dark. Just as she had previiously. She didn't want to live in a marriage filled with secrets. Not ever again.

Still, she tried to give him quarter. To accept that maybe he had needed another ex-military guy who was also happily married to serve as his sounding board. "Does anyone else know?" she asked, hoping like hell he would say a definitive *no* this time.

Zach paused in that telltale way.

Her heart sank again.

"Your parents?" she asked, feeling painfully excluded once again.

"Yes."

And he isn't even that close to them! "Both?"

"Yes."

She studied the closed expression on his face. "Anyone else?"

The corners of his lips slanted downward. "The guys on my SEAL team. My officer in charge."

So now they were up to what...more than ten people? she thought incredulously. "Anyone else?" she asked, thinking there better not be, or she really would feel at the very bottom level of the totem pole.

"The guys at Laramie Gardens. Your brother-in-law Griff. Ian Baker. They all know I've been thinking about it."

She jerked in a shaky breath, realizing too late the signs had all been there. She just hadn't paid attention to them!

"Is that the real reason you bought a pickup truck last week?"

Zach paused. "Not entirely, since I hadn't one hundred percent made my decision yet, but it factored into the purchase. I did want something to drive when

I was in Texas and I also wanted to be ready to jump into full-time fatherhood at a moment's notice."

Of course, he would want that. He might not be proving to be the best husband, but he certainly was one of the world's best dads.

"So when were you going to tell me?"

"Christmas morning." Zach released a long, frustrated breath. "I thought it might make a nice present to go along with the one I bought you. I guess not."

She could see that his intentions about that were sincere. It still stung, though, knowing how thoroughly he had shut her out. Shouldn't she have been the first person he shared his dilemma with…not the very last? Tears sprung to her eyes. "This decision impacted me, too, Zach." She gritted her teeth and pushed out the words. "Shouldn't I have had a say in it? Or at least heard about it, before you went ahead and decided?"

Irritation creased his handsome features. "Honestly? No. It's *my* career. I'm the one who had to decide whether to stay or go. The ironic thing is—" he jammed his hands on his waist "—I thought you would be happy when you found out I planned to be here, with you and Quinn, from here on out."

If she thought he knew what he was doing, that he had given it the proper consideration, she would be. Unfortunately, for her, it was history repeating itself. Her husband acting out of honor and duty, trying to keep promises made in the heat of the moment, without considering how that would really feel, later on. She couldn't be with anyone who felt so miserable again.

Maybe it wasn't too late to rectify this.

If he went to his OIC, explained…

Not sure she could suggest that yet, she jerked in a bolstering breath.

"It's not that I don't want you here with us," she said carefully. Reminded what he had told her about Annette, never really minding seeing him go, she vowed to keep true to her promise.

To be a good military wife this time.

He uttered a hoarse, mirthless laugh. His eyes gleamed with cynicism. "It sure seems like you want to get me out of here."

Faith shoved her hands through her hair. She dug deep into her heart, searching for the words to explain. "I just… I had one husband who was filled with regret when he suddenly parted from the military."

Zach's scowl deepened. "You can't really compare our two situations. Harm's resignation wasn't voluntary."

Faith knew that now. Thanks to Zach. She hadn't back then. "But a lot of what Harm went through is typical for guys who are getting out of the service, Zach." She knew that from talking to other military wives.

She stepped closer and spread her hands beseechingly. "You know that. When a soldier finally resigns, it's like a death to this huge part of his or her life…for a lot of you, the only life you have had for years. And then you get home, and you have no idea what you're going to do with the rest of your life, and you're miserable and everyone around you is miserable as a consequence."

Zach shook his head in exasperation. "What are you saying?"

Frustrated he wasn't taking her concerns seriously, Faith angled her chin at him. "I'm saying that you need to stay a SEAL until you have really had time to consider this. And make a plan. And have some idea of what the rest of your life looks like."

He stared at her for a long, debilitating moment. She felt like she hadn't a single defense left inside her. Then he moved purposefully closer, his eyes shimmering with hurt. "You don't think I already know any of that?" he rasped.

She recalled Harm's half-assed plan about going into construction, a job he quickly found out he loathed. She swallowed around the growing knot of emotion in her throat. "I think you're acting strictly on emotion, Zach." She took his hand in hers and looked into his eyes. "And that's never good."

He stared back at her for a long, grim moment. "Well, maybe you're right." He sighed and pulled back his hand. "Maybe I have been. No more."

He turned and went upstairs, looking colder and more remote than she had ever seen him.

She stayed where she was and tried to calm down. They could work this out. They *could*. They just needed to talk. Take their time. Figure it out together, instead of alone.

Short minutes later, Zach came down the stairs, the duffel he had brought with him zipped up and ready to go. He had both his cell phones—the government-issued one and his private one—in hand.

Her voice caught. "What are you doing?"

Looking even more betrayed, he reached for his coat and shrugged it on. "Making your most fervent wish come true. I'm leaving."

"To go to the Laramie Inn?"

"Back to Virginia."

Her spirits sank even lower. "Before Christmas? Zach, you can't miss that!" She gasped. "Quinn…"

"Won't even know what day it really is, not this year, anyway." Zach stared at her like she was a complete stranger. "But if you want, on the big day, we can do what all military families do when it's just not feasible for them to be together and FaceTime. That is, if you pick up your phone," he added sarcastically.

Aware she barely recognized him, either, she countered, "Of course, I would pick up my phone!" The tears she had been holding back began to fall. "Zach, come on, be reasonable."

"Worried about what everyone else is going to think?"

That was the least of her worries!

He came closer, his gaze roving her face, as if memorizing it one last time. "Just tell them I had to leave even earlier than expected," he advised morosely. "Which is true."

She balled her hands into fists, wishing he wasn't being so damn stubborn. "Except you don't have to, Zach!"

He shook his head in soulful resignation, sorrow creasing the handsome lines of his face. "Listen to me, Faith. I spent more holidays than I can count, after my parents' divorce, and even before, being where I wasn't wanted. I don't want to live like that. Not ever again." He walked out.

Chapter Twenty-One

The following evening, Zach was welcomed into his father's study, in his DC high-rise. He had spent the afternoon with his mom and stepdad before they headed to Aspen.

"Zach. Good to see you, son."

Zach shook his father's hand. "Same, Dad." He had been surprised to realize how much he needed the support of family, since realizing he had a son. Even more stunned to realize how ready they were to give it, even on a moment's notice. Up to now he had always felt like an uncomfortable reminder of a failed marriage.

Had that been more in his heart than theirs?

His expression serious, Ezekiel gestured for him to take a seat in one of the leather wing chairs before the fire. "You didn't bring the family?"

Zach sat down opposite his father. "Not this time."

The general steepled his fingers. "I look forward to meeting them."

Zach nodded.

Would that even happen? At least as far as Faith went...?

"Something wrong?"

Zach grimaced. He must be wearing his heart on his sleeve because his dad wasn't usually one to ask something like that. The general preferred to see emotions stuffed as deep inside as they would go.

Realizing if anyone would know when it was time to call it quits on a union, it was his dad, he admitted, "I think I might have made a mistake with the marriage."

Ezekiel's glance narrowed. "Why?"

Not sure how to articulate it, Zach swallowed. "It's just…"

His dad waited. Also, unusual.

"I didn't expect her to be glad to see me deployed again."

Ezekiel's shoulders relaxed. "Ah. She put on a brave face?"

Zach remembered their bitter argument. With a frown, he conceded, "A little more than that."

"Said she couldn't wait for you to leave?"

"Said I *had* to leave, for all our sakes."

His dad nodded. "Nothing really unusual about that, son. Departures are hard. On everyone. Always have been, always will be."

Who was this man? "It never seemed to bother you when you had to say goodbye to me and Mom."

Ezekiel's unflinching expression hardened even more. "That's because it was my job as head of the household to be strong."

"I didn't think you missed me," Zach blurted out before he could stop himself.

A suspicious glint appeared in his dad's eyes. "Well, then you were wrong about that," the general said in a rusty-sounding voice. "I missed the hell out of you, Zach. Always have, always will. No matter how old you get. When you're not with me, a part of me just aches."

For the first time, Zach realized his dad had worried about him every bit as much as his mom, when he was deployed. Even though his dad would have had an easier time finding out if he and his unit were okay. "What about Mom? Did you miss her?"

Again, that unflinching honesty. "We weren't suited for each other. Ever. You know that. Our divorce was a relief to both of us. But I did miss, and do miss, your stepmother because we are suited for each other."

Zach could see that. Iris was the model military wife. "Do you tell Iris that?" Zach asked, curious.

Ezekiel waved off the question. "She knows."

Funny thing was, Zach bet his stepmother did. "Does she tell you?" he persisted, even more curious.

Another dismissive wave of the hand. "Doesn't have to," his father huffed. "I know."

Zach wished he had his dad's confidence in the romance arena. But nothing came to him. He mumbled his frustration and pressed his hands against his aching temples. Suppressed emotion roiled through him like a category five hurricane. "I don't know what I'm going to do, Dad."

The general stood and walked over to put his hand on Zach's shoulder. His touch was warm and reassuring. "Yes, you do."

His head still bowed, feeling suddenly near tears, Zach croaked out, "What I want..."

"Isn't always what you get. At least not right away." His dad's grip tightened; familial love flowing between them. "That doesn't matter. Only *you* know what you need. What is worth going after...from your mother and I, from your son and, most of all, from the woman you married."

* * *

Faith had always found solace in work because she loved helping others, especially the seniors at Laramie Gardens. But after her big blowup with Zach the day before, she was having trouble concentrating. Fortunately, her mediation skills weren't really needed, after all.

"So this was all just one big misunderstanding," Faith observed, from her place at the conference table. She had come into the meeting on December twenty-third prepared to have to do mediation and or damage control, only to find out that Ted and Tillie Tarrant and their son, Eddie, had already worked everything out.

"I was upset," Tillie explained, "because I checked on our investment portfolio and found all the accounts had nearly been emptied out."

"She knew I was in charge of the accounts," Eddie said. "So she thought I stole from them—"

"No," Tillie interrupted. "*Mismanaged* maybe. Unintentionally, of course. Which is why I went to Ian Baker. I knew, as a former investment banker he would be able to make sure what I was seeing online was actually what was in the accounts."

"And it was?" Faith asked, thinking back to that day when she'd seen Tillie and Ian on the bench outside. Tillie crying, Ian consoling her, papers being exchanged…

"Only because I moved their retirement funds to more stable accounts," Eddie said.

"With my permission," Ted added, giving his son a grateful look.

"The problem was, no one told me!" Tillie protested, still a little upset about that.

"Because you never wanted to be involved in finances!" Ted and Eddie said in unison.

"All you had to do was tell me what you'd found," Ted told his beloved wife gently, "and I could have cleared it up straight away. Instead of looking for ways to cut expenses that didn't need to be cut."

"I should have come to you." Tillie held Ted's hand tightly. "I promise, I won't ever make the mistake of not trusting in you again."

Faith smiled at them in relief, glad they had cleared up the confusion and worked everything out. And could now enjoy a stress-free holiday. She wished them all a merry Christmas.

The meeting broke up soon after.

In an effort to keep her mind off Zach, Faith went to the dining hall to get a coffee. She saw Nessie Rogers, seated at a table alone, staring down into her teacup.

She joined her, beverage in hand. "May I join you?"

Nessie, who had been doing better with every day that passed since coming to Laramie Gardens, shrugged indifferently. Faith sat down. "What is it?" she asked.

Nessie's gnarled hand trembled slightly. "I can't believe I am going to miss my first Christmas Eve at the ranch in ninety years. But they're saying I can't possibly go home and manage on my own yet." Tears sparkled in her faded blue eyes.

Faith squeezed her hand. "That's true. You aren't strong enough yet." She brainstormed the kind of solutions that hadn't been needed in her previous meeting. "But maybe there is something we can do. Let me check..."

Half an hour later, she was back. A fresh cup of tea for Nessie, another coffee for herself. "Okay. See what you think about this. I talked to the director, your doctor, your physical therapist and your social worker. I explained to them how much it would mean to you to be at the ranch tomorrow. They all said it would be okay if it was a short visit. And you came back here after. So how would you like it if I drove you there myself?"

Nessie sat up straight. Her lips quivered with excitement. "But it's Christmas Eve! Don't you get the day off?"

"I do." But with Zach gone, and no word from him, the holiday was turning out to be excruciating for her, too.

"My sister Emma is going to babysit Quinn while we run out there and check on the property and do what you want or need to do. So as long as we could get back before early afternoon…?"

"We could!" Nessie clapped her hands joyfully. "Oh, Faith! You don't know how much this means to me!"

Faith hugged the retired rancher. "I'm glad I could help."

Glad I could think about someone else's problems instead of my own.

The next day, Nessie was ready for her when she arrived at 10:00 a.m. to get her. They settled her in the passenger seat and put her walker in the back of her SUV. Faith played Christmas music on the radio as they drove out. Nessie perked up visibly with each passing mile. Finally, they arrived at the cattle ranch where she had lived all her life.

The meticulously maintained one-story adobe ranch house with the red tile roof looked, Nessie declared happily, just as she had left it.

Together, they went inside.

A month had passed since anyone had been there, so it had a slight musty smell. With no lights on it, it was a little dark, too. Nessie walked through the rooms, a pensive look on her face. Moving slower and slower. "Would you like me to put on a pot of tea for you?" Faith asked, not sure how she could help.

"No, dear," Nessie replied thoughtfully, a distant expression on her face. "I don't think so. In fact..." She turned her walker toward the door. "I think I'd like to get my favorite afghan, my favorite picture of my late husband and the family bible and then go."

"Are you sure?" Faith asked as she collected the items under Nessie's direction.

"Yes." Hands gripping the bars of the walker, Nessie stood a little straighter. "I think I've seen what I needed to see."

"Which was...?" Faith asked, confused.

"That sometimes, no matter how painful it is, you have to let go of the past and move on."

Faith returned Nessie to Laramie Gardens, and then headed home herself. Emma was flushed with excitement when she walked in.

"What's going on?" Faith asked.

"Can't tell! It's a Christmas present!"

Faith had about had enough of secret Christmas presents to last a lifetime. Although she would have liked a chance to give Zach his before he left.

She suspected Emma was just trying to cheer her up—a near impossibility given how her heart was aching for her husband. "Okay." When she had a moment alone, she was going to call him. They couldn't leave it like this. They had to talk before he went out on a mission! Or was in danger again.

She put her computer bag down and shrugged out of her coat. “Where’s Quinn?”

“Out at the ranch with Mom and Dad.”

“What?” That hadn’t been in the plan! Plus, she had been hoping if she could get ahold of Zach, they could FaceTime with Quinn, too.

Emma looked at her phone, then grabbed her purse. “Just drive out there later and we’ll, um, talk.” She rushed out the door.

Frowning, Faith turned back to the Christmas tree.

Well, she thought, maybe this was a blessing in disguise. Since she had made a decision on the drive back to town. And knew after dealing with the Tarrant family and Nessie Rogers what she had to do…

She was just gathering her courage when her doorbell rang. She walked over to open the front door. Zach stood on the other side, broad shoulders flexed resolutely. Pulse pounding, she took a second to assess him.

He was in his camouflage utility uniform again. Just as he had been the first time they’d met. And, as always, he looked damn good. His sea-blue eyes were intent, his short dark hair was brushed neatly into place. It looked like he had shaved earlier in the day, but the hint of scruff was already edging his roughhewn jaw. But it was the cautious smile curving his lips that turned her heart upside down.

“Hey,” he said softly. “Merry Christmas.”

“Oh, Zach!” She had never been so glad to see anyone in her life. “Merry Christmas to you, too, soldier!” She threw her arms around his neck and hugged him close. The tears she had been holding back for what seemed like forever flowed.

Zach held her until her shoulders stopped shaking,

then wordlessly lifted her face to his. "Aw, darlin'," he murmured gruffly, "I missed you, too."

And to prove it, he kissed her, hot and passionately, soft and deep. Finally, he lifted his head. The look in his eyes reminded her they had other responsibilities, too. "Quinn…?" he asked.

Wondering where this all was going to lead, Faith took a stabilizing breath. "He's with my folks at their ranch."

His gaze drifted over her, as if he was memorizing every detail. "Good. We need to talk." He stared down at her with the quiet resolve she loved so much. "And just for the record, I did ask Emma and your folks to help me out with this."

The lump in her throat was back, as another wave of anxiety sifted through her.

He clasped her hands in his. "Because more than anything I want us to have a very good first holiday together."

Her heart filled with hope for their future. "I want that, too. And I also want you to know, Zach, that I was wrong to compare you to my late husband and lash out at you for keeping me in the dark about what you were wrestling with."

He stopped her with an understanding glance. "Hey. You were right to force me to take a step back and really consider things." He squeezed her hands and his voice dropped a notch. "I needed to do that, Faith."

She blinked in surprise, the strength of his touch imbuing her with warmth. "You really mean that."

He nodded. "I hadn't had my moment," he admitted, regret tightening the corners of his mouth. "The one where I really knew deep down in my gut what I really needed to do."

Clearly, he had it now. She took his hand and led him over to sit on the sofa, by the beautifully lit and decorated Christmas tree. As they settled, side by side, she searched his face. “When did it come?”

“After I left Texas. I went to see both my folks, but it was when I was talking with my dad—about some of the regrets we both had…and later, about how we wanted things to be different between the two of us, more open, going forward—that I finally had *that moment* everyone talks about. And I knew. That even though I loved every minute of my service to my country, I was done. I needed to be here with you and with Quinn. So I went to see my OIC this morning, and we talked, and I signed my exit paperwork.”

His heartfelt admission prompted a self-effacing one from her, too. “Oh, Zach, I know I could have handled our first argument a whole lot better, too. I’m sorry if it felt like I was pushing you away. That I didn’t want you here with us, because nothing could have been further from the truth, then or now. Or in the future.”

“Hey.” He shifted her closer, so her bent knee was pressing against his thigh. “I’m glad you forced me to do some more soul-searching.”

Their glances held for a long, palpable moment. The need she felt was reflected in his eyes. “That’s all I was trying to do.”

He nodded. “I know that now. But…” He swallowed, letting her know in that instant how hard their falling out had been for him, too. “At the time it felt like history repeating itself.”

She knew how Annette had pushed him away, at the end. The same way Harm had shut her out.

It was easy to see why they had both been so angry and resentful. She sighed. “For me, too.”

He brought her all the way onto his lap and ran a hand tenderly down her spine. “But what we have is not like what either of us had with anyone else.”

She snuggled against his hard, strong body. “You’re right about that.” They had their own very special story. She sifted her hands through his hair. “Because I love you, Zach, with all of my heart and soul.”

“I love you, too, Faith.” He bent his head to kiss her, sweetly and evocatively.

Tenderness wafted through her, fueling an even deeper reverence and need. Aware of the vows they had taken, and pledged to honor, she took another deep bolstering breath. “As far as the rest of your life…whatever you want to do, however long it takes you to figure things out, career-wise, is okay with me. From this day forward,” she told him intently, marveling at the wonder of the moment, “I will be here to support you.”

He answered her with a Texas-sized grin. “Good. Because things might be a little uncertain initially. As I get my new business off the ground.”

She blinked. “What new business?”

“Callahan Custom Carpentry. I’m going to resurrect my granddad’s old company. And base it in Laramie County.”

“That’s…incredible,” she murmured. And meaningful, too, in the way it honored his grandfather.

Eyes dark with emotion, he pulled her closer still. “I think it will be. I realized when I was working on your study how much I still loved working with wood. Building things that made people happy, their lives easier.”

He traced the back of her hand. “Learning the woodworking trade with my granddad was one of the most amazing times of my life. The hours and pay are both good. And, best of all, I'll be able to be with Quinn while he grows up. Take him to school. Help him with his homework." He winked. "Teach him how to read a compass. Identify the stars."

Once a SEAL, always a SEAL. She laughed softly. "I don't think he will ever feel lost with a daddy like you around."

"The only time I've ever been lost is when I walked out on you. It's not going to happen again, Faith. Because as you know, that was a quitter move, and SEALs never quit."

"No, they don't." She was glad he was holding on to that. His years of service had made him into the gallant man he was now. They shared another leisurely kiss that made her feel as if their whole world was suddenly right.

When they finally drew apart, he pulled a velvet box from his pocket. "And now for the present I've been wanting to give you."

Faith opened the lid, saw the sparkle of a beautiful diamond ring. "Oh, Zach," she breathed as he put the ring on her finger.

He smiled. "It's the engagement ring you should have had."

"Thank you, it's stunning!" She hugged him fiercely then went to the tree and returned with a four-by-four-inch package. She felt suddenly shy. "Mine isn't nearly as expensive..."

"But just as heartfelt," he said, as he opened it and found a pocket-size leather photo wallet, filled with pictures of Quinn, from birth to six months, and one of their wedding.

His eyes gleamed. “I love it,” he claimed in a rusty-sounding voice.

The tears she had been holding back finally came. Spilling down, over her lashes. “I got it so you could carry it with you, whenever you were away…”

“And I will carry it with me. Always. No matter where I am.” He kissed her sweetly, meaningfully. “As a reminder that love and family always have been and always will be the most important things in life.”

Epilogue

Two Christmases later...

"Quinn, can you help Daddy?" Faith held out an ornament from the box.

"Yes!" Two-and-a-half-year-old Quinn raced over to where she sat on the sofa. Once there, he stopped dead in his tracks, and slowly and carefully held out his hand. Just as carefully, she put the stuffed, cloth Santa Claus in the palm of his hand.

His little chest puffed out, he marched over to where Zach stood, next to the tree.

"Here, Daddy. Put this one on," he said.

Zach squinted down at his son. "Do you want to show me where it should go?"

Quinn nodded importantly. "Up top!" He pointed high.

Grinning, Zach scooped him up in his arms. Together, they selected just the right spot while Faith took a photo with her phone.

Father and son were a handsome pair. In fact, Zach looked more and more like his daddy every day.

"Look, Mommy!" Quinn pointed to the lone ornament on the pretty lit tree that they had put up the evening before, and were just now getting around to finishing decorating. "Isn't it gorgeous?"

Faith chuckled at his use of one of her favorite words when it came to anything her son and husband did. "It is."

Zach set Quinn down. "Go get another one," he said.

As Quinn enthusiastically rushed to comply, Tinkerbelle got off her cushion and came over to curl up next Faith's feet.

"I want Christmas train!" Quinn said.

"Then the Christmas train it shall be." Faith exchanged affectionate glances with her husband, and then handed over the chosen ornament.

As Quinn marched carefully back to the tree, she reflected on the last two years. A lot had happened. All good. She had officially petitioned to adopt and been granted full parental custody of Quinn, along with Zach. Meanwhile, Zach had received a lot of advice from the retired businessmen—and women—at Laramie Gardens. As a result, Callahan Custom Carpentry had gotten off to a grand start, and he now had so much work, he was hiring ex-veteran apprentices, and teaching them woodworking, too.

Ted and Tillie Tarrant were once again the resident sweethearts of Laramie Gardens. Living happily in the same suite and vowing never to let a misunderstanding get in the way of their happiness once again.

Nessie Rogers had sold her family ranch to a young couple with small children, who vowed to keep it in their family for generations, and moved permanently into Laramie Gardens. She and Russell Pierce had become even better friends and were working together on collecting more antique ornaments, and then outfitting them with batteries that would light them from the inside.

Quinn was still one of the beloved "mascot kiddos" at the assisted-living facility, but these days he attended preschool five mornings a week, too, and went home in the afternoon to nap while his daddy worked, then came over in the late afternoon to visit with the seniors, before heading home to dinner with Faith and Zach.

And speaking of their family…

Quinn returned and climbed up beside her. He put his hand on her swollen tummy. "Can baby sister see tree, Mommy?" he asked.

Only if she had X-ray vision… "I know she can hear us talking about it and decorating it."

Quinn frowned. "I want her *see* it, Mommy!"

"She will, next year, I promise. And I took a picture so when she is born, we will be able to show it to her."

"When hospital?"

"The first of April, four months from now."

Quinn's brow furrowed in confusion.

Zach came over to snuggle beside them on the sofa, too. "In the springtime, buddy. When it gets warm outside and the trees get all their new green leaves, and all those *gorgeous* Texas wildflowers come out."

Faith chuckled at *his* use of one of her favorite words, too.

"Baby sister be *gorgeous*," Quinn said seriously.

"Yes, she will be." Smiling down at her son, Faith tickled his tummy. "Just like you, you little lovebug!"

He erupted in giggles that proved infectious. When they had all stopped laughing, Quinn looked at them and sighed, already prepared to move on to the next event of the day. "Can I play toys now?" he asked hopefully.

Clearly, the group-decorating was going to be a long

process, Faith thought, realizing she was in no hurry, either. She wanted to enjoy every second of their third holiday together.

She nodded. The little boy gave them both a hug, then climbed down and raced over to his wooden blocks. Her tail wagging, Tinkerbelle followed along to lie beside him and watch.

Zach shifted her over onto his lap and stroked her hair lovingly. "So where are we going to put the mistletoe this year, Mrs. Callahan?" he drawled.

"I don't know, soldier…" Faith returned playfully, wreathing her arms about his shoulders and looking deep into his eyes.

Gosh, she loved this man, and he loved her right back.

Aware life was more perfect than she had ever imagined it could be, she gently kissed his lips. "I guess you're going to have to surprise me…" she murmured, waggling her eyebrows at him. Loving the fact that after two years, things were still as hot between them as ever.

He laughed and hugged her close. "Sounds like I've got my orders, then…"

* * * * *

Watch for the next book in
Cathy Gillen Thacker's
Lockharts Lost & Found miniseries,
coming spring 2022, only from
Harlequin Special Edition!

COMING NEXT MONTH FROM

HARLEQUIN

SPECIAL EDITION

#2881 THEIR NEW YEAR'S BEGINNING

The Fortunes of Texas: The Wedding Gift • by Michelle Major

Brian Fortune doesn't think he will ever find the woman he kissed at his brother's New Year's wedding. So when the search for the provenance of a mysterious gift leads him into a local antique store a few days later, he's stunned to find Emmaline Lewis, proprietor—and mystery kisser! Brian has never been the type to commit, but suddenly he knows he'll do anything to stay at Emmaline's side—for good.

#2882 HER HOMETOWN MAN

Sutton's Place • by Shannon Stacey

Summoned home by her mother and sisters, novelist Gwen Sutton has made it clear—she's not staying. She's returning to her quiet life as soon as the family brewery is up and running. But when Case Danforth offers his help, it's clear there's more than just beer brewing! Time is short for Case to convince Gwen that a home with him is where her heart is.

#2883 THE RANCHER'S BABY SURPRISE

Texas Cowboys & K-9s • by Sasha Summers

Former soldier John Mitchell has come home after being discharged and asks to stay with his best friend, Natalie. They're both in for a shock when a precious baby girl is left on Natalie's doorstep—and John is the father! Now John needs Natalie's help more than ever. But Natalie has been in love with John forever. How can she help him find his way to being a family man if she's not part of that family?

#2884 THE CHARMING CHECKLIST

Charming, Texas • by Heatherly Bell

Max Del Toro persuaded his friend Ava Long to play matchmaker in exchange for posing as her boyfriend for one night. He even gave her a list of must-haves for his future wife. Except now he can't stop thinking about Ava—who doesn't check a single item on his list!

#2885 HIS LOST AND FOUND FAMILY

Sierra's Web • by Tara Taylor Quinn

Learning he's guardian to his orphaned niece sends architect Michael O'Connell's life into a tailspin. He's floored by the responsibility, so when Mariah Anderson agrees to pitch in at home, Michael thinks she's heaven-sent. He's shocked at the depth of his own connection to Mariah and opens his heart to her in ways he never imagined. But can an instant family turn into a forever one?

#2886 A CHEF'S KISS

Small Town Secrets • by Nina Crespo

Small-town chef Philippa Gayle's onetime rival-turned-lover Dominic Crawford upended her life. But when she's forced together with the celebrity cook on a project that could change her life, there's no denying that the flames that were lit years ago were only banked, not extinguished. Can Philippa trust Dominic enough to let him in...or are they just cooking up another heartbreak?

SPECIAL EXCERPT FROM

HARLEQUIN

SPECIAL EDITION

Brian Fortune doesn't think he will ever find the woman he kissed at his brother's New Year's wedding. So when the search for the provenance of a mysterious gift leads him into a local antique store a few days later, he's stunned to find Emmaline Lewis, proprietor—and mystery kisser! Brian has never been the type to commit—but suddenly he knows he'll do anything to stay at Emmaline's side—for good...

Read on for a sneak peek of the first book in the The Fortunes of Texas: The Wedding Gift continuity, Their New Year's Beginning, *by* USA TODAY *bestselling author Michelle Major!*

"I'd like to take you out on a proper date then."

"Okay." Color bloomed in her cheeks. "That would be nice." He leaned in, but she held up a finger. "You should know that since Kirby and the gang outed my pregnancy at the coffee shop, I'm not going to hide it anymore." She pressed a hand to her belly. "I'm wearing a baggy shirt tonight because it seemed easier than fielding questions from the boys, but if we go out, there will be questions. And comments."

"I don't care about what anyone else thinks," he assured her and then kissed her gently. "This is about you and me."

HSEEXP1221

Those must have been the right words, because Emmaline wound her arms around his neck and drew closer. "I'm glad," she said, but before he could kiss her again, she yawned once more.

"I'll walk you to your car."

She mock pouted but didn't argue. "I'm definitely not as fun as I used to be," she told him as he picked up the bags with the leftover supplies to carry for her. "Actually I'm not sure I was ever that fun."

"As far as I'm concerned, you're the best."

After another lingering kiss, Emmaline climbed into her car and drove away. Brian watched her taillights until they disappeared around a bend. The night sky overhead was once again filled with stars, and he breathed in the fresh Texas air. He needed to stay in the moment and remember his reason for being in town and how long he planned to stay. He knew better than to examine the feeling of contentment coursing through him.

One thing he knew for certain was that it couldn't last.

HSEEXP1221